What lurks in the

MW01615527

High in the Andes, Dane Maddock and Bones Bonebrake discover a secret prison cell where a Spanish explorer lived out his final days. The words carved into the wall seem like the ravings of a madman, but they are the key that opens the door to an ancient mystery.

Hidden somewhere in the depths of the Peruvian Amazon is the Inca's lost City of the Serpent, the gateway to the underworld. Boundless treasure and unimaginable power lie in wait for those who are clever enough to follow the clues left by the mysterious Cloud People. But Maddock and Bones are not the only ones searching for the city, and to get there they must brave the perils of the jungle and the deadly guardians of the underworld as they come face to face with the giant serpent of the Amazon.

Praise for David Wood
and The Dane Maddock Adventures!

"What an adventure! A great read that provides lots of action, and thoughtful insight as well, into strange realms that are sometimes best left unexplored." Paul Kemprecos, author of *Cool Blue Tomb* and the *NUMA Files*

"Dane and Bones.... Together they're unstoppable. Rip roaring action from start to finish. Wit and humor throughout. Just one question - how soon until the next one? Because I can't wait." Graham Brown, author of *Shadows of the Midnight Sun*

SERPENT

A DANE MADDOCK ADVENTURE
DAVID WOOD

ADRENALINE PRESS

BOOKS BY DAVID WOOD

THE DANE MADDOCK ADVENTURES
Blue Descent
Dourado
Cibola
Quest
Icefall
Buccaneer
Atlantis
Ark
Xibalba
Loch
Solomon Key
Contest
Serpent

DANE AND BONES ORIGINS
Freedom
Hell Ship
Splashdown
Dead Ice
Liberty
Electra
Amber
Justice
Treasure of the Dead
Bloodstorm

DANE MADDOCK UNIVERSE
Berserk
Maug
Elementals
Cavern
Devil's Face

Herald
Brainwash
The Tomb
Shasta
Destination: Rio
Destination: Luxor
Destination: Sofia
Aztlan (short story)
Urban Legend (short story)

JADE IHARA ADVENTURES (WITH SEAN ELLIS)
Oracle
Changeling
Exile

MYRMIDON FILES (WITH SEAN ELLIS)
Destiny
Mystic

BONES BONEBRAKE ADVENTURES
Primitive
The Book of Bones
Skin and Bones
Venom

JAKE CROWLEY ADVENTURES (WITH ALAN BAXTER)
Sanctum
Blood Codex
Anubis Key
Revenant

BROCK STONE ADVENTURES
Arena of Souls
Track of the Beast (forthcoming)

FROM THE AUTHOR

A few years ago, Matt James and I wrote a Bone Bonebrake novella called VENOM for the Kindle Unlimited program. When that program closed down and we took a second look at VENOM, we decided that the legend of Yacumama and Sachamama really demanded a deeper story. Consequently, we've started over with that particular legend. If you read VENOM in its previous incarnation, please know that SERPENT is a completely different book. The only similarities are that both take place in the same part of the world, they deal with the legend of Yacumama, and Bones is a character in both.

At the last it bites like a serpent
and stings like a viper.
Proverbs 23:32

PROLOGUE

1531- The Mountains of Peru

The midday air was cool high in the cordillera the natives called the Andes. Not for the first time since his arrival in the wilderness some called New Spain, Fray Marcos de Niza looked to the sky and wondered at God's plan for his life. The young priest had left Spain in search of adventure, but instead found himself tasked with molding savages into civilized men. He closed his eyes and let the sound of the fast-flowing waters of the Urubamba calm his frayed nerves.

"Fray Marcos!" a familiar voice called. "Where are you?"

Marcos winced. Rimaq was an exceptionally bright young boy with an aptitude for languages. He was already fluent in Spanish and Marcos was now teaching him Latin. In his native tongue, Rimaq's name meant "One Who Speaks" and Marcos could not help but wonder if the boy's mother had been blessed with the gift of prophecy.

"There you are." Rimaq sat down beside him. "How are you, today?"

"I am well, just as I was when you asked me earlier today."

Rimaq cocked his head. "Are you thinking about gold again?"

Marcos put a finger to his lips. "Do not forget. That is between us."

"I haven't told anyone."

"Has your grandfather remembered any more of the story?" Marcos asked.

"Only one thing."

Marcos' heart raced. For all his constant chattering, Rimaq had proved a fertile source for accounts of lost treasure. If even a fraction of the legends were to be believed, this part of the world was overflowing with gold. Men would write their names in the history books with their monumental discoveries, and Marcos was determined to be one of those men. He just needed to know where to look.

"What did he tell you?" Marcos asked.

Rimaq scratched his head. "I can't remember now."

"Remember what we talked about. Stop and think before you decide that you can't remember."

The boy scowled at the rushing water. Finally, a smile spread across his face. "She lies on a bed of..." He frowned.

"Gold?" Marcos asked.

Rimaq shook his head. "The glass that you Spanish love."

"Glass? Do you mean diamonds?"

"Yes."

Despite the cool weather, sweat trickled down the back of Marcos' neck. A princess laid to rest on a bed of diamonds!

"You would like to find this treasure, no?" Rimaq asked.

"Yes, for the glory of God, of course," Marcos said. "Does your grandfather remember the location of the tomb?"

"Up in the sky under the ground."

Marcos let out a growl of frustration. That was all the

old man ever said, and he had no idea what it meant.

"I am sorry, Fray Marcos."

"It is all right. You have done well." Marcos paused. "Why were you looking for me?"

"Fray Carlo sent me. He wants to see you right away."

Marcos sprang to his feet. There was no point chastising Rimaq. The boy did his best. He hurried to the makeshift hut that served as a monastic outpost, where Fray Carlo was waiting.

"I apologize for the delay," Marcos said. "Rimaq found me several minutes ago, but it took him until now to tell me I was needed."

Fray Carlo de Vargas raised a bushy eyebrow. "If you say so, Fray Marcos."

"How may I serve?"

"A stranger arrived in the village. A soldier, burning up with fever and raving mad. Do what you can for him."

"Where will I find him?"

"In the cell under the mountain."

Marcos forced a thin smile. Fray Carlo stood higher in the ranks, so it was Marco who would be forced to put his own health at risk tending to the fever-addled soldier.

"You fear the spread of his fever?"

Fray Carlo made a dismissive wave. "I fear the spread of his profane lies. A Spaniard who believes in primitive gods! He could completely undermine what we are doing here."

Marcos scratched his chin thoughtfully. It was highly unusual, and that interested him.

"Anything else I need to know?"

"He had this." Fray Carlo held up a map.

It took Marcos a moment to realize what he was seeing. "Is that human skin?"

"Mummified."

"Did he say where the map leads?"

"Do not turn this into another of your treasure hunts. The man went into the jungle, witnessed some unspeakable horror, and returned raving mad." Fray Carlo laid the map down. "I will see to it that this is placed in safe hands."

Marcos tried not to stare at the map. He knew he would never get the chance to study it. Fray Carlo disapproved of his hunger for discovery. But there was another way he could learn about the map.

"I will do everything I can for him. Given time, we will bring him back to the light. God's will always prevails."

Fray Carlo gave a sage nod.

Marcos paused as he was turning to leave. "By the way, how do you know he saw something horrifying in the jungle?"

"He must have," Fray Carlo said gravely. "He tore out his own eyes."

1

The train rumbled along the track, carrying its passengers deeper into the Peruvian mountains. Its path wound alongside the churning waters of the boulder-choked Urubamba River. Dane Maddock let his eyes drift, taking in the distant, snow-capped peaks. He was eager to reach their destination, mostly because the man in the seat beside him was driving him nuts.

Bones Bonebrake, Maddock's best friend and his business partner since they'd left the Navy SEALs, sat slouched in his seat, pounding out the drumbeat from what he said was a song by Five Finger Death Punch. Maddock didn't know the band, so he took Bones' word for it.

"Not much longer, right?" Bones asked, tapping away at the seat in front of him.

"We'll get there when we get there," Maddock said. Searching for a distraction, he turned his attention to a man who sat a few seats in front of them. He was a fleshy, broad-shouldered fellow with a sunburned neck and close-cropped red hair. He wore a khaki shirt, fresh off the rack judging by the creases that hadn't yet been ironed out. He was speaking animatedly to an attractive young woman with big brown eyes, full lips, and long chestnut hair. She was seated across the aisle from him, nodding along but not meeting his eye.

"They were called the Cloud People," the man said. His accent carried the nasal harshness of Boston. "The Incas considered them to be their most ferocious enemies. They had white skin and light-colored eyes. The Spanish even formed an alliance with the Cloud People because they had so much respect for their power, their nobility, and their beauty."

Maddock rolled his eyes. The Chachapoya, or "Cloud People," were a tribe that had, at times, been an enemy of the Inca. Like most nations oppressed by the Incas, they had briefly allied with the Spanish invaders against their native oppressors until their own tribe was largely wiped out by diseases carried to the Americas from Europe by their new allies. They had no written language, so the only surviving accounts of them were those recorded by the Spaniards. Consequently, many farfetched legends had grown up around the long-dead civilization.

The red-haired man took out a smartphone, opened a document, and scrolled through. "An explorer named Pedro Cieza de Leon wrote that the Cloud People were 'the whitest and most handsome people of all that I have seen' and Orellana wrote that they were definitely European."

"That's a pile of crap." Bones had stopped drumming. While he did not have the same level of interest in history and sociology that Maddock did, he loved myths and legends, and doubtless had some familiarity with the Chachapoya. "They were lighter-skinned than the Inca, but they were natives."

Ginger turned around, looked Bones up and down, and smirked. "You were there?"

"Were you?" Bones asked.

"Orellana was, and he said they were tall and blonde with extremely white skin. Their women were so desirable that the Inca preferred them as wives."

"More like slaves," mumbled the woman whom Ginger had been regaling with his tales.

"History tends to be biased in favor of the victors,"

Maddock said.

Ginger gritted his teeth in something just short of a grin. "That's the way it should be. The only thing the losers care about is erasing history."

"Look, genius," Bones said. "DNA and linguistics indicate that the Chachapoya were a distinctive race, genetically diverse from the Inca, but they were not Anglo."

Ginger blinked and Maddock stifled a laugh. Bones wasn't as dumb as he sometimes pretended to be, and when it came to the stuff of conspiracy theories, he occasionally surprised with his depth of knowledge.

The ginger-haired man turned to Maddock. "Why don't you tell your friend to shut up?"

"I've been trying to shut him up for as long as I've known him," Maddock said truthfully.

The man bared coffee-stained teeth in a wolfish grin. "If you don't shut him up, I'm gonna do it myself." He cracked his knuckles for emphasis.

Maddock arched an eyebrow. The fellow was large and muscular, but he was carrying about fifty extra pounds of body fat. If he had ever been fully fit, it was a long time ago.

The woman who had been sitting with her back to them finally stood and turned around. Maddock was immediately struck by her beauty. Her downcast brown eyes and full lips gave her an air of poutiness.

"Leave them alone, Boyd," she said.

"Stay out of this, London," he replied

"You work for me," London reminded sharply.

Boyd rolled his eyes. "We both work for your father."

"And he put me in charge."

Boyd ignored her. "Listen, smart guy," he said to

Bones, "you don't want to mess with me. I used to be a bouncer."

"Wow, that's impressive," Bones deadpanned. "Which nursing home? Or did you mean that your moobs bounce when you move too fast?"

"What are moobs?" Maddock said.

"Man boobs. Dude needs a sports bra."

Boyd lurched to his feet, fists clenched. His face was now nearly as red as his hair. "Why don't you stand up and say that again?"

Bones flashed an easy smile, stretched luxuriously, then rose to his full six and a half feet. The powerfully built Cherokee stood half a head taller than Boyd. The train had gone quiet. The other passengers were all watching the two men.

Boyd's eyes went wide. "You're the biggest damn Indian I've ever seen."

"That's what your old lady said last night," Bones replied. Silence reigned for a full three seconds as Boyd stared at Bones, clearly trying to decide whether or not to punch him. Finally, Bones barked a laugh. "Just kidding, dude. I won't keep talking if facts are going to trigger you." He paused, leaned down until the two men were almost nose to nose. "But next time you want me to keep my voice down, it wouldn't kill you to ask nicely," he added slowly, then punctuated his statement with a wink.

Boyd's shoulders sagged and the tension left his body. He grinned with obvious relief. He gave a curt nod. "My ma says I got a temper." With that, he returned to his seat.

"You showed a great deal of restraint," Maddock said to Bones as his friend sat down.

Bones shook his head. "I just saw that the station is coming up. Why bruise my knuckles on his face when we're almost there?"

London approached them with an air of nervousness about her. "Sorry about that," she said softly. "Mister Boyd works for me, but he wasn't my hire."

"You can buy me a drink when we get to Aguas Calientes and we'll call it even," Bones said.

London smiled. "I don't know if that would be a good idea. I'm stuck with that guy, and he doesn't play well with others." She inclined her head in Boyd's direction. "Maybe I'll see you around?"

"Shame about that," Maddock said to Bones as London walked away.

"It's cool," Bones said. "It's a small town. I'm sure we'll bump into them again." He froze, then suddenly laughed.

"What's the joke?" Maddock asked.

"London looks like she's in pretty good shape, but I cannot wait to see Boyd lumbering around at altitude. If they're headed up to the ruins, he might have to be carried back down. Or just tossed over the edge."

Maddock laughed and shook his head. "Bones, you are one of a kind."

Bones smiled and sagely nodded. "And don't you ever forget it."

2

The town of Aguas Calientes was nestled deep in the Urubamba Valley, at the base of the mountain upon which Machu Picchu, the legendary city of the Incas, was built. Accessible only by rail, this remote town was the gateway to the historic site which stood atop a mountain a little less than four miles away. Named for the hot springs in the area, Aguas Calientes had grown up along the walls of a deep gorge. Flanked by high cliffs, a rainforest, and the Urubamba and Alcamayo rivers, it was an island of civilization isolated in the wilderness. It was easy to feel like they had left the world behind.

A gentle breeze ruffled Maddock's short blond hair, carrying with it the savory aroma of roasted meat and exotic spices.

Bones tilted his chin and sniffed the air. "I smell food. That's a good sign. You think there's any kind of nightlife in this place?"

Maddock chuckled. "I doubt there's much of a party scene, but there are bars, restaurants, live music. But the bus to the ruins leaves at five-thirty in the morning. Choose wisely."

"Always tossing the wet blanket," Bones said. "Do you do it on purpose, or is it instinct?"

"Somebody has to remind you not to touch the hot stove since you never seem to learn from experience."

Bones heaved a tired sigh and fixed Maddock with a pitying look. "Maddock, you can't go through life afraid of getting burned."

"Tell that to Joan of Arc," Maddock said.

"Yeah, but we still remember her name," Bones said

with a grin.

"A lot of good it's doing her now," Maddock said, "but point taken."

They passed a covered market area then followed the main avenue, a narrow street that was open only to foot traffic, into the town's center. The town had an air of colorful incompleteness about it, with brightly painted, tourist-friendly shops and restaurants, and lots of exposed concrete and rebar.

"So, tell me about the blonde who Spenser is bringing along," Bones said.

Maddock kept his expression blank. Spenser was his girlfriend, a social media influencer who was making the transition to travel adventure show host. They had met during an adventure race in the Mohave, and she had assisted Maddock and Bones in their search for the Lost Ship of the Desert. It was she who had invited Maddock and Bones to Machu Picchu and was even footing the bill.

"You did say she was bringing a blonde. I'm supposed to be sharing a room with her." Bones paused. "What's wrong with her? Halitosis? New York Mets fan?" His eyes narrowed and he lowered his voice. "Tell me she's not a redneck," he said dangerously.

"No, definitely not that." Maddock cleared his throat. He'd been dreading this moment. "A genuine, easygoing, southern California blue-eyed blond, enjoys a good time."

"Nice!" Bones said. "Does she look anything like Spenser?"

Maddock felt his ears burning, but Bones didn't seem to notice. "A lot of people say there's a strong resemblance."

They crossed a bridge that spanned Rio Aguas Calientes, a narrow river that bisected the town, and made their way to the town square. At the center of the square, a tall, bronze statue of an Inca warrior stood among fountains behind a sign that read *Bienvenidos a Machupicchu.*

"That's Pachacuti," Maddock said, trying to change the subject. "Also known as Pachacutec. He was one of the greatest Inca emperors. It's believed that Machu Picchu was built as one of his estates."

"Cool," Bones said blandly, looking around the square.

"He also built houses called Acllahuasis, or 'Temple of the Chosen Virgins,'" where future wives of leading Incas resided."

Bones shrugged. "I never understood the fascination with virgins. I prefer a woman who knows her stuff. Speaking of, I wonder where the girls are? Aren't they expecting us?"

"Namaste, my amigos!" a familiar voice called out.

Maddock's heart skipped a beat. The moment of truth had arrived.

Bones looked in the direction from which the voice had come. A slender young man with shoulder-length blond hair waved to them. He was clad in Birkenstocks, cargo shorts, and a cheap knockoff of a traditional Inca-style poncho. Bones did a double-take, then slowly turned to glare at his friend. At a hair over six feet tall and solidly built, Maddock was not a small man, but right now he felt three feet tall standing beside the angry Cherokee. He could sense Bones' barely contained rage.

"You have got to be freaking kidding me." Although Bones spoke barely above a whisper, frost coated his words. "Dakota is the blonde?"

"I never said Spenser was bringing a girl." Maddock

took a step back, palms up in a placating gesture. Dakota was Spenser's twin brother. He had a big heart, but he was all Tin Man and no Scarecrow.

Bones puffed out his chest, but deflated almost immediately, a rueful grin spreading over his face. "I would have done the same thing to you."

"You *have* done the same thing to me. More than once."

Bones didn't have time to reply, because just then, Dakota barreled into the big man and grabbed him in a bearhug. Bones was nearly a foot taller than the young man and outweighed him by at least fifty pounds, so he didn't budge when the pair collided. Awkwardly, he patted Dakota's back, a helpless expression painting his face.

Maddock barely paid them any mind. His attention was now fully on the beautiful young woman who had draped her arms around his neck and was kissing him thoroughly.

When they finally broke the kiss, Spenser turned and greeted Bones. "Are you guys ready for an adventure?"

"I was," Bones said resentfully.

Dakota draped an arm around Bones' shoulders. "Cheer up, bro. We have got a dope trip planned! We don't even have to wait in line for the tour buses in the morning. We've got a private vehicle lined up for four-thirty sharp. An hour before the first tour buses depart."

"We get to wake up extra early. That's great," Bones deadpanned.

"And they're letting us stay after hours so we can do some filming without all the tourists around," Dakota continued.

"An extra-long workday. Even better." Bones was

replying to Dakota but staring daggers at Maddock.

"Did you know that Machu Picchu was pretty much the Playboy Mansion of the Inca Empire?" Dakota asked. "It was party central!"

Suddenly, Bones was interested. "Seriously?"

Dakota nodded. "The Emperor used it as a retreat. Most of the year it was empty, except for a small staff that cared for the grounds and structures. But when the Emperor visited, all of his sycophants and hangers-on followed." He lowered his voice. "Some even say it was where the most exotic of his mistresses were kept."

"I wasn't aware that you knew so much about Machu Picchu," Maddock said, impressed.

"He's been memorizing his lines for tomorrow," Spenser said quietly. "I can't trust him to ad-lib."

Maddock grinned. He had no desire to burst Dakota's bubble. Life was hard enough for the young man. Not long ago, he had attempted to market a product he called "raw water." The venture had failed because raw water was only a small step above sewage. Most of it turned green within a day or two of bottling, and anyone who drank it ended up with major intestinal distress.

A trio of men stalked toward them, speaking loudly and pointing at Dakota. At first glance, they appear to be natives of the region. They had the typical facial structure and dark hair, but they were above average in height, had broad shoulders, and skin a few shades lighter than that of the locals Maddock had encountered so far. He was forcefully reminded of the conversation on the train regarding the so-called Cloud Warriors.

"Why are you wearing that?" one of them asked in heavily accented English. He tapped a finger at Dakota's chest. "It is an insult."

"Oh, sorry, dude," Dakota said. He immediately began removing the poncho.

The three young men exchanged scornful glances. One of them spat on the ground while another muttered something under his breath. Maddock didn't understand the words, but he got the gist. *Asshole tourists.*

As the men turned and walked away, Maddock noticed that all three had matching tattoos on the back of their necks. Green and gold serpent scales. He frowned, remembering an encounter he and Bones had had with a group called the Serpent Brotherhood in Guatemala. He glanced at Bones who looked at him and nodded. He had noticed it too.

"What's their problem?" Dakota asked, his voice muffled by the poncho he was struggling to remove. It was stuck halfway over his head.

"Judging by the tattoos, they're part of the Amaru, a nationalist movement among young people in some of the more remote parts of Peru," Spenser said. "They take pride in their traditions and tend to get defensive about it."

"Oh, not cool," Dakota said. He gave up trying to remove the poncho and tugged it back down into place, then took a moment to smooth his disheveled hair.

"How come that's not cool?" Spenser asked. "They're proud of their history and culture."

Dakota scratched his head. "Okay, gotcha. But back home, I thought nationalism was a bad thing."

"I think that's a longer discussion than I feel like having at the moment," Maddock said. He slipped an arm around Spenser's waist. "Right now, I want a meal and a beer."

"Sounds good to me," Bones said.

As Dakota led the way through the small town, they soaked in the atmosphere. From the open-air cafés, mouth-watering smells and gentle strains of music drifted through the air. Maddock was surprised to see that the local eateries were not limited to Peruvian and Spanish cuisine but included foods from all around the world. He only hoped Bones didn't find a burger joint.

"Look, Bones, there's a boulangerie," Maddock said.

Bones glowered at him. "Screw the French."

"The Elvis statue is right over there." Dakota pointed to another statue of Pachacuti. A condor perched on the emperor's shoulder, and at his feet were a puma and a serpent.

"Doesn't look like Elvis," Bones said. "Too thin, no sideburns, and not a sequin in sight."

"I think that was the name of the sculptor," Spenser said, pointing to a name engraved on the base. "Elvis is a popular name in Peru."

"This represents the Inca Cosmological Trilogy," Maddock said. "The condor is the messenger of the gods, and it represents the heavens. The puma represents the land of the living."

"It's believed that Machu Picchu was designed to honor the condor and the city of Cusco was built in honor of the puma," Spenser said.

"There's no city for the serpent?" Bones asked.

Spenser shrugged. "There probably was one, but it would have been built in the lowlands. Wherever it stood, it was most likely reclaimed by the jungle long ago."

"Why would it necessarily be built down in the jungle?" Dakota asked.

It was Maddock who answered his question.

"Because the serpent symbolizes the underworld."

3

They selected a restaurant specializing in Peruvian cuisine and chose a table overlooking the Urubamba River. The décor was heavy with local flavor, and the air heavy with the scent of spices. Maddock hadn't enjoyed authentic Peruvian cuisine since his last visit to New York City.

While Dakota asked their server about the restaurant's vegan options, Maddock looked around, taking in the scene. His eyes fell on a painting in the corner. It was of a pale, goblin-looking man with long skinny arms and legs. He crouched in the jungle, tipping a bottle to his lips. Maddock frowned. It looked out of place here.

"Who is that guy?" he asked.

"Looks like a guy my sister dated in high school," Bones said. He flashed a nervous glance at Spenser and frowned. Maddock and Bones' sister had once been engaged.

Spenser paid him no mind. "That is the Chullachaqui. He is a shapeshifter and guardian of the Amazon rain forest."

"Yeah, I've heard of him," Bones said. "He leads people into the forest and then loses them. And you can't follow his tracks because one of his feet faces backward."

Maddock looked again at the painting. Bones was right. He had not noticed at first glance, but one of the Chullachaqui's feet did point backward.

"In some versions that's the case," Spenser said. "In others, one foot is simply larger than the other."

Maddock looked at Spenser and quirked an eyebrow.

"It concerns me that you and Bones are familiar with the same weird legends. I guess working for Grizzly has had a detrimental effect on you."

Don "Grizzly" Grant was a television presenter and an even greater purveyor of obscure legends than Bones. He had once aided them on a treasure hunt in Scotland and the trio had become friends. And it was through Grizzly that Maddock had met Spenser.

Spenser laughed. "Researching local myths and legends is an important part of my job. It adds spice to our travel videos. Besides, it makes for interesting conversation."

"I'll drink to that," Bones said, raising his beer.

"What else can you tell us about Chullachaqui?" Maddock asked.

"He is also the guardian of the Chullachaquicaspi tree," she said.

"I've never heard of it," Maddock said.

"Dude, it's amazing!" Dakota said. "Its resin is used to heal cuts, stop heavy bleeding, to treat strained muscles, it's even good for the joints."

Maddock looked to Spenser for confirmation. She smiled and nodded.

"How do you know that?" Maddock asked, trying to keep the surprise from his voice.

"A friend of mine is really into it," he said.

"Your friend is into healing?" Bones asked.

Dakota shook his head, his blond locks falling over his eyes. He brushed them back and grinned. "No, that's just the boring stuff you can do with the tree. My friend is a shaman."

Maddock and Bones exchanged glances. Bones gave a little shake of his head.

"Here we go," Bones mumbled.

"The Chullachaquicaspi is the Teacher Tree. If you eat it regularly or take the capsules that my friend sells, it will bring you closer to nature. It can even guide you to plants that will cure mental illness."

"Well, I hope you find some soon," Bones jibed.

"Thanks, bro," Dakota said, the joke going right over his head. His expression suddenly grew serious. He leaned in close and lowered his voice. "But I need to warn you, most of the legends you hear about the Amazon are not true. I would hate for you guys to get taken advantage of. People will try and sell you all kinds of crazy stuff that they claim comes from the rainforest."

Maddock had half a mind to tell him what exactly he and Bones had found deep in the Amazon just a few years before. Of course, the truth was so unlikely that it made Dakota's story about a Teacher Tree seem downright plausible. He glanced in Bones' direction and saw a twinkle in his friends' eye that told him the Cherokee was thinking the same thing.

Dakota droned on about the other benefits of the fabled Amazon tree, and about his plans for a line of skincare products utilizing its bark. Spenser, however, had not missed the shared glance between the two treasure hunters.

"Okay, you two," she said softly. "What was that look for?"

"What do you mean?" Maddock said blithely.

"I'm not stupid. You two were thinking about another of your mysterious adventures. What's the story?"

"We were just remembering a conversation we had on the train," Bones said, inventing on the fly. "Maddock and I were talking about how the Boiling River was considered a legend until someone actually found it." He began to describe a river fed by geothermal springs so hot that a person who fell in would be boiled to death. Dakota found this fascinating and peppered Bones with questions about how long it would take to cook various items in the boiling river.

"Dude, I'm not Gordon Ramsay," Bones said.

Spenser leaned over until her lips brushed Maddock's earlobe. "Fine, don't tell me. I will get the truth out of you sooner or later."

Their meals arrived and they dug in. Maddock was ravenous after a long day, and had to force himself not to devour his plate of saltadito, a dish of sliced beef tenderloin stir-fried with garlic, tomato, and potatoes, and served with a side of rice. Bones went with tacu-tacu, beans, rice, and a fried egg served atop a pan-fried steak. After a few bites, he proclaimed the dish "almost as good as huevos rancheros," a beans and egg dish popular in the southwestern United States. Spenser and Dakota opted for vegetable and rice dishes that smelled better than they looked. They washed it down with bottles of Cristal, a popular beer in the region, and not bad for a mass-produced brand. As they dined, Dakota regaled them with more wild tales of the Amazon.

"My shaman friend has also mastered the song of the Huancahui," he said around a mouthful of peppers. Maddock was unfamiliar with the name, but there was no need to ask Dakota to elaborate. The man was fully capable of carrying on a lengthy conversation all by himself. "The Huancahui is a magical bird that lives somewhere deep in the rainforest. It's called the Huancahui because its cry sounds like a person yelling, 'Huancahuiii, huancahuiii.' His cry has the power to captivate snakes, which are his prey. According to legend, if a shaman masters the song, or icaro, of the Huancahui, he can also dominate snakes just like the Huancahui does. But if he gets it wrong, the snake will turn on him."

"Have you seen it done?" Bones asked.

Dakota nodded enthusiastically. "My friend bosses his boa constrictor around all the time. I tried it and the thing bit me." He held out his left hand, revealing a scar on his palm. "I've got an audio file of him doing the call. I'll send it to you guys. It's really cool." He took out his smartphone and tapped the screen. A few moments later, Maddock's phone buzzed.

"Thanks, I'll check it out later," Maddock said. Just then, something out in the street caught his eye. Boyd, the burly, red-haired pseudo-archaeologist, was standing in an alley, glancing furtively up and down the street. As Maddock watched, the Amaru who had confronted Dakota sidled up to him.

"What are they up to?" Maddock said quietly. As the others turned to watch, Boyd and one of the Amaru engaged in an animated conversation. Boyd shook his head and gestured wildly. Finally, he dug several bills out of his pocket and handed them to the man who appeared to be the leader of the group. The man counted the bills, said something to his friends, and then pocketed the money. He motioned for Boyd to follow as the group headed down the street.

"Either something bad or something interesting is about to happen," Bones said. "Either way, I want to be there to see it."

"I think we should follow them," Maddock said. He turned to Spenser. "We'll meet you back at the hotel," he said, laying some cash on the table.

"Hold on," Dakota said. "No offense, but Bones kind of stands out. Maybe Spenser and I should go. We're kind of ordinary-looking."

"You're not in Cali anymore. In Peru, I'm the one who blends in," Bones said. "Maddock can come along because he so boring that no one takes notice of him in any country."

"Don't be too long," Spenser said. "We have reservations for the Hot Springs. Cold drinks served by attractive young women," she added for Bones' benefit.

"You're sure they're women?" Bones said. Spenser smiled and he nodded. Bones grinned. "In that case, I'll make sure we're back in time."

4

Maddock and Bones made their way slowly down the street. Boyd was easy to spot. A big, white man stood out in Aguas Calientes. He and the three tattooed men hurried along through the throng of foot traffic. It was late afternoon but the tall mountain peaks that surrounded the town cast Aguas Calientes in deep shadow. And with the darkness had come the revelers. Tourists packed the restaurants and wandered the streets. Aguas Calientes was a sparsely populated town, with a modest number of year-round residents, but the tourist trade swelled the population to the point of overcrowding during the peak season.

Maddock was grateful for the cover that the crowds provided. His instinct told him that the wannabe archaeologist was up to something and he was dying to know what it was.

They passed through the town square and headed in the direction of a modest church.

"An old cathedral," Bones said quietly. "That's promising. These places all have secrets to hide."

"I doubt they're going to mass," Maddock agreed. The small house of worship was built in the shadow of one of the high cliffs, nestled against the dense forest. As their quarry crept around behind the church, Maddock and Bones sought the shelter of the trees. To their surprise, Boyd and the Amaru did not try to break into the church. Instead, they moved into the forest.

"Idiot," Bones whispered. "The Amaru are probably going to lure him into the woods to rob him, maybe even murder him."

Before Maddock could reply, Bones hurried away, moving like a shadow through the forest in the direction the men had gone. Maddock followed behind, wishing he could move half as quietly as his friend.

They quickly caught up with Boyd and his party. Bones had apparently been wrong. The Peruvians did not appear intent on murder. Instead, they pushed aside a tangle of vines to reveal an old, moss-covered rock pile. Each stone was the size of a bowling ball. While one man watched, the others quickly moved the boulders aside until they revealed a narrow crevice in the rock wall.

Maddock and Bones exchanged glances. Bones was grinning from ear to ear. Hidden passages were right up their alley.

"I don't think I can fit in there," Boyd said, eyeing the narrow passageway nervously.

"It opens up after a few meters," one of the men said, holding his hands a few feet apart. "We can give you a shove if you get stuck." Everyone laughed except for Boyd.

"It is not very far," another said. "In and out in a minute." He clapped his hands once for emphasis.

"I still say murder is on the table," Bones said in a low voice. "Boyd goes in, but he doesn't come back out."

"I don't know. Disappearing tourists are bad for the local economy," Maddock said.

"Twenty bucks," Bones said. They shook on it.

Boyd appeared to be having second thoughts. "And you are sure he was in there?" The men nodded gravely. "All right, but you guys go first."

Smiling and shaking their heads, the Amaru slipped into the small opening. Boyd hesitated only a second before following them. He had to suck in his gut, but he made it through without much difficulty.

"Do we follow them?" Bones asked.

"Not yet. If the way is narrow and the distance to wherever they're going short, we might meet our unwitting guides on their way back."

"That could be fun," Bones said, cracking his knuckles. "Boyd seems like the kind of guy who could do with a punch in the face."

"I haven't seen Spenser in weeks," Maddock said. "I'm not going back to the hotel battered and bruised if I can help it."

"Rub it in," Bones said. "You got your hot California girl, and I'm stuck sleeping with her brother."

"You don't have to sleep with him. I'm pretty sure there are two beds in your room." Maddock held up a hand. "I know, I know. 'Screw you, Maddock.'"

Bones quirked an eyebrow. "You know, everybody was wrong about you. You are capable of learning."

They waited only a few minutes before Boyd returned. His khakis were dirty and soaked with sweat, but he was all smiles. As he emerged into the evening light he looked up at the darkening sky and raised his fist in triumph.

"It's real!" he said to no one.

"You don't tell anybody," the leader of the Amaru warned as the other two put the stones back in place and concealed them beneath the foliage. "If the wrong people found out we showed it to you, all of us are dead."

Boyd threw his head back and laughed heartily, his meaty hands pressed to gut. Finally, he wiped his eyes and took a moment to regain his composure. "Relax, Alejandro. I promise you I don't want anybody else in the world to know about this." With that, he turned and hurried back in the direction of the church. The men followed a few seconds later.

Maddock and Bones smiled at one another. And then Bones' expression fell. Soon he was scowling.

"What's with you?" Maddock asked. "It looks like we just stumbled onto some deep secret. This should be right up your alley."

Silently, not breaking eye contact with Maddock, Bones reached into his pocket, took out his money clip, and peeled off a twenty-dollar bill. "I hate losing a bet."

It took very little time for them to clear away the stones that blocked the entrance to the hidden passageway. It was nearly dark now, and the space beyond was pitch black. Fortunately, they had brought their Maglites.

"If I had a dollar for everyone who's made fun of me for always carrying one of these," Bones said.

"What do you need more dollars for? You going to lose another bet to me?" Maddock said, taking out his own flashlight and flicking it on.

Bones shook his head. "You get cocky when you have a woman in your life. No pun intended.

"Not cocky," Maddock said. "I just have a very good feeling about this trip. I mean, we've been here a few hours and already we've stumbled onto a mystery." He squeezed through the narrow entrance and took a step into the open space ahead.

His foot hadn't touched the ground before he felt Bones shove him hard in the back. He flew through the air and hit the ground hard. His breath left in a rush and the coppery taste of blood filled his mouth. He rolled over and shone his light up at Bones.

"What the hell was that?"

"Get that out of my face," Bones said, shielding his

eyes from the glare. "You almost missed a booby trap." He pointed down at his feet, where the stone in front of him was smoother and darker in color than the cave floor. "If you stepped on that, I'm pretty sure something pointy was going to come shooting out from there." He directed the beam of his light at a waist-high hole in the wall. He squinted his eyes and peered inside from an angle. "Sharp point, rusty metal. Looks like the head of a spear."

"Thanks, Bones," Maddock said. He spat blood on the floor, rose to his feet, and looked around. The passageway in which they stood took a sharp turn to the left up ahead. Maddock looked around carefully for more traps or pitfalls. "Looks okay to me."

"I'm taking the lead." Bones slipped by him, casting a scornful glance back over his shoulder. "I told you, you get cocky."

The way grew narrower and steeper as they went. Soon the confines were growing uncomfortable.

"It can't be much farther," Maddock said. "Those guys came back quickly."

"Looks like there's a cave up ahead," Bones said.

It was not a cave, but a prison cell carved out of the rock. Rusty iron bars ran from floor to ceiling. The door stood ajar. Inside was a stone bench carved in an alcove in the wall. The place appeared to have been swept clean.

"If there was anything here, Boyd must have taken it," Bones said.

"I don't think they took anything," Maddock said. "I think they were here for the graffiti."

Bones brought his light up to shine it on the walls of the cell. "Holy crap."

Every inch of the alcove above the bed was covered with images scraped into the stone. There were odd shapes, a few words in Spanish, but mostly there was the letter *S*. Again and again, a large S with a small loop at the top.

"Today's episode of Sesame Street is brought to you by the letter *S*," Bones said.

"I'm surprised to learn you watched educational programming."

"Of course I did. Maria was hot. And the chick from Mister Rogers' Neighborhood?" He whistled and waggled his eyebrows.

"You are a piece of work," Maddock said.

They took up their phones and made a thorough photographic record of the strange chamber. Then they gave everything a quick search, just to make sure they had missed anything. No luck.

"I wonder what it was in all of this that Boyd was excited about," Maddock said.

"I don't know," Bones said. "You know what else I'm wondering?"

"What kind of prisoner requires a secret prison cell under a mountain?"

"Exactly," Bones said. "But we'll have to figure that out later." He turned his phone around so Maddock could see the screen. Bones pointed to the time. "We've got an appointment at the Hot Springs. I'm not about to miss the good-looking servers."

5

"**Machu Picchu was** built in the year 1450 and is believed by many to have served as an estate for the Inca emperor Pachacuti. It is often referred to as the 'Lost City of the Incas,' but it was never truly lost. It was abandoned by the Incas during the time of the Spanish conquest, a century after its construction. Because of its remote location, the outside world was unaware of its presence, but the site was well-known to the locals."

Maddock rubbed his eyes and tried to focus on Spenser's narrative. They'd been here several hours, had seen all the sights, and now they watched as Spenser and Dakota filmed segments for their travel adventure show.

"Late night last night?" Bones flashed a knowing smile.

"No comment," Maddock said. He was far too groggy to deal with Bones' innuendos.

"Let me guess. Your little Navy SEAL couldn't stand at attention? I've heard that happens to guys with low testosterone levels." Bones nodded wisely.

Maddock rolled his eyes and returned his attention to the filming.

"In the Quechua language, 'machu' means 'old,'" Spenser said, "while 'pikchu' means 'pyramid' or 'portion of coca being chewed.' I think we know which one is more likely the accurate translation." She flashed a dazzling smile. Her blue eyes sparkled.

"The stones from which Machu Picchu was built are cut so precisely that no mortar was needed in the construction of the city," Dakota chimed in.

"Which was important because earthquakes are a

common occurrence here," Spenser added. "With no mortar, the stones move during a quake and then fall back into place once the shaking stops. It's truly a marvel of engineering."

"And one of the many gifts given to the Inca by the space aliens that visited this area so many centuries ago," Dakota said.

Spenser forced a laugh but her eyes burned with anger. Evidently, this was not in the script. Dakota went on.

"And the use of the word 'pyramid' once again proves pre-Columbian contact between the Old and New Worlds," Dakota added.

Out of the corner of his eye, Maddock saw Bones nodding in approval. That sort of legend was right up his alley.

"Well, I don't know about that," Spenser said. "It's more likely that the shape of Huayna Picchu Mountain reminded the Inca of a pyramid." She pointed in the direction of the cone-shaped peak that loomed over Machu Picchu.

Bones leaned close to Maddock and lowered his voice. "She's just like you. Always has to rain on the parade."

Dakota raised a finger. "But how did they even know the word 'pyramid' unless they'd had contact with the Old World?" He smiled triumphantly.

"That's not what it… it's not the same..." Spenser pressed her fingertips to her temples. "Cut!" she groaned. The local cameraman they had hired chuckled and turned off the camera.

Dakota made an exploding sound with his mouth, accompanied by a 'mind blown' gesture. His twin sister rounded on him angrily.

"Stick to the damn script or we'll never finish," she said.

"I'm going to go talk to her," Maddock said.

"I wouldn't get involved if I were you," Bones said. "Brother and sister stuff. And twins, no less."

Maddock knew exactly what he meant. Each of them had dated the other's sister and had discovered how tricky those relationships could be. Still, Spenser looked like she could use some moral support.

She made up his mind for him, stalking over to where he and Bones waited.

"This is going to take all day," she said. "We've got several locations to hit and everything is taking twice as long as it should, thanks to Dakota."

At that moment, Dakota joined them.

"How did I do, Bones?" the young man asked.

"Good." Bones spoke in a clipped tone and flashed a tiny frown. He suddenly appeared nervous.

"I added in the alien stuff just like you told me to."

Spenser's tone was as icy as her glare. "You told him to do that?" She advanced on Bones and poked him in the chest with a lacquered fingernail. "Maybe you don't care, but this is my job and I take it seriously. Your little pranks are not funny."

"Hey, the pyramid stuff was all me," Dakota said, showing for the first time a touch of annoyance. "Did you like that logic bomb I dropped?"

"My bad. But I didn't exactly tell him to do it," Bones said slowly. "We just talked about conspiracy theories and I said that all my favorite travel shows include that kind of stuff. It's not all my fault."

"Come on, Bones. If you take a dog to the dog park, you know he's going to sniff some butts." Maddock froze, realizing he had just compared his girlfriend's brother to a canine. It was an easy mistake to make. Privately, he thought of Dakota as a golden retriever—affable, enthusiastic, but perhaps not as bright as some other breeds.

"They had a dog park here?" Dakota asked, turning to look down at the main square. "We should definitely film there."

"I think Bones and I will let you two get to work," Maddock said as Spenser slowly turned her glare in his direction. "We'll just explore the citadel."

"That's a great idea," Spenser said in a neutral tone.

Maddock wasn't sure whether he or Dakota was in Spenser's doghouse at the moment. Probably both. He didn't try to give her a kiss goodbye before he and Bones began the climb down to the main site.

"Don't tire yourselves out!" Dakota called after them. "Tomorrow we start our hike down the Inca Trail."

Maddock winced. The other shoe had finally dropped.

"What the hell is he talking about?" Bones asked.

"We're not taking the train back." Maddock kept his eyes on the steep steps in front of him. He didn't have to look to picture the angry expression on Bones' face.

"The Inca Trail is a six-day hike. No hotels, no bars..."

"I know," Maddock said, still not meeting his friend's eye.

"You promised me food, booze, and a blonde, not in that order."

"I no more promised you those things than you forced Dakota to change his lines."

Almost as if he had heard his name, Dakota shouted at their backs. "Bones, you and I are going to be tentmates!

Hope you don't mind my white noise machine."

"You're a white noise machine," Bones said back, though only loud enough for Maddock to hear.

"Sorry, Bones." Maddock could not quite keep the note of amusement from his voice.

Bones sighed loudly. "Screw you, Maddock."

6

Maddock and Bones made their way down the slope to the main citadel where tourists milled about. He and Bones had not yet taken part in any guided tours so they looked around for a group to join. A group was gathered nearby. Bones chatted up the tour guide, an attractive middle-aged woman, who was more than happy to allow them to join the group on the condition that Bones buy her a drink later that evening.

The guide, whose name was Margarita, led them first to the Palace of the Princesses. She explained that the place served as home for the special virgin princesses of the Inca Empire who were known as Ñustas, or Princesses of the Sun. She added that most of the bodies found in the burial chambers at Machu Picchu were female. When she asked for questions, Bones raised his hand like an eager schoolboy.

"Why were so many civilizations obsessed with controlling female sexuality? I mean, nobody built a palace for virgin boys, did they?" Bones asked.

Laughter rippled through the crowd. Margarita smiled and nodded.

"That's a fair question without a simple answer. Historically, a daughter who was not a virgin had no economic or political value to her father. There was also a matter of preserving bloodlines for people who value that sort of thing. And, in many religions, only a virgin womb was considered to be sacred enough to be gifted to a deity."

"I'm impressed," Maddock said. "I didn't think you devoted much thought to things like that."

"I don't," Bones said. "But Margarita seemed to like it."

Maddock shook his head. He was about to remark when someone else spoke up from within the crowd.

"Didn't Hiram Bingham refer to Machu Picchu as the last refuge of the virgins of the sun?" The voice was abrasive, nasal. Maddock turned to see Boyd and London standing on the far side of the group.

"Yes," Margarita said. She glanced at Bones. "Proving that men in the 1900s were just as obsessed with female virginity as their historical forebears."

Several people laughed but Boyd was not one of them. His face turned a delicate shade of crimson. "Has DNA analysis been done on the princesses?" he asked.

"DNA analysis has been performed on remains unearthed at Machu Picchu and has revealed that the people who lived here came from all over what is now Peru, although most were from the Highlands. However, since the Inca had no written language, we can't say for certain which remains were those of nobility and which were servants. In fact, the idea that this palace was devoted to the princesses is not a certainty, although researchers are confident." Margarita hurried on before Boyd could ask another question. "Speaking of princesses of the sun, that leads us to our next location." She turned and led the way out of the palace.

Adjacent to the Palace of the Princesses stood the Temple of the Sun. This structure was so named for its two windows, one of which marked the summer solstice, the other the winter. It was also, Margarita explained, a site where sacrifices might have been performed. She pointed out a few of the interesting features, including the Serpent Gate, which led to Torreon, the temple's main tower.

Boyd shoved his way to the front of the group and asked another question. "Is there anything odd or unusual about this place?"

Bones and Maddock perked up. They suspected this had something to do with the prison cell to which Boyd had unwittingly led them the previous day. They had scrutinized the images carved on the walls but could make no sense of them. Perhaps Boyd could offer a clue.

"There is a natural cave under the Temple of the Sun. Originally, it was believed that this cave may have contained the remains of the Inca Pachacutec, but more recent studies indicate that it was likely devoted to ceremonies in honor of Pachamama, Mother Earth."

"Is the cave open to the public?" Boyd asked, far too casually.

"No," Margarita said. "It's very small and difficult to access. Not much to see there."

"Have there been any laser scans made of the various parts of Machu Picchu?" Boyd pressed.

Beside Maddock, Bones let out a low groan. "Crackpot," Bones mumbled.

Maddock arched an eyebrow. "I assume you know what he is talking about?"

Bones nodded. "There's one self-described archaeologist who is been trying for years to get permission to excavate a restricted part of Machu Picchu. I don't know where, exactly. He claims he performed laser scans that showed a temple, a tomb, the bodies of children, and steps lined with gold."

"Why would anyone look for gold here?" Maddock asked.

Margarita answered his question for him. "If you're

wondering about El Dorado," she said to Boyd in a tired voice, "it is not unusual for conspiracy theorists to try and attach that legend to any site of historical interest in South and Central America. In this case, it is all absolute nonsense." El Dorado was a legendary Central or South American city of gold, the story of which sprang up shortly after Spanish explorers arrived in the new world. Most likely, the story had been fabricated and perpetuated by natives of the region as a way of diverting the European intruders away from their own settlements.

"Not El Dorado," Boyd began. He cut off in midsentence when London elbowed him in the ribs.

"That is interesting," Bones said. "What is he really after? An undiscovered burial tomb?"

"We should keep an eye on those two," Maddock said. "Did you see anything in the engravings from the cell that might connect to this place?"

Bones took out his phone and began swiping through a series of photographs. "Besides the letter S, which is here over and over? There's the word *flor*, which means flower, and over here is *blanca*, which means white, like your pale ass. *Quilla*, which means keel. I don't see anything on the map that would correspond to any of them." He continued to swipe through the images. "This one looks kind of like the setting sun. Maybe there's a connection to the Temple of the Sun?" He pointed to a circle with five lines coming out of the top half.

Maddock thought the circle looked too small for the sun, and the lines too wavy to be sunbeams. But it was possible.

"It's pretty thin, but maybe." He glanced at Boyd. "The way he acted when he left the church last night, he was borderline triumphant. What does he know that we don't?"

"He knows how to dress like an idiot," Bones said. The crowd had parted, and they could finally see what Boyd was wearing. He was dressed in Victorian-era safari clothing, olive green in color, and he was fanning himself with a straw pith helmet.

Maddock covered a laugh with a cough. "At least he stands out in a crowd."

Margarita instructed the group to make their way to the Royal Palace. As the tourists filed out, Bones and Maddock hung back. Margarita caught sight of Bones and flashed a shy smile.

"Follow my lead," Bones said.

"When has that ever worked for us?" Maddock asked as he followed behind.

"Sorry about that guy," Bones said, sidling up to Margarita. "He's an idiot. Made a big scene on the train yesterday. He thinks he's Percy Fawcett or Doctor Livingstone."

"He doesn't dress like any archaeologist I've ever seen. He looks like he's going on safari," Margarita said.

"I agree. Especially since my friend and I really are archaeologists."

She made a show of looking them up and down before folding her arms and smirking. "Okay, if you say so. Are you also going to ask me about lost treasure?"

Bones laughed. "Hardly. We'd like to show you some photos. It will only take a second."

Maddock frowned. He didn't love the idea of showing these pictures to anyone else, but he trusted Bones' instincts, so he held his tongue.

"Do any of these petroglyphs remind you of anything at Machu Picchu?" he asked as he held up his phone for her to see and began swiping through the images.

"What is this for?" she asked nervously.

"We're just trying to connect some dots," Maddock said. "Purely academic."

"I could perhaps believe *you* are an academic, but him?" She eyed Bones with a twinkle in her eye.

"He's the brains. I'm the muscle." Bones winked.

Margarita laughed. "Now it makes sense." She frowned and pursed her lips as she concentrated on the images. When she had seen all of them, she scratched her chin. "I don't know. *Quilla* could be a Spanish phonetic representation of the name Keel."

"Keel is a person?" Bones asked. "We thought it meant the keel of a boat."

Maddock clapped the palm of his hand to his forehead. He should have remembered.

"Keel is the moon goddess, wife of the sun. She protected the women of the Inca empire."

"How was I supposed to know that?" Bones asked.

"Because she also controls the wind and the sea. A sailor should know these things."

"So now you guys are sailors? And don't tell me that you are marine archaeologists, because there's nowhere here for you to dive," Margarita said.

"Well actually," Bones began.

Margarita held up a hand, forestalling the explanation. "I need to catch up with my tour group. You can explain tonight over dinner."

"One more question," Bones said as they followed her out of the temple and onto the path that ran through the center of the citadel. "Suppose that word does mean keel. Does that mean anything to you?"

"I don't know. Maybe the temple of the moon," she

said.

"Where is that?" Maddock asked.

Margarita pointed to the peak of Huayna Picchu Mountain.

"All the way up there."

By the time Maddock and Bones caught up with the tour group, Boyd and London were gone. Margarita had also noticed the pair's absence. She stood at the entrance to the Royal Palace, looking around and wringing her hands. Behind her, the tourists were becoming annoyed with the delay.

"You will make us wait how much longer?" A tall man with curly hair and a big nose demanded in a strong German accent.

"Quit your squawking, parrot," Bones warned.

The man glared at Bones and tapped his own forehead.

"I know what that means, buddy. I hate the French, too."

The German man frowned, cocked his head to the side, and then burst out laughing. "Ja! Hate the French." Still laughing, he waggled his hand at Bones and turned away, muttering, "Arschgeige."

Bones turned to Maddock. "What did he just say?"

Maddock grinned. "He called you an ass violin."

"Ass violin." Bones repeated the words slowly, savoring them, a faraway look in his eyes. And then his face split into a broad smile. "That is awesome."

"I'm sorry to interrupt... whatever this is," Margarita

said. "But that annoying man has disappeared. I worry he has gone back to the Temple of the Sun. I would look for him myself, but the tourists are growing impatient." She flashed a hot look at Bones. "Your fault."

"We will take care of it," Bones said. She thanked him and they hurried away.

When they got to the temple, no one was there. They looked around, but Boyd was nowhere in sight.

"I would say that his questions about this place were just a diversion, but I don't think he's that clever," Bones said.

"He's not, but I'll wager London is," Maddock said. "What do you say we check out this Temple of the Moon?"

7

The pathway leading up Huayna Picchu was steep, narrow, and busy with tourists, most of whom had to stop frequently to catch their breath. Machu Picchu stood at eight thousand feet above sea level, and Huayna Picchu stood nearly two thousand feet higher. Even Maddock and Bones, who kept their bodies in good physical condition, were feeling the burn as they made their way up the steep path. They had been fortunate to get tickets at all. Only four hundred tourists were permitted to climb Huayna Picchu on any given day — two hundred in the morning and the same number again in the afternoon. Fortunately, Spenser had a hunch Maddock and Bones would not be able to resist conquering the peak, and had booked tickets in advance for both time slots. As the way continued to grow steeper, Maddock wondered if she hadn't been wise to skip the climb.

"There's no way in hell Boyd has kept ahead of us," Bones said. "He can't be that fast a climber."

"We're not exactly able to set a fast pace," Maddock said as they stopped to give way for yet another pair of tourists who insisted on stopping and exchanging pleasantries.

"What kind of Indian are you?" an elderly man asked.

Bones gritted his teeth in what was not quite a smile. "Cherokee."

"That's wonderful!" The old man reached out and patted Bones on the shoulder. "I didn't know you all was interested in each other like that." With that, he continued on his way.

Bones scratched his head. "I feel like I ought to be

offended."

"I'm impressed that he knew there was a difference between your nations," Maddock said.

"Fair point. Look at you, being the optimist for once." Bones reached out and gave Maddock a condescending pat on the shoulder.

"Speaking of my pessimistic nature, I'm wondering if maybe Boyd didn't come this way after all."

Bones closed his eyes. "I knew it was too good to be true." He opened his eyes, gave his head a shake. "No. Like you said, Boyd is an idiot, but London is smart. The Temple of the Moon is the only connection we've found between Machu Picchu and the prisoner's carvings. If this were a poker game, we'd be making the smart play right now."

"My dad used to play poker," Maddock said as they continued their way up the trail. "Whenever he lost a big pot of money, he would always say the same thing."

"What was that?" Bones asked.

"The math said it was the right bet, and I would do it again!"

Bones laughed. "Now I'm the one defending the math and you on the side of gut instinct? Did you forget I'm a poker player, too?"

"Do you play by the math or by gut instinct?" Maddock said.

"You know. A little of this, a little of that."

There was no need to continue the debate. They rounded a curve in the path and spotted a large, sweat-drenched, redhaired man up ahead. To their surprise, Boyd was still trudging along, keeping a good pace.

"You know what *my* dad used to say?" Bones said.

"No," Maddock was stunned. Bones' father was a

topic that was off-limits in the family.

Bones smiled. "Never underestimate an ass violin."

Maddock blinked and nearly stumbled, then had to bite the inside of his jaw to keep from laughing out loud. "Don't do that when we're stalking somebody."

"You thought I was serious? That son of a dead goat never said one thing worth remembering." That ended the conversation.

They finally reached the Stairs of Death. Here the steps rose at a sixty degree angle up the side of the cliff At the end, the steps were mere flat stones jutting out from the terraced walls of the cliff face, giving climbers a spectacular and dizzying view of the citadel far below. Here they encountered fewer tourists. Most people, it seemed, never made it to the top. That was good for them, but also good for Boyd.

Upon reaching the summit they paused to take in the spectacular view. Here, high above the clouds, Maddock felt a sense of awe as he looked down upon Machu Picchu far below. He caught a glimpse of Aguas Calientes, scarcely visible in the gorge below. Boyd and London, however, did not pause to enjoy the scenery. Instead, they headed off in a different direction, ignoring a sight that few people would ever experience.

"I knew they were up to something," Bones said. "Let's go."

The trek to the temple of the moon was a further forty-minute hike. The distance was not great, but the path was challenging at times, with lots of sharp drops and ascents. They continue to shadow Boyd and London, keeping just out of sight. Maddock had hoped they would be able to learn something by eavesdropping, but the pair kept a space between them and barely spoke to one another. All of that changed when they reached a sheer cliff face. The only way down was a wooden ladder.

"I think I should go on alone," London said to a profusely sweating Boyd.

"No way," he huffed, fanning his face with his pith helmet. "I'm the only one who knows the way in."

"Why don't you just tell me?" London said. "You and I are on the same side."

"No way. You are not cutting me out of this. Not after all the work I've done."

"There's one way in and out of this place, so it's not like I could ditch you. You don't have to give me all of your precious clues. Just tell me enough so I can scout ahead and see if we are on the right track."

"I've been working for this all my life. I am going to do this."

London folded her arms beneath her breasts. Maddock felt like a jerk for noticing how the fabric of her tank top clung to her body.

Bones had no such compunction. "She's hot, even if her buddy is a tool," he whispered.

"All right, Boyd," London said. "Have it your way. But if you exhaust yourself, I can't haul your ass out of here."

"I don't need your help."

"No, you just needed my dad's help."

"That makes two of us." Boyd took a deep breath then planted his pith helmet firmly on his head. "Let's do this."

Maddock winced as he watched Boyd mount the wooden ladder. The man's hands were slick with sweat and he was obviously running on fumes. He was trembling from head to toe as he slowly descended. London waited for about ten seconds, then followed him down. She moved with a grace that her companion sorely lacked.

A few seconds later they heard a shout of surprise followed by a cry of pain from Boyd. "Help me!"

"Hang on!" London shouted. "I'm coming."

"I can't hang on!" he shrieked. "The damn thing bit me!"

"What bit you?"

"A giant ant!" Boyd howled. "It looked like a black widow!"

"I'm sure it wasn't a black widow ant," London said calmly. "Just hold on."

"I don't think I can."

Maddock rushed to the edge of the precipice. He didn't like Boyd, but he wasn't going to let someone fall, possibly to his death, if he could help it. Unless, of course, he had a very good reason. He had a length of nylon rope in his backpack. It wasn't ideal, but he could make a loop at one end and secure it with a bowline knot so it didn't clamp down on Boyd like a noose when he put his weight on it.

He didn't come close to making it in time. He was still formulating his rescue plan when a long, loud cry split the air. He reached the ledge to see Boyd hit the ground hard, his leg buckling underneath him. He let out a grunt of pain and rolled over onto his back.

"It's not my fault! That thing was huge!" Boyd shouted. The fall had not knocked the wind out of him, much to Maddock's disappointment.

Bones appeared at Maddock's side. "Of course, he lived," he said, with a note of disappointment.

"Let's go down there and see if we can help," Maddock said.

They made a quick descent of the wooden ladder.

When they reached the bottom, they found London kneeling over Boyd. It seemed to Maddock that the expression on her face was one of anger rather than concern.

"Now I *have* to go alone," she said.

"No way. I'm in charge of this expedition," Boyd grunted as he pushed himself up to a seated position.

"You work for me," London said.

"I'm the lead archaeologist, and the only *real* scientist on this expedition. That puts me in charge."

Neither of them noticed Maddock or Bones until the pair dropped down onto the ground alongside them.

"It's you two!" Boyd's jaw dropped. "Why are you following us?"

"Don't flatter yourself," Bones said. "There aren't that many places to visit in Machu Picchu. It's not exactly a surprise that tourists would bump into each other."

"How badly are you hurt?" Maddock asked.

"I'm fine. This bite hurts like hell." Boyd held up his left hand to show a swollen red spot the size of a quarter. "Other than that, I just twisted my ankle." He reached down and began unlacing his boot.

"I wouldn't do that if I were you," Bones warned. "If take your boot off, your foot could swell up so big that you won't be able to get it back on."

Boyd nodded begrudgingly and retied the lace of his boot. "How am I going to get out of here?" he asked, glaring at the wooden ladder as if it had caused his fall.

"There's only one way out of it," Bones said. He pointed up.

"I was afraid of that," Boyd said. "I don't know if I can make it."

"I don't think you have a choice," Bones said.

Boyd glared at him. "I'll be fine after I rest my ankle for a while." His eyes flicked to London for a moment, then down at the ground. "So, where are you two headed?"

"Just hiking," Maddock said in an offhand manner. "Down to the Temple of the Moon, going to take a few photos. Maybe we'll see you on the way back." He looked at Bones and inclined his head down the path. He sensed this would be a good time for them to move along. Boyd had no idea that Maddock and Bones were aware of his search. He thought it would be a good idea to keep it that way. "If I were you, I'd start back as soon as I felt able. It's going to be a difficult hike back and you'll need to take your time with your ankle."

"I agree," London said. She cast a meaningful look at Boyd, who glanced away. He sat, staring at the ground for a long time.

"Thanks for the advice," he said, not meeting Maddock's eye.

They wished London and Boyd good luck and headed away down the path.

"Twenty bucks says he caves within ten minutes," Bones said.

Maddock grinned. "That's a bet I won't mind losing."

8

A sign reading *Templo de la Luna* marked the entrance to the Temple of the Moon. Also known as the Grand Cavern, the temple stood beneath a rock overhang. Guarded by high stone walls and terraces, it was much smaller than Maddock had expected. Inside were a few false doors and windows, none more than a meter deep. It was hard to believe that anything could be hidden here, but he knew from experience that sometimes the most remarkable discoveries were hidden in plain sight.

They gave the site a quick inspection, but nothing caught their eye. After a few minutes, they found a spot nearby out of sight and waited. It wasn't long before their patience was rewarded. London came strolling down the path, trying just a bit too hard to appear casual.

"Six minutes," Bones whispered. "I want my twenty bucks back."

London paused several times to snap photographs of nothing in particular, each time casting a furtive glance back up the path before continuing. When she reached the entrance to the temple, she paused and looked around, then peered inside. She stood there for a full five seconds, head cocked to the side, listening. Then, after one final look around, she entered the temple.

Maddock and Bones followed, moving silently. But when they reached the temple, London was nowhere in sight.

"She disappeared fast," Bones said, looking around.

Maddock nodded. Obviously, Boyd and London were aware of some sort of secret passageway. Something hidden from plain sight. Once again, they made a quick inspection of the temple but found nothing. The recesses in the wall were small and hid no obvious trapdoors.

"It's hard to believe there could be anything here that hasn't already been discovered," Bones said.

"Whatever it is, I doubt it has completely escaped notice. It's probably nondescript, something you'd pay little attention to unless you knew exactly what you were looking for."

They moved away from the false doors and windows and headed off to the right. The ceiling sloped downward until they had to hunch as they moved into the darkness. The Inca had walled off the sides of the cavern, but there was nothing else to interest the casual tourist.

"It looks unfinished," Bones said.

"Or maybe someone wanted it to appear that way." He took out his Maglite and clicked it on; Bones followed suit. The ceiling grew lower as they explored the cavern's depths until they were forced to drop down and crawl on all fours. Soon they were barely able to squeeze through.

"See anything?" Bones asked. "If we don't find something soon, I vote we get the hell out of here. I'm tired of looking at your fat butt."

Maddock didn't reply. He couldn't say for certain that they were on the right track, but this seemed to be the only part of the temple that was likely to conceal a secret. The problem was, they were running out of space.

"I think the moment of truth is upon us," he said. "Much farther and we won't be able to move at all."

"If this is the right place, then Boyd must not have known what to expect," Bones replied. "No way he could fit through here."

"Even better for us." As the way grew more difficult, Maddock was forced to hold his Maglite in his teeth as he slithered forward. If this proved to be a dead-end, it was going to be a huge pain to get back out again, mostly because Bones would complain the entire time. And then he spotted something out of place – a spot of color among the unrelenting gray. It was a scrap of blue fabric caught between two rocks. He pulled it free. It was tee-shirt material. Someone had come this way and gotten snagged as they squeezed through the tight passage. "Do you remember what color shirt London was wearing?" he asked Bones.

"It was a blue tank top," Bones said immediately. "Snug and low cut."

"For the record, I only asked about the color." He handed the scrap of fabric back to Bones. "I think she came this way."

"Okay, but where did she go?"

Up ahead, a meter-high wall of stones barred the way. Like all the other constructions they had seen at Machu Picchu, these were stacked together without mortar. But unlike the other stone walls, these were not fitted together with the usual precision. Or maybe they had been at one time.

"I think the way we want to go is behind this wall," Maddock said. He scooted forward until he could touch one of the stones. He gave it a tentative shove and the entire structure wobbled. "I think this is it, but there's no space for us to move the stones aside."

"Just knock the damn thing down. We can stack it up again afterward. That's probably what London did."

Although it went against his instincts, Maddock saw the wisdom in Bones' advice. He gave the wall a shove. It came crashing down, revealing a large, empty space on the other side. He hastily moved enough blocks aside that they could squirm through.

On the other side, they stood, stretched, and worked the kinks out of their muscles before hastily replacing the blocks. As Maddock was setting the last stone into place, he noticed something scratched into its surface. He held it up and shone his light on the marking. It was a capital *S* with a loop at the tip, just like the letters carved on the wall of the hidden cell.

"I love it when a plan comes together," Bones said.

The chamber in which they stood was featureless, unimproved. At the far end, only a narrow crack in the wall provided egress. They squeezed through and found themselves in a narrow passageway that wound down into the darkness.

"I guess there's only one way to go," Bones said. "It's my turn to take the lead. I'm sick of looking at you."

"Be my guest," Maddock said, stepping aside for his friend. "Just watch your step and don't bang your head on any low-hanging objects."

"Okay, Mom," Bones said as he trudged off into the darkness.

Several times the way became so narrow that, if they had not been certain that London was somewhere up ahead of them, they would have turned back.

"This could explain how this place, whatever it is, might still be a secret," Maddock said. "No one with any common sense would keep going. There would be no reason to believe this passageway leads anywhere."

"Funny you should say that." Bones came to a halt.

Up ahead, the passageway ended at a deep shaft that ran straight down into the earth. They moved to the ledge and shone their lights around. There was nowhere to go from here.

"You don't think she fell in, do you?" Bones asked, shining his light straight down.

Maddock didn't want to think about that. As he stared down into the darkness, he imagined falling into what looked like a bottomless pit. He couldn't begin to guess how long someone would have to fall before hitting ground. It turned his stomach just to think about it. Then he had an idea. He lay down, hung his head over the ledge, and shone his light on the wall beneath them.

There was an opening just below them.

"I found it," he said. "It's right beneath our feet. We just couldn't see it because the wall is recessed here."

"I'm liking this even better," Bones said, joining Maddock at the ledge. "Even if someone were to come all this way, which is unlikely, they would probably stop here. They wouldn't have any idea what was right beneath them."

Maddock nodded. It was a simple but effective form of concealment. It was for this same reason that the cliff dwellings at Mesa Verde had gone undiscovered for many years.

"Now we just need to get down there without falling," Bones said.

Maddock smiled. "You are the risk taker in this partnership. You go first."

Bones fixed him with a long, level stare. Finally, he turned, slipped his legs over the ledge, and swung down.

Maddock held his breath as his friend vanished from sight and released it a moment later when he heard the sound of boots striking hard stone.

"Made it," Bones' voice said from the darkness.

"Do you see anything?"

"Oh, yeah. Come down here and check it out for

yourself."

9

When Maddock's feet hit the ground, he immediately felt a sense of alarm as his eyes fell on a tall figure standing no more than a few paces away. He quickly recognized it as a statue of Pachacuti, the Inca Emperor. The legendary leader stood holding a spear aloft. Behind him stood three more statues: a condor, a puma, and a serpent. Each guarded an arched doorway.

"Which way do we go?" Bones asked.

Maddock frowned. "It would help if we knew what we were looking for." He thought about the clues and then a thought struck him. "You know what? That symbol we thought was the letter *S*... what if it was actually a serpent?"

Bones scratched his chin and nodded thoughtfully. "I think you might be right. But I want you to go first just in case you're wrong."

"Fair enough," Maddock said.

They chose the doorway guarded by the serpent. The winding corridor descended at a steep angle, taking them deeper into the earth.

"You know what sucks?" Bones asked. He didn't wait for Maddock's reply. "When this is done, we've got to climb all the way back to the top of the mountain." He pointed up for emphasis. "And then we've got to climb back down again."

"You need the exercise," Maddock said. "You've been looking a little pudgy lately."

For a moment, Bones' hands went to his midsection, then he stopped and frowned. "Screw you, Maddock."

It seemed as if they had walked forever. Maddock

began to wonder if he had been wrong about the serpent clue. Then again, the serpent was the symbol of the underworld, and it wouldn't make sense for the underworld to be at the top of the mountain. If the snake was guarding something, it would make sense for that thing to be deep within the mountain. Finally, they saw a light up ahead. They slowed down, turned out their own flashlights, and crept forward.

London stood before a stone door. It looked very much like the doors they had seen in the Temple of the Moon, except the surface of this one was carved with the serpent symbol that they had originally taken to be a capital S. She was alternating between shoving it and throwing her shoulder into it. Finally, she let out a low groan and sank to one knee, her head in her hands.

"Need some help?" Bones asked.

London gasped and sprang to her feet. "Who's there?" She directed the beam of her flashlight at them. Maddock and Bones hastily shielded their eyes.

"Chill. It's us," Bones said.

"Oh. What are you doing here?"

"Same thing as you, I imagine," Maddock said. "Following the clues from the prison cell behind the church."

"How do you know about that?" she demanded.

"We're archaeologists."

"Real ones," Bones added. "Unlike your friend, Boyd."

"He's not my friend." London rolled her eyes. "Like I told you before, he is my father's man."

"You always do what daddy says?" Bones asked.

"Not most of the time. But when he's footing the bill, I have to make some concessions."

"So, what…" Bones paused at a sharp glance from Maddock. No sense in revealing how little they actually knew. He cleared his throat. "What's the holdup?" He pointed at the door.

"I can't open the door, obviously," she said. "I don't suppose either of you has any dynamite?"

Maddock looked the door up and down. It was very much like those they had seen above—less than two meters tall and a meter across, set back in a recessed area. He saw no hinges, levers, or release buttons.

"Boyd said he 'had the key,'" London said, a touch of bitterness in her voice. "I thought he was referring to the location of the hidden passageway at the back of the cave, but now I'm wondering if he meant it more literally. Like, he has a physical key. He always holds things back from me."

"We're looking for a keyhole, then?" Bones asked.

London shrugged. "Maybe, but I haven't found one yet." She ran her fingers over the smooth stone block that barred their way.

"It's not likely to be a door key in the traditional sense," Maddock said. "Something this heavy typically requires a mechanism to raise and lower it, or in rare instances, slide it from side to side."

London rested her hands on her hips and raised a speculative eyebrow. "You've had a lot of experience with hidden doors among ancient ruins?"

"Once or twice," Maddock said, flashing a grin at Bones.

"Great," London said. "A couple of bros who like their inside jokes. I don't suppose you'll let me in on it."

"There's no joke, really," Maddock said. "This place just brings back memories."

"Okay, since you're such experts, let's see you open this door."

"Did Boyd give you any information at all beyond the location of the secret door?" Bones asked.

"Just that he found the key in the prison cell." She brushed a stray lock of hair from her face. "He refused to say more, even when it was obvious that he was physically unable to continue. I thought if I found the door, I could figure the rest out."

"What do you expect to find on the other side?" Bones asked.

"You mean you don't know?" London asked sharply.

"Do you want our help or not?"

She tensed, clenched her fists, then relaxed.

"Fine, I'm looking for the tomb of an Inca princess. One of Pachacuti's mistresses."

"That's odd." Maddock scratched his chin. It was highly unusual for an Inca, especially a beloved one, to be entombed in such a secret and secure location. "The Inca believed that biological and social death were distinct. The body might die, but the deceased remained alive in the souls and the minds of the living."

"That's what most people believe today," London said.

"No, the Inca meant it much more literally. They believed that on some level, the dead still lived among them. They would literally dress up and bring out the mummified remains of a revered ancestor for special events, like marriages or harvest festivals. They would offer the mummy food and drink, even ask them for advice."

"Man, you could never get rid of your judgmental mother-in-law," Bones said.

"They needed easy access to the remains of their ancestors, so they didn't hide their tombs like the Egyptians did," Maddock continued. "Which is why it has been so hard to find undisturbed Inca tombs."

"I guess Pachacuti wanted to keep this one to himself." London didn't quite meet his eye as she spoke.

Maddock sensed she wasn't quite ready to let them into her confidences, so he took out his phone and once again reviewed the photos they had taken of the prison cell. London moved in for a closer look.

"Boyd didn't show me any photos," she said. "He only said he found the key."

"He didn't say anything else?" Bones asked.

"When I pressed him for details, he just waggled a finger at me and made a weird hissing sound."

Maddock cocked his head. An idea had just struck him. "Is there any chance he was forming this shape?" He pointed to one of the many rough serpent shapes carved on the wall.

She pursed her lips, narrowed her eyes. "I don't know. Maybe."

"You've got that look in your eye, Maddock. What are you thinking?" Bones asked.

"This passageway descends, but it's also S-shaped, with a loop at the end, just like this symbol. I think the serpent is the key. See if you can find the symbol engraved anywhere in here."

They immediately began to search. In a matter of minutes, Bones called them over to a spot a few paces back up the passageway.

"Found it! The moisture on the walls makes it hard to see, but it's here."

Maddock and London joined him. The mark was at

eye level for Bones, which meant it would have been nearly a foot above the average Inca's head. Maddock immediately noticed that the thumb-sized space inside the circle that represented the head of the serpent was slightly sunken. Bones noticed, too. In typical Bones fashion, he didn't stop to think; he simply pressed his thumb into the sunken spot. Gradually, a fist-sized section of stone sank back into the wall. A loud click reverberated through the passageway, and with a dull grinding sound, the door began to rise.

"I guess you guys weren't kidding when you said you've done this before." London looked at them as if reassessing her opinion of them. "But I want to be the first inside." She turned and headed for the door.

"Hold on!" Maddock said sharply.

London ignored his warning and stepped through the doorway. Maddock made a lunge for her and managed to grab her by the belt and yank her back just as a stone spear shot out from the wall at waist level. It just missed skewering her.

"Holy Mother of Earth!" she gasped as she stared wide-eyed at the booby trap. "That nearly got me."

Maddock took a closer look at the spear. The head was made of bone, sharpened to a fine point, and tipped with a deep red substance.

"Poison," Bones said. Carefully, he took hold of the shaft and began pushing the spear back into the wall. After a few inches, he released it and the trio watched as it retracted and locked into place with a click. "In case Boyd followed us." He smiled and winked.

"Let's make sure we watch our step on the way out," London said.

"We need to watch every step in a place like this,"

Maddock said.

Bones smiled down at London.

"You'll get used to Maddock. He takes the fun out of everything."

"We'll all have more fun alive than dead," Maddock said with a wry grin. "Now, let's see what secrets this place is hiding."

They kept a close eye out for more traps. The passage formed the now-familiar S- shape, ending in a walled, oval-shaped chamber. What they saw there elicited a gasp from London and a curse from Bones.

At first, Maddock thought the walls were moving. But then the beams of their lights revealed shiny, dark creatures scurrying over everything. They were everywhere.

"What are they?" London whispered.

"Dinoponera," Maddock said, an icy tension rising up his spine.

London frowned. "In English?"

"Giant Amazonian ants."

10

The walls were alive with giant ants. They were black with diamond-shaped red markings on their abdomens. To Maddock's relief, the creatures seemed to have no interest in intruders to their domain.

"Do these things eat people?" London asked.

"Depends," Maddock said. "Some ants are predators; others are carrion eaters. Hopefully, if we don't mess with them, they will leave us alone. Still, I say we get in and out as quickly as possible."

"That's what she said," Bones quipped.

"More like *he* said," London replied.

Bones gave a sad, slow shake of his head. "You're hanging out with the wrong dudes."

The trio hastily examined the chamber. Oddly, the ants stuck to the walls, and didn't venture onto the floor or ceiling. Beneath the crawling layer of ants, the walls sparkled in the beams of their lights. All of the blocks were rich with thick veins of quartz. It was a magnificent sight, but nothing to compare with what stood at the center of the room.

A two-meter-tall step pyramid constructed from blocks of translucent stone. As the light struck the pyramid it began to glow. A statue stood at each corner— the now familiar quartet of an Inca warrior, a condor, a puma, and a serpent. The pyramid was guarded by the skeletal remains of an Inca warrior, its dead hands clutching a spear. Maddock's eyes climbed the three steps to the top of the pyramid, where a mummy lay in the fetal position.

"I think we found her," Maddock said.

"This is really freaking weird," Bones said. "And I don't just mean the tomb itself. She's an Inca. Why wasn't she buried with her possessions?"

Maddock nodded. The Inca believed that a person retained possession of their property even after death, which is why people of means were entombed with their valuables.

"She *was* a possession," London said, a trace of resentment in her voice. She hurried ahead to examine the body. Maddock and Bones followed behind.

They rounded the statue of the warrior, stepped over the skeleton guard, and climbed the three steps to the top of the pyramid, which still shone with a dull glow. Its faint white light cast the mummy lying atop it in a pale sheen. But it wasn't only the glow from the pyramid that gave the corpse a ghostly aura.

"She really does have white skin," London said.

The mummy was female, with long, light brown hair and fair skin, now dry as old leather. Her eye sockets were large, and her skull had been elongated as was the fashion among certain branches of Inca society. She wore a flimsy gown of a loose weave. She lay in the fetal position, typical of an Inca burial.

"She's pale, but she's not Anglo," Bones said.

"The Chachapoya? One of the Cloud People, maybe?" Maddock said. He turned to London. "Is this what you expected to find?"

London bit her lip. "Hopefully," she said.

"What is that supposed to mean?" Bones said.

"This is T'ika Yuraj, or 'White Flower', the most beloved of all of Emperor Pachacuti's mistresses. Even in death he insisted on keeping her all to himself. But it's not her I'm looking for. It's what was reportedly buried with her."

Maddock and Bones began snapping photographs of the amazing find. They recorded the mummy, the remarkable pyramid upon which she lay, and the surrounding chamber. Directly above White Flower another small pyramid made from the same translucent stone dangled from a golden chain. Maddock scrutinized it, but it seemed to be purely for decoration.

The statues that guarded the mummy were rendered in exquisite detail. One by one, he pushed, pulled, and prodded them to see if any hid a deeper secret. When he came to the puma, he noticed a gap at one corner of the base. There was an open space underneath it.

Maddock turned to tell the others what he had found. He was surprised to see London standing over White Flower's mummy with a knife in her hand.

"What are you doing?" Maddock asked. She didn't reply.

A loud cry of pain pierced the quiet of the tomb, followed by low, urgent voices.

"Somebody must have followed us, and the booby trap caught them," Bones said. "Boyd?"

"I don't think he would have made it, even without his injured ankle," Maddock said. He keenly felt the absence of the Walther he had carried for years. He had only his Recon knife for self-defense.

"Do you have any idea who it might be? Friends of your dad?" Bones asked London.

She shook her head but did not reply. She sliced open the back of the dress. Her blade cut a ragged line in the brittle fabric, and when she pulled the halves apart, it crumbled at her touch.

She let out a gasp. "It's really here!"

DAVID WOOD I 82

11

The circle of light from London's flashlight revealed a bizarre tattoo in the center of the princess's back. It was no pattern Maddock recognized—just a series of lines forming odd shapes.

London wasted no time. She deftly carved out a rectangle of mummified flesh and pulled it free.

"I can't risk anyone else seeing this," she said, slipping it into a protective pouch and tucking it into her backpack. "Now, we just need to get out of here."

"Easier said than done," Bones said. "Looks like we're out of time."

A group of men entered the tomb and paused, staring at the trio surrounding the mummy. Maddock recognized the man in the lead.

"I saw you yesterday. You guided Boyd to the prison chamber," Maddock said.

"That's right," the man said. "We thought your friend was a fool, but he actually knew what he was talking about. To think the White Chamber actually exists!" He looked around in wonder.

"Who the hell are you?" London said.

A huge man with a broad face shook his fist. "We are the Amaru, and you will show respect."

"Buwis! You speak of things you should not!" the leader snapped.

"What does it matter, Alejandro?" the man said. "They will be dead soon."

"So, Boyd actually told you how to find the chamber," London said. "What was he thinking?"

"He was thinking he didn't want us to cut off any

more of his fingers," Buwis said.

Maddock's gut twisted in a knot. He didn't like Boyd; the fellow was a buffoon. Still Maddock didn't wish torture on the man.

"What are you talking about?" London asked.

Alejandro chuckled. "We shadowed the two of you. Once you and your partners left him alone, we escorted him off of the trail and had a little chat."

Maddock didn't bother to correct the man's impression that he and Bones worked for Boyd. That meant the Amaru were unaware of his link to Spenser and Dakota.

"You are sick," London said.

"We are the protectors of the sacred." He pushed up a sleeve, displaying the serpent scales tattooed along his arm.

"Where is Boyd, anyway?" Bones asked. His tone suggested that he didn't particularly care but wanted to keep the men talking as they searched for a way out of this predicament.

"Dead," Alejandro said indifferently. "He won't be found. We know where to hide bodies around here. Besides, who is going to report him missing? Are you truly sorry he is not here?" He grinned at London.

"Like you're actually going to let us leave," she replied.

"Give me what you took, and I will consider letting you go." Alejandro drew a long-bladed knife from his belt and smiled.

"Give you what?" Maddock said.

"Ask your friend. I get the impression she is the one in charge."

"I don't know what you're talking about," London said. "We're archaeologists. We've been searching for this tomb for years."

"You are grave robbers," a lanky man with a lazy eye hissed.

"Quiet, Diego," the leader said.

Alejandro flashed a tight smile. "Hand over your bags and turn out your pockets. If you are telling the truth, I will let you go."

Maddock heard the lie in the man's voice. Even if London had not defiled White Flower's corpse, the man would want to keep this place a secret. His mind working quickly, he considered their options.

There were seven men barring their way. All of them looked physically fit and carried weapons, knives and cudgels. He didn't know if London could handle herself in a fight, but even if she could, he still didn't like their odds.

"Got any ideas?" Bones whispered.

Maddock remembered the open space underneath the puma statue. He'd only caught a glimpse of it, just a sliver of darkness, but the opening had appeared to be deep. Could they possibly escape that way?

"We need to buy time," Maddock said, just as quietly. "And we need to keep them on this side of the pyramid, away from the puma statue. Kill the flashlights. The less light the better."

They turned out their Maglites and pocketed them. The pyramid still emitted a faint glow that cast the chamber in twilight. A couple of the Amaru also carried flashlights, but visibility was low.

"I'm on it." Bones stepped forward, and removed the small day pack he wore. "Okay, fine," he said loudly to the newcomers. "I stole some artifacts off of the corpse. Here you go."

Without warning, he flung the backpack underhanded like a fast pitch in softball. The pack flew through the gloom and smacked one of the men in the face. He let out a grunt and fell backward.

"Best I could do," Bones said, then charged.

Everything was chaos. Bones ducked a wild punch from the first man he encountered, then drove a right cross into his chin, sending him falling rubber-kneed to the ground. Maddock found himself facing two knife-wielding adversaries. He could tell by the way they held their blades that neither had been in a real knife fight before. Maddock circled away from the small pyramid, drawing them away from London, who held her own knife out in front of her with both hands.

"What do I do?" she asked.

"There's an open space underneath the puma statue. It might be a way out. See if you can dislodge it," he said as the men closed in.

London made a beeline for the jaguar statue, but Maddock didn't get the chance to keep an eye on her progress. The boldest of the attackers charged in. He made a clumsy swipe aimed for Maddock's throat. Maddock dodged it and struck the man on the wrist of his knife hand. The blade clattered to the ground and Maddock followed with a right cross to the temple that put him to sleep.

The second man seized on the opportunity to attack, but he was cautious after seeing the fate that had befallen his friend. He danced in like a fencer and thrust at Maddock. The blade fell woefully short, and when the attacker drew back, Maddock replied with a side kick to the chest that sent him flying into the wall. His head struck solid stone with a hollow thud and he slumped to the ground. Dazed, he wobbled, trying to get back to his feet. And then his eyes went wide and he let out a scream of sheer terror.

Giant ants swarmed over him. In seconds, his body was covered in an undulating armor of shiny black and red carapaces. His cries grew more strident as the voracious insects began to devour him.

Maddock turned to see that Bones had taken down another of the attackers, and now faced off with the three remaining men—Alejandro, Diego, and Buwis. All of them were circling, weapons at the ready, but keeping their distance. They seemed to be trying not to look at their friend.

"Who's next?" Bones shouted. "Anybody else want to join the human ant farm over there?"

As if on cue, the dying man staggered to his feet and made a run for it. Completely covered in biting ants, he ran blindly toward his companions.

"How are we coming, London?" Maddock said.

"Almost there," she grunted.

Maddock's eyes fell on the skeletonized Inca warrior and the spear it still clutched. He snatched it up, took three steps, and flung it at Buwis, the largest of the men. It buried itself in his chest. Buwis looked down with wide eyes at the spear haft sticking out from his body. His lips moved, but only a bloody froth came from his lips as he staggered backward and fell against the wall.

Once again, the ants did the dirty work. They swarmed all over the big Amaru. Buwis tried to scream, but he managed only a wet, frothy wheeze. In a matter of seconds, he was covered from head to toe with angry insects.

"Nice throw for a white guy," Bones said.

"I had practice at Grizzly's adventure race," Maddock said.

"That's five down, two to go!" Bones said loudly. "I think we can finish these two and be home in time for dinner."

Alejandro and Diego eyed the two men nervously. Now that the odds were even, they were suddenly hesitant to continue the fight.

"We could seal them up inside here," Diego said to Alejandro. "Come back in a few days when they have run out of food and water."

Alejandro considered, then shook his head. "Go get the others, those who are standing guard. We will regroup in the corridor and then we will deal with these grave robbers." He and Diego beat a hasty retreat.

"You better come back with harder men than these," Bones shouted, pointing at the fallen Amaru, now twitching in their death throes. "Otherwise, you're all going to end up as human ant farms."

"Laying it on a little thick, aren't we?" Maddock said.

"They don't seem too bright to me," Bones said as the two ran for the back side of the pyramid. "More balls than brains. You know the type."

"Absolutely I do," Maddock said.

"If that was directed at me, I'm going to pretend I didn't hear it."

London had managed to pivot the puma statue, revealing a manhole-sized opening in the floor with a short drop down to a large empty space. A small tunnel led off to one side. Maddock couldn't see where the tunnel led, but at least they wouldn't have to deal with armed cultists. London dropped in first, then moved out of the way as Maddock and Bones followed. The way out was low and narrow. They would have to crawl.

Maddock glanced up at the opening through which they had just dropped, just inches above his head.

"Bones, do you think you can shift the statue back over the hole?" Maddock said.

"Sure, make me do the heavy lifting."

"You're the only one tall enough to reach the thing," Maddock said.

Bones let out a tired sigh. "I hate short people."

London cleared her throat. "Wouldn't it be easier to pull that lever?" She pointed to the wall behind Bones. A tarnished copper handle stuck out from the wall.

"At least someone here has got some brains," Bones said.

"Wait," Maddock warned. "We don't know what that thing does."

But Bones was already pulling the lever. It made a series of rusty clanks, and then loud clacking sound filled their ears. Bones ducked as the puma statue swung back into place. He turned to Maddock and smiled.

"See? You were worried about nothing."

Maddock didn't have a chance to admit he had been wrong. The stones beneath his feet shifted, and then the floor collapsed beneath them. He had only a moment to realize what was happening before he was falling into darkness.

12

Maddock felt a fluttering sensation in his gut as he hurtled down into nothingness. Unable to see their surroundings, it almost felt as if he were motionless. But that was not the case. They were falling and who knew what lay at the bottom?

London's screams and Bones' curses rang in his ears but Maddock was surprisingly calm. If this was to be the end, he supposed it was a fitting one. He had never really expected to die quietly in his bed.

Cold arms enveloped him. A chill swept up his spine. His body was numb, his eyes sightless.

Damn! I'm dead and I didn't even feel a thing.

A sharp shock brought him back to reality. Icy water filled his nose and he began to choke. He had fallen into deep water. He braced himself to hit bottom and seconds later his feet struck a hard, rocky surface. The water had slowed his descent but still the impact sent a jolt of pain shooting through him.

He pushed off and swam for the surface. His boots, wet clothing, and day pack dragged him down. In the complete darkness it was difficult to know if he was swimming in the right direction, or if his friends were okay. He remembered the waterproof flashlight he'd tucked into his pocket before the fight with the Amaru. Getting it free from the pocket of his sodden pants was no easy task. His lungs began to burn, and he struggled to resist his instinctive urge to take a breath.

He flicked the light on and shone it all around. It was only a narrow flashlight beam, but it seemed like the light of day. Relief flooded through Maddock when he saw

Bones and London alive and swimming hard for the surface. Calmly, Maddock blew out a breath of air and let the bubbles show him which way was up.

As he swam, he shone his light down on the pool in which they swam. It was steep-sided, maybe ten meters deep. The bottom was flat, rocky, and strewn with the skeletal remains of many humans. Maddock saw no artifacts, not even weapons or armor. Perhaps these were the workers who had built the White Chamber. In the ancient world, it was not uncommon to execute construction workers in order to protect a secret location.

He emerged in an underground cavern. Stalactites hung from the low ceiling. Maddock sucked in a deep breath of damp, stale air and swam for shore. Bones and London were also bobbing along. When they reached the rocky ledge, they sat catching their breath.

"What the hell is this place?" Bones finally asked.

Maddock told them about the remains he had spotted at the bottom of the pool. "I guess the booby trap was for people who tried to enter the chamber from that side tunnel we saw."

A quick search revealed a corridor that led upward. That being the only exit, they took it. Silence hung in the air as they climbed. Several times, Maddock caught Bones and London staring at him.

"Are you waiting for one of us to say you were right about not pulling that lever?" Bones finally asked. "Because you know I will always pull the lever. Well, almost always."

Maddock gave a small shake of his head. He stopped climbing and turned to face them.

"No, I'm waiting for London to tell us what she took off of that mummy. What is so important that those men were willing to kill for it?" The two men looked at London, who stared back defiantly.

"We saved your life," Bones said.

"And almost killed me in the process," she shot back.

"Hey, you're the one who told me to pull that lever!"

"Cut the crap!" Maddock said. "You need to come clean with us. What was on that mummy?"

London removed her backpack and clutched it to her chest. Her big brown eyes burned with anger, but then they softened. "I suppose you could just take it from me if you wanted to."

"We wouldn't do that," Maddock said quickly.

"I know. I had a sense about you from the start." Maybe it was a trick of the light, but there was a look in her eye that said her words were meant especially for Maddock. "But if you also want what's inside here," she tapped the side of her head, "you two have to be honest with me as well."

"I don't think we've lied to you about anything," Bones said.

"I want the whole truth. Who are you guys, really? I've known archaeologists and none of them are like you."

"It's the hair," Bones said, tugging at his ponytail. "The ladies can't resist it."

London ignored him. Her eyes bored into Maddock. "I can keep a secret," she said. "In the corporate world, I deal with confidential issues all the time."

"It's not so much a matter of trust," Maddock said. "It's just that, in our case, the truth is sometimes stranger than fiction."

"What is that supposed to mean?" London asked.

"We've been face to face with Nessie and lived to tell about it," Bones said with his usual lack of diplomacy.

"Aliens are real, and ghosts aren't total crap. Still want to work with us?"

London bit her lip, looked from one man to another. "And where did you learn to fight like that?"

"Navy SEALs," Maddock said. "He and I go way back. Not that I'm happy about it."

"Screw you, Maddock."

London leaned back against the cavern wall and looked the men up and down. "Are you also archaeologists?"

"We are," Maddock said simply. His patience was wearing thin.

London gave a single nod, as if making up her mind. "I don't know if I'm buying your Nessie story, but at least what I have to say won't seem too insane." She opened her pack and took out a transparent bag containing a large square of leathery flesh. Faint lines covered it.

"The princess was tatted up," Bones said.

"This tattoo is part of a map," London said.

"A map to what?" Maddock said.

"Akakor." She held up a hand. "Not *Akator* from the Indiana Jones movie. I'm talking about the actual story that inspired it." She held her breath and waited.

"The underground city of the Amazon?" Maddock asked. According to the legend, Akakor was a lost underground city that had once been the home of extraterrestrial "gods" who departed Earth twelve thousand years ago. When the aliens left, they appointed the Uhga Mongulala tribe as Guardians of the city and as keepers of Earth's records. The natives were given special stones by which they could watch events transpire around the world and keep records of world history.

"I thought Boyd was crazy at first, but I soon became

convinced. And it turns out he was right! A map to the underground city, preserved in the flesh of the emperor's most beloved princess." London held up the map. "It's probably not a city of the alien gods that the legend claims, but I'm convinced there's an undiscovered city there that is the source of the legend."

"We're open-minded about this sort of thing," Bones said.

"Why risk your life to find it?" Maddock said.

"Trust me. If I had known I might die, I would have brought more than just Boyd." She winced. "Do you think they were telling the truth? Is he dead?"

"Wouldn't surprise me," Maddock said. "They certainly had no qualms about killing us."

"Trying to kill us," Bones corrected.

London chuckled. "I should probably feel sorry about Boyd, but he was a nasty piece of work."

"Didn't you say he was your father's hand-picked man?" Maddock asked.

She nodded. "It's complicated. Boyd gained my father's trust and convinced him to fund the expedition. I managed to worm my way in."

"You said this is part of a map. Do you know where the other part is?"

"Yes." She didn't elaborate.

The tunnel came to a dead end against a sheer wall. Bones cursed and London let out a sigh. Maddock shined his light on the ceiling above. There was a square like a trapdoor.

"We might not be out of luck just yet," Maddock said. "Bones, see if you can open this."

"This is just like the library when you can't reach the books on the top shelf," Bones grumbled as he moved into place.

"Like you've ever gone to a library… for reasons other than meeting women," Maddock added hurriedly.

Bones gave the trapdoor a shove, but it didn't budge. He took out his knife and began working it around the edges.

"There's a groove here. It ought to move," Bones said.

London cleared her throat and they turned to look at her.

"I hate to suggest this after what happened inside the tomb," she said, "but I'm wondering if we should pull this lever." She directed the beam of her light on a cleverly disguised handle set in the rough stone wall.

Bones stepped back, turned to look at Maddock.

"You make the call."

Maddock considered for a moment. "Do it."

London took a deep breath and pulled the lever. The trapdoor swung down. They stood there in silence until London heaved a sigh of relief.

"I was waiting for the ceiling to come crashing down on our heads."

"You're as optimistic as Maddock," Bones said, shining his light through. "Looks like a small cave."

"I'll go first," Maddock said. "We'll need somebody strong to pull your fat butt through." He jumped up, grabbed the ledge, and lifted himself up. Bones gave him a boost up and over the ledge.

He recognized this place from photographs. It was the chamber underneath the Temple of the Sun. He helped the others up.

They were in a confined space. The walls were finished with the distinctive Inca style masonry. There was nothing to see, really, but London seemed entranced.

"This is where they worshiped Pachamama," she said, a beatific smile painting her face.

"Whose mama?" Bones asked.

"Mother Earth. Remember from the tour?" Maddock asked.

"Can't you just let me make a bad joke every now and then?" Bones asked.

"I could, if it were only every now and then," Maddock said.

They made their way out into the Torreon, the main tower of the Temple of the Sun. The sun had sunk behind the mountain peaks and dusk was swiftly approaching.

"What are you doing in there?" a voice called as they exited the tower. They spotted Margarita, their tour guide from earlier, approaching them.

"I've got this," Bones whispered. He smiled and strode forward. "I was looking for you, actually."

Margarita pursed her lips. "The park is closed. You shouldn't be here."

"We're with the travel show that's been filming here," Bones said. "We've got permission to stay after hours, and then we'll be hiking down the Inca Trail."

Margarita relaxed and flashed a coy smile. "And why where you looking for me?"

"I was hoping you could give me a private tour of one of the ruins."

"Really? Which one?"

Bones reached out and took her hand. "Whichever is the most secluded." The pair waved goodbye to Maddock and London and strolled away.

"You should probably come with us," Maddock said. "The Amaru know who you are. You shouldn't be alone."

"I agree," London said. "That's why I want to hire you

to help me find Akakor. I've got resources. I'll pay you well."

"You don't even know us."

"The two of you have already saved my life once today. That puts you head and shoulders above anyone else I might hire."

"Hire the wrong person and you'll end up dead in the jungle, either through malice or incompetence," Maddock said.

"I know. That's why I want someone who knows what he's doing." She tapped him on the chest, stepped in a little closer than necessary. "I know I can trust you."

"How do you know that?" Maddock asked, trying to subtly inch away. The last thing he needed was Spenser wandering up at the wrong time and misinterpreting things.

"You're an honorable person. The two of you could have just taken the map from me and left me for dead. But you didn't. You helped me get free, and you haven't asked for anything in return...yet." She emphasized the last word.

"This is a bad idea," Maddock said. He wasn't sure if he meant the search for the city, or the fact that London was standing so close that he could feel her breath on his neck. He pivoted away and looked up at the rapidly darkening sky, pretending to think. "Any expedition in this part of the world is potentially deadly, and I'm not talking about serpent cults. Mundane things like viruses, parasites, infected cuts, broken bones, snakebites can be a death sentence in the wilderness. And then there are the predators, animal and human. Not that there's always much difference between the two."

"See? This is exactly why I need you. I've actually

spent a lot of time in the field and I'm aware of the potential dangers. I can deal with the mundane. It's the fighting cultists and finding ancient ruins that I could really use some help with."

"You should go home," Maddock said.

She laughed, but there was no mirth in it. "Put yourself in my shoes. Would you stop now, just when we've discovered the map to Akakor?"

Maddock shook his head.

"I'm not going to quit," London said. "So, if you truly are concerned for my well-being, why don't you come along and keep me safe? I understand if you can't answer for your partner."

"Don't worry about Bones. He'd do it for the spare change in your pocket."

She cocked her head. "And what about you?"

Maddock let out a long, slow breath. Of course he wanted to join a search for Akakor! But there was a problem... Spenser. Either he pissed her off by abandoning their vacation, or he joined her on the Inka Trail hike, thus putting her life, and that of her brother, in potential danger should the Amaru make a connection between them.

Maddock felt the beginnings of a headache coming on. He closed his eyes and grimaced.

"What is that face for? Is that a no?" London asked.

"That face is me trying to figure out how to tell my girlfriend that I'm skipping out two days into our vacation."

13

Maddock took his time making his way to the camp where the Inca Trail hikers had gathered. He wasn't eager to break the news to Spenser. She understood his passion for the undiscovered, so maybe she would cut him some slack. He almost laughed at the thought. He was about to head into the jungle with a drop-dead gorgeous woman. Spenser would make him pay for this one way or the other.

It was well after dark when he and London stopped just outside of the camp. From his hiding place among the trees, Maddock could see Spenser sitting beside a campfire chatting with other hikers. A moment later, Bones arrived.

"That was quick," Maddock said.

Bones brushed the sweat from his brow and took a long look at the night sky. "I don't know what happened. We found a quiet spot with a nice view. Ten minutes later, things are getting friendly, moving along at a nice pace, so I go in for a kiss. Next thing I know, she wants to introduce me to her parents." He shook his head, gave his ponytail an annoyed tug.

Maddock pretended to check his watch. "Still, that was one of your longer relationships."

"Screw you, Maddock. At least I don't fall in love with every girl who gives me the time of day." Maddock winced and Bones frowned. "Just messing with you. What's the problem?"

Maddock told him about London's offer. As expected, Bones was eager to join the hunt. He also understood why Maddock was worried.

"Don't worry about Spenser. You need to do something to make her mad from time to time. Women love complaining to friends about their relationships, and if you're too nice, they've got nothing to talk about. Pretty soon, there's 'something missing' from the relationship." He bracketed the words in air quotes.

"That's the dumbest thing I've ever heard," London snapped.

"Every girl I've ever dated did nothing but complain about me to her friends," Bones said.

"Right data, wrong conclusion," London said, rolling her eyes.

"Back to the issue at hand," Maddock said. "The Amaru don't know about our connection to Spenser and Dakota. I'd like to keep it that way for their own safety."

"You think there are Amaru among the Inca Trail hikers?" London asked.

"You never know," Maddock said. "The guides are locals. Even if they aren't Amaru, they might have friends who are. Better safe than sorry."

"You ought to have that saying tattooed on your ass." Bones heaved a tired sigh. "You two hang back. I think I can slip into camp, get Spenser, and bring her back out without being seen." Seconds later, he had vanished into the darkness.

"Can he really do that?" London asked doubtfully.

"Probably, but it could take a while."

London quirked an eyebrow. "Why are you grinning like that?"

"Because the tour group we're with has a portable router, so I should actually have a signal here." Maddock took out his cellphone. Sure enough, he had a weak signal. He had a pair of text messages from Spenser—one when she had left Machu Picchu for the day and another from a short while ago asking if he was all right. He typed out a quick message to her.

Meet me on the north side of the camp. Avoid being seen. Don't tell Dakota.

He watched as Spenser read his message. She played it cool, pocketing her phone and continuing to chat for a while before excusing herself and heading off in the opposite direction. Maddock and London moved back into the trees and waited until they heard her approach.

"I was trying to sneak up on you," she said as Maddock greeted her with a hug and kiss. "What's with all the cloak and dagger?" Before he could reply, she caught sight of London. "And who is this?"

Maddock introduced London. The women exchanged a tense greeting and then both turned their eyes on Maddock. He quickly outlined the events of the day, leading up to the discovery of the map.

"As long as the Amaru are unaware of our connection, you and Dakota will be safe from them," he finished.

Spenser looked at him doubtfully. Maddock tensed. The two had not yet had their first really big fight, and he sensed one coming.

"Are you about to tell me that, for my own safety, you're going to go off *with her* in search of a lost city?" Spenser's blue eyes, always so bright, now burned with anger.

Maddock didn't miss the emphasis on the words 'with her.' He held his breath and nodded.

"Let me see the map," she said tightly. London carefully took out the map and handed it to Spenser. When her eyes fell on the tattooed flesh, her entire demeanor changed. "This is unbelievable," she breathed. "You have to tell me about Akakor. I want to hear the whole story."

"As soon as Bones gets back," Maddock said. "He went to find you."

"We're here!" someone called. The voice was not that of Bones but Dakota. He stepped out of the forest, followed by a sullen-looking Bones.

"I told you to bring Spenser," Maddock said.

"By the time I got there, she was gone," Bones said, casting an annoyed glance at Spenser.

"And then I busted my big red buddy trying to sneak out of camp." Dakota pointed over his shoulder at Bones.

Maddock let his jaw drop in mock surprise. "I thought you were good at sneaking," he said to Bones.

"I wasn't sneaking at that point. I was well outside of camp. But this genius was…" He turned to Dakota. "What did you say you were doing out there?"

"Moonbathing. You guys should try it. It would help with those wrinkles." Dakota pointed at the corner of London's eye. Instinctively, her hands went to her face, and then she dropped them a moment later, her face red.

"Keep your voice down," Maddock said. "You and Spenser can't be seen with us. Have a seat and I'll explain."

Like an obedient hound, Dakota immediately dropped to the ground. He assumed a full Lotus position, sitting cross-legged with each foot resting on the opposite thigh. His hands rested on his knees, with thumb and forefinger forming a circle. "I listen better this way," he said simply.

London adopted the same cross-legged sitting position. "What? It's comfortable," she said when Bones cast a quizzical look at her.

The rest of them sat down in a circle. Maddock quickly brought him up to speed, then turned to London.

"Start with the map. What's the story there?"

"Among the Inca, the ancient city we now know as Akakor was a taboo subject. But six hundred years ago, an Inca priest had a vision that led him to permanently mark the map to Akakor on the backs of his twin daughters. One of those daughters was White Flower, who became Pachacutec's mistress. The other was Black Thorn, who went on to become a priestess of the serpent god. Two hundred years later, a Spanish explorer found her tomb somewhere in the jungle and took the map from her body. That map eventually fell into the hands of the church. Acquiring it will be next on our list."

"Tell me about Akakor," Spenser said.

Maddock cleared his throat. "The popular version of the Akakor story can be traced back to the 1960s, when a plane carrying a group of Brazilian government officials crashed in the jungle. The survivors were aided by a man called Tatunca Nara, a name which means 'big water snake.' He claimed to be a member of the Ugha Mongulala tribe, who lived in a vast underground city called Akakor somewhere in the western part of the Amazon rainforest. He claimed to have left his home behind long ago and had been wandering the rainforest since then, living off the land and communing with the Earth."

"Like, Mother Earth?" Dakota asked.

"Don't start with that," Spenser said.

"Most ancient religions believe in some sort of Earth mother." London turned to Bones. "Don't most Native Americans believe in Mother Earth?"

Bones shrugged. "It's more of a metaphor these days, but I suppose so."

"Back to Akakor," Maddock said in a raised voice. It was easy to get Bones off-track, so it was best to shut him down before he got started. "The story of Tatunca Nara made its way to a German explorer and journalist named Karl Brugger. Brugger tracked him down deep in the Amazon. But Tatunca Nara wasn't what he expected."

"What do you mean?" Spenser asked.

"He was a white dude with a German accent," Bones said.

"He had an explanation," Maddock said. "According to Tatunca, the Uga Mongulala were white-skinned. And among their residents were Nazis who fled to South America in the aftermath of the war. Some of them found their way to Akakor. Tatunca claimed his mother was German and his father a native of the city."

"Some Nazis wandered into the jungle and just happened to find an underground city full of white people?" Dakota asked.

"It was no accident," London chimed in. "Hitler created a think tank called the Ahnenerbe, the purpose of which was to prove the existence of the so-called 'Aryans,' godlike descendants of an advanced civilization. Their research included everything from archaeological expeditions, to witchcraft, to psychic research, to human experimentation."

"That stuff was real?" Dakota cocked his head to the side. "It wasn't just made up for the movies?"

Bones shook his head. "They traveled the world looking for anything they could use as proof of a white master race. Everything from the Norse gods to Atlantis."

"Which means the Nazis would have been aware of the legends surrounding the Cloud People," Spenser said.

Maddock nodded. "According to Tatunca, the people

he called Ugha Mongulala were appointed by a godlike race to be the record keepers of world history. Before the gods departed our world, they gave the natives magical stones that let them see faraway places. Some said they could even see the future."

"Stones have power," Dakota said. He took out the crystal he wore on a thick cord around his neck and held it up. "My crystal always brings me good luck."

Maddock had a sudden sense of déjà vu. He couldn't remember Dakota wearing a lucky crystal before, but there was something familiar about the words and the gesture. He couldn't quite place it. It was like an itch he couldn't scratch.

"Who were these gods?" Spenser asked.

"Tatunca called them the Former Masters, and he said they were from another solar system," Bones said. "It was said that they had ships that could move without sails or oars, and flying ships faster than birds, and they could find their way at night as well as they could in daylight."

"So, a crazy white guy cosplays as a native and goes full Ancient Aliens?" Spenser asked.

"I know how it sounds, but Brugger found him convincing. He even wrote a book about it," Bones said.

"Couldn't Tatunca have guided Brugger to the city?" Spenser asked.

"He tried, but he claimed he hadn't been there for a long time, and in the rainforest, things change quickly. Landmarks disappear," Maddock said. "A week and a half into their journey, they had an accident and lost their cameras and most of their supplies, so they turned back. There were other expeditions over the year. He even led Jacques Cousteau into the jungle once, but they didn't find the city."

"And then, explorers started disappearing," London chimed in. "In 1980, Tatunca led an American explorer named John Reed into the wilderness. Reed never came back. The same with Swiss adventurer Herbert Wanner in 1983. Brugger was murdered the same year while he was putting together another expedition. There were other deaths on Tatunca's watch, but he denied involvement and was never prosecuted or even charged."

"This doesn't sound sketchy at all." Spenser rolled her eyes.

"It gets better," Maddock said. "Tatunca Nara turned out to be a German ex-pat named Günther Hauck, who had fled to Brazil in 1967 to avoid alimony payments. He had a fascination with adventure stories, so he gathered bits of myths and legends and crafted the Akakor story, which he turned into a profitable wilderness guide business."

Spenser folded her arms beneath her breasts and looked Maddock in the eye. "Do you really think there could be an undiscovered lost city out there?"

Maddock nodded. "There are parts of Peru that haven't even been fully mapped. I've seen topographical maps with sections labeled,= 'Insufficient Data.' Nothing more."

"And if the city is underground, the entrance could be hidden in plain sight," Bones said. "Out in the jungle, even if you know exactly where a ruin is supposed to be, it's possible to walk right past it and never know."

"Next question," Spenser continued. "If the guy was a con artist, why do you believe Akakor is real?"

"I didn't until I saw the map," he admitted. "But I doubt it bears much resemblance to the tale Tatunca crafted. Maybe London can fill in some gaps for us."

London sat up a little straighter.

"Tatunca really was Hauck, and he actually was the son of a Nazi, but he wasn't born in Akakor, nor had he ever been there. His mother was a member of the Ahnenerbe and part of a mission to find a lost white race in South America. When Hauck, or Tatunca, stumbled across her research, he came to the Amazon region and embarked on his own quest to find the city. He had no money to fund expeditions, so he created the Tatunca Nara character and put out a fanciful version of the Akakor legend. Pretty soon, he was a legend in his own right and explorers were eager to not only foot the bill for the expeditions, but also pay him to guide them."

"And with each failed search, he murdered his employer so word wouldn't get out that he didn't know where he was going?" Spenser asked.

"Or they found out about his Nazi connections and had to be silenced," London said.

"How did you become involved in all this?" Maddock asked.

"It's a long story. My father has been dealing in illegal artifacts for a long time. Several years ago, he acquired something truly bizarre—a simple gold ring set with a gem that defies the laws of physics."

Maddock and Bones exchanged glances. Spenser nodded knowingly. He had shared a few of their stories with her.

"This gem stores light and shines in the darkness," London continued.

"A glow-in-the-dark ring!" Dakota said. "I had one of those when I was a kid."

"It doesn't just store light; it amplifies it somehow. Expose it to a few minutes of candlelight and it will shine brightly for hours. The Pharaoh whose tomb it was taken from believed it was magic. In fairness, my father's best scientists can't figure out how it works. And it's just a tiny thing. I can't imagine what a large stone could do."

Maddock had seen such gems and crystals and knew their power very well. They were extremely dangerous.

"How does this relate to the map?" Spenser pressed.

"For my father, the gem was a gateway into the more esoteric realms of archaeology. He figured if a borderline magical artifact actually existed, so might other unexplained phenomena. He started delving into myths and legends and working with increasingly sketchy people. That's where Boyd comes in.

"Boyd had been researching legends of a lost white race in the Amazon. He believed he had found the clues to the city Tatunca called Akakor, but he didn't have the funds. He came to my father looking for financing, and the story of magical stones was all it took to get Daddy on board."

"How did you personally end up joining the hunt?" Bones asked.

"I've long been fascinated with the Amazon and the potential discoveries it holds, both historical and pharmacological. I was familiar with the legend of Akakor long before Boyd showed up charming my father with his arcane knowledge and his talk of secret societies. I had done enough of my own to know that Boyd was on to something. His evidence was compelling, but he was holding a lot back. I wanted to know what he knew, and I wanted to be part of the expedition, even if it meant putting up with Boyd. I also suspected he had a hidden agenda."

"Why do you say that?" Maddock asked.

"He's been in contact with a group called Heilig Herrschaft."

Bones swore and Maddock covered his eyes.

"I take it the name is familiar to you?" London asked.

Heilig Herrschaft was the German branch of the Dominion, a shadow organization with extreme religious leanings. They regularly sought out artifacts of great power or of cultural significance—anything that could advance their aims. The Dominion had largely been rooted out in the United States thanks to the work of their friend Tam Broderick and her Myrmidon squad, but it was still going strong in other parts of the world. If there was any truth at all to Tatunca's story, Akakor was definitely a place Heilig Herrschaft would be interested in. Maddock explained what he and Bones knew of Heilig Herrschaft and the group called the Dominion. "They are very dangerous," he concluded. "If they are looking for Akakor, it's essential that we get there first."

He turned to Spenser, expecting a sharp rebuke. Instead, she reached out and gave his hand a squeeze.

"I understand," she said. "You have to do this. I won't tell you to be careful. Just promise me you'll come back."

"We will," he said.

"We'll be fine," Bones said. "Maddock is useless, but I always get us home safe." He sprang to his feet. "I guess we should get started."

"Not so fast," Spenser said, squeezing Maddock's hand. "You can leave first thing in the morning. Tonight, he's all mine."

14

It was nearly midnight but tourists still wandered the streets of Aguas Calientes. Music and laughter filled the air, but Bones was on high alert. Since Maddock would be occupied for the rest of the night, he and London had decided to return to town under the cover of darkness to retrieve their belongings. They also wanted to get their hands on Boyd's notes.

The hotel where London and Boyd were staying sat just off the main square. The lobby was empty when they arrived. The desk clerk scarcely glanced up from his cellphone as he greeted them.

"We misplaced our room key, could we get another?" London said to the clerk. She provided Boyd's room number and the man handed her a key, no questions asked. He immediately returned his attention to his phone, where he was playing an updated version of the old Snake mobile game.

Boyd's room was on the third floor. A sign reading *Privacy Please* hung from the door handle. Bones entered first in case they encountered trouble.

The room was completely empty.

"What the hell?" London shouldered past Bones and stood with her hands on her hips.

"Maybe the maids cleaned up?" Bones offered.

"Boyd told me he always declines maid service. He's too paranoid. Also, he's a slob."

They checked the closet, dresser, and desk, but there was nothing there. The safe in the closet stood empty as well.

"The Amaru must have gotten here first," London

said. "But how did they get in? The window doesn't open."

"The front desk guy didn't seem too particular about who he gave a key to," Bones said.

"I was really counting on gaining access to Boyd's research. I've picked up a few tidbits here and there but he hasn't trusted me with all of it."

Bones opened the door to the bathroom. He stopped, frowning. Discarded towels and washcloths lay on the floor. The latter were soiled with streaks of dirt and blood. He touched one and found it was soaking wet. Someone had showered here very recently. In the waste basket he found an empty hydrogen peroxide bottle and the wrapper for a roll of gauze. He called London into the room and showed her what he had found.

"Someone was here tonight. They were dirty and bleeding. They cleaned themselves up, gathered everything, and left."

London frowned and then suddenly paled. "Let's check my room."

They hurried to the top floor. London opened the door and uttered a curse. The room had been ransacked. Clothing was strewn everywhere. Drawers stood open. A briefcase had been upended. Even the safe stood open.

"I don't get it," London said. "No one could know my code. It was just a set of random numbers."

"A lot of these brands of hotel safes have a master code. Watch." Bones locked the safe. Next, he hit the lock button twice, then entered 999999. The safe opened.

"That's good to know," London said ruefully.

"What was in there?" Bones asked.

"A decoy notebook filled with meaningless numbers and symbols. Anyone who tries to decode it will be wasting their time. All of my important notes I've kept on my person with copies stored in the cloud."

"At least there's one bright spot," Bones said. A lacy black bra was draped over the desk lamp. He held it up. "This is nice, too."

"Give me that." London snatched it away and tossed it into her suitcase.

While she collected and packed her belongings, Bones sat down at the desk and mulled over the situation. It seemed likely that the Amaru were responsible for the break-ins. The fact that they had not lain in wait for her suggested they believed London was dead, and by extension, Maddock and Bones. That could work to their advantage.

"Don't check out of the hotel," Bones said. "Pack the essentials and leave your suitcase behind."

"Why?" London asked, stuffing items into the suitcase.

"In case the Amaru are keeping tabs on you. If you check out of the hotel tonight, they'll know you're alive and are still on the search for Akakor."

"Makes sense," she said. She began sorting through her possessions, putting a few things in her backpack and the rest in the suitcase.

"What do you think is the Amaru's agenda?" Bones asked casually. "Do you think they are searching for Akakor or just trying to keep people away?"

"Both." London closed her suitcase and carried it to the closet.

"What makes you say that?"

"You're familiar with the Inca's cosmological trinity?" When Bones nodded, she went on. "The Amaru take their name from a mythical giant serpent that dwell in the underworld. The serpent has two heads—the head of a condor and the head of a jaguar. Sometimes it is also has wings and legs."

"So, it's a symbol of the trinity?"

London nodded. "There were once three great cities, one for each aspect of the trinity."

Bones nodded, remembering something Spenser had told them. Machu Picchu was the city of the condor and Cusco the puma. Bones suddenly understood. Akakor was an underground city, perfect for honoring the symbol of the underworld.

"You think Akakor is the City of the Serpent."

London nodded. "There are numerous connections to serpent lore, lots of overlap in the clues, and Akakor is in the right place."

"Fair enough. I suppose we need to find the other part of the map. You said you know where it is?"

London smiled. "Yes, I do."

15

Mayra Arizmendi stopped beside a gaggle of tourists who stood gazing at the Convent of the Holy Rosary, more commonly known as the Convent of Santo Domingo de Lima, in the heart of Lima, Peru. It was one of the first churches built in the Americas, and one of the most beautiful. No matter how many times her work brought her to Lima, Mayra never tired of seeing it.

She took out her phone, snapped a couple of pics for appearance's sake, then typed out a quick text message.

I'm here.

She waited. The reply came ten seconds later.

Top of tower. 56 minutes from now.

Mayra rolled her eyes. The man was running late and he was trying to cover it by giving her an oddly precise time, as if it were all part of a carefully orchestrated plan. And why meet at the top of a tower that had been closed to the public for many years when they could make this exchange in any busy bar or restaurant and no one was likely to pay them any mind? Her eyes drifted to the bell tower. It stood nearly fifty meters high and shone white against the blue sky. The tower was surmounted by a sculpted figure holding a trumpet, symbolizing the angel that would someday proclaim God's final judgment.

Now having time to kill, she fell in with the tour group and followed along as the guide led them into the church. Paolo, their guide, gave them the highlights of the church's history, which mostly consisted of being destroyed or damaged by earthquakes and rebuilt over and over again.

"Clearly, God has been trying to tell us something,"

Paolo said with a wink.

Several tourists laughed, but not Mayra. The world was what it was, natural disasters included. The people of this church had never given up, and she respected that kind of determination.

Paolo next led them to the Chapter Room, underneath which lay the crypt where members of the convent's religious order were buried.

"Among them is Santa Rosa de Lima, the Patroness of the Americas," Paolo said. "She was known for her great beauty, but she rubbed pepper on her face and lime on her hands to avoid vanity."

Probably to avoid the groping hands of perverted men, Mayra thought. Several members of the tour group whispered praises to God for Rosa's acts of self-mutilation. It was a shame, really. Weren't beautiful things a part of God's creation? She chose that moment to slip away before she dropped a sarcastic comment that would only serve to draw unnecessary attention to her. She didn't want to be noticed or remembered.

She made her way, unnoticed, to the top of the tower with two minutes to spare. She peered out onto the small balcony and saw a man standing there, tapping his foot and checking the time on his phone. She smiled and took a step back into the shadows.

"You were the smartass who specified fifty-six minutes," she whispered. "You can wait."

The man began to pace. She looked him up and down. He was a tall man with a big nose and curly hair. An odd-looking fellow, to be sure.

She let her eyes drift to the city below. She didn't care for Lima. One of the most populous cities in the Americas, it was crowded and polluted. Frequent earthquakes and their aftermath gave the city the feel of being constantly under construction.

Five seconds before the appointed time, she stepped through the doorway. Although he was expecting her, the man jumped when she suddenly appeared.

"What do you have for me?" she asked, seizing on the moment. "Make it fast. You're late."

"There were a lot of arrangements to make in a short period of time," he said in a thick German accent.

"Not my problem. And step away from the edge of the balcony."

"No one is watching us up here," he replied.

"Every tourist who visits this place gazes at the tower, takes photographs."

"Arschgeige," the man muttered. He moved away from the ledge and into the shelter of the recessed doorway. He reached into his jacket and took out a thick envelope. "Here is your new driver's license and passport, along with a credit card with the same name. You will also find airline and bus tickets there. The credit card works but there is a thousand-dollar limit. It is mostly for show. You will also find the necessary information about the target, her itinerary, and her objective."

She removed the contents of the envelope and pocketed everything except the instructions, which she scanned. Her chest tightened and her heart raced. The further she read, the more puzzled she became.

"This is quite detailed. How did you come by all of this?"

"We have our ways. I assume this will be sufficient for you to do the job."

"It should be."

"Good. There is another task we would like you to

perform if the opportunity arises. There is a man who betrayed us. We would like to buy his thumbs. The rest of him you can do with as you please." He handed her another envelope.

"As you say, if the opportunity arises, and only if it doesn't compromise the mission."

"It shouldn't be a problem for you. They say you are the best, and you had better be for what we are paying you."

Mayra smiled. If the man only knew for whom she really worked.

"Who is 'we'?" she asked offhandedly.

"You do not need to know that."

"Fair enough." Mayra pocketed the instructions, smiled, and punched the man in the throat. He gasped, stumbled backward, and drew a switchblade.

Mayra kicked his knife hand, sending the switchblade clattering to the ground. She followed with a knee to the groin and a solid left cross to the head that stunned him. She drove her fist into his gut, and he doubled over, gasping for breath. A well-aimed punch to the jaw sent him slumping to the ground. She snatched the switchblade and pressed it to his throat.

"Who do you work for?"

Fear shone in his glassy eyes. "Heilig Herrschaft."

"And why does Heilig Herrschaft want to find Akakor?"

The man frowned. "Isn't it obvious?"

The pieces fell into place. This man and his organization had no idea what Akakor really was. He would be of no further use to her.

She punched him twice in the head, stunning him, then used the switchblade to slash his left wrist. His eyes fluttered open, but he was still too dazed to struggle. She covered his mouth and nose with her left hand and held his bleeding arm in place with the right until he expired. She wiped down the knife, pressed it into his right hand, then let it fall to the ground. With luck, the authorities would think he had come up to this balcony for one last look at the city before taking his own life.

She made her way down from the tower, being careful not to be spotted, and out into the street. She hailed a taxi and headed for the airport. The clock was ticking.

16

The three doorways of the Basilica Cathedral of Lima loomed up ahead. Occupying nearly a full city block, the massive cathedral dominated the capital city's famed Plaza de Armas. Known to many as the Plaza Mayor, the spot was known as the birthplace of Lima. It was here that, in 1535, the famed Spanish conquistador Juan Pizarro had selected this site to be the center of the city, and construction of the cathedral had begun. And it was here Pizarro had been laid to rest.

"I'm a decent burglar, but do you really expect me to break into Pizarro's tomb in broad daylight?" Bones asked.

"Don't say that out loud," London hissed. "We're going to scout things out and then make a plan to get the map."

According to the information London had obtained through Boyd, Black Flower's map had fallen into the church's hands and been lost. It was found by a young priest in 1891 on the day Pizarro's mummified remains were to be put on permanent display in the cathedral. Taking it as a sign, the priest had hidden the map with the conquistador's remains. He had told no one, but had recorded it in his journal, which eventually fell into Boyd's hands.

"Chill, I'm just joking. Besides, nobody's paying any attention to us."

He was correct. The few tourists in their vicinity were captivated by the sheer scope and magnificent architecture. The interior of the cathedral was no less impressive, with its polished dark wood, gleaming marble, and shining gold adornments. The cathedral contained fourteen side chapels. The one to the right housed the tomb of Juan Pizarro.

The tomb of Pizarro stood atop three marble steps. A lion slumbered atop it, and behind it was a mosaic of golden scrollwork. On its face was a memorial to Pizarro. The entrance to the chapel was blocked by velvet ropes, and a group of people were huddled around the tomb.

"May I help you?" a tall man in a clerical collar asked from behind them.

"Just enjoying your beautiful cathedral," London said. "What is happening over here?"

The priest smiled sadly. "That is the tomb of Juan Pizarro. It was vandalized last night."

"What happened to it, exactly?" Maddock asked.

"Someone opened it and defiled his corpse."

"Defiled?" Bones cocked his head.

"Disturbed his remains."

"Why would someone do that?" London asked bitterly.

"These days, people like Pizarro are viewed as invaders who brought death, disease, and suffering to our world," the priest explained.

"It's not an unfair assessment. The Europeans wanted riches and power," London said.

"But they also brought the Word of God."

Maddock held his tongue. When it came to persecution, some of the missionaries to the New World were the worst offenders. They enslaved the natives and frequently used violence to force people to convert to their faith. He sensed that was not a conversation the priest was interested in having.

"Was anything taken?" Bones asked.

"Not as far as we can tell. Pizarro suffered a violent death. His remains are not in good condition. They have not always been well cared for as they have been moved from place to place."

"They haven't always been here?" Bones asked.

"Pizarro was assassinated in 1541. Because he was notorious for beheading his enemies and displaying their heads on stakes, his friends feared the same fate would befall his corpse. They buried him behind the cathedral that same night. Over the years, as the cathedral was expanded and renovated, the body was moved and reburied many times. Finally, in 1891, the body was disinterred and his mummified remains were placed in a glass coffin here in the cathedral in recognition of the 350th anniversary of his death."

"He was mummified?" Bones asked.

"After a fashion. The body was preserved with salt and the dry climate did the rest. For more than eighty years, people visited here to view what they believed were Pizarro's mummified remains."

"What do you mean by that?" London asked.

"In 1977, workers broke through a wall beneath the crypt and found a lead box. On it was inscribed, *Here is the skull of the Marquis Don Francisco Pizarro who discovered and won Peru and placed it under the crown of Castile.* The skull they found inside showed damage consistent with the accounts of Pizarro's extremely violent death. They also found a wooden box containing the remains of several people. They were eventually able to identify Pizarro's skeletal remains, which also showed signs of being hacked and stabbed to death."

"Why have I never heard about this?" London asked.

"It was highly controversial. People didn't want to

accept that their beloved mummy was not that of Pizarro. Even after the remains were switched, many people refuse to accept it."

Maddock nodded. Humankind had a remarkable ability to deny the truth when it conflicted with their own beliefs and biases, even when the evidence was right in front of them. In this case, it might have worked to their advantage.

"Whose remains were actually on display?" Maddock asked.

"We don't know. Probably a church functionary whose remains were confused with that of Pizarro some time before 1891, when his body was put on display."

"Once Pizarro's actual remains were put on display, the original mummy was quietly retired."

Maddock's heart pounded, but he maintained his exterior calm.

"Where is that mummy now?"

It was after midnight when Maddock and Bones returned to Lima's historic district. This time, their destination was the Convent of Santo Domingo. They had tried to visit it earlier in the day after learning that the mummy they sought had been laid to rest there, but had found the place surrounded by police due to a suicide on the grounds.

"This place is a convent?" Bones asked, gazing up at the tower that loomed above them. "Do you think there might be some lonely nuns hanging around?"

"Can we focus?" Maddock asked. "We need your sharpest burglary skills."

"Piece of cake. It's a church, not Fort Knox." True to his word, Bones quickly found an out of the way door, disabled the alarm, and picked the lock. As a teenager, Bones had run afoul of the law on a regular basis. He had turned things around in the service, but had retained and honed some of the skills he had developed during that time, including breaking and entering.

"They really need better security," Bones said as he closed the door and locked it behind them.

"Yeah, but who in their right mind breaks into an old convent?"

Bones grinned. "Nobody."

They crept through the dark church. Their soft footsteps echoed in the cavernous sanctuary.

"Which way to the catacombs?" Bones asked.

"Underneath the altar." It was common for cathedrals to include a space beneath the chancel for treasured objects and the remains of church functionaries. It was here that the mummy once believed to be Pizarro had been secreted away.

Near the altar they found the narrow stairwell that led to the crypt. The way was barred by a retractable gate. Bones picked the lock in short order and slid it back

"Not exactly heavy security," Bones whispered.

"Probably not much need for it," Maddock said. "It's not like they've got the remains of Saint Peter stored down here."

"Been there, done that," Bones said.

The space beneath the altar was small and they quickly found the crypt. Maddock hesitated before opening the stone vault.

"I never feel good about disturbing someone's remains."

"The church put this guy's body on display for what? Nearly a century? They turned him into a carnival side show because they thought he was someone else. That's a million times more disrespectful than us taking a peek at his body."

Maddock nodded. He took a breath and opened the vault. A surprisingly small coffin lay inside. They slid it out and carefully removed the lid. Bones shone his light down on the mummy.

The mummy was dry and leathery, the skin distended and few features visible. The Spaniards had attempted to preserve it with salt, and the results had left much to be desired. The man was clad in a simple monastic robe and clutched a bone cylinder.

"Want to do the honors?" Maddock asked.

Bones removed the cylinder from the mummy's hands. He unscrewed the cap and peered inside. "There's something in here, all right!" With great care, he removed a tightly-rolled sheet of parchment and unrolled it. "Holy freaking crap."

"Is it a map?"

"Yes, but not the one we're looking for." He held the map out for Maddock to see.

"Dammit!" Maddock swore. It was a treasure map—a paper placemat from a seafood chain back in the States.

"Somebody left us a note," Bones said.

At the bottom of the page someone had scrawled in block letters I GOT HERE FIRST!

"Either Boyd is still alive, or there's something about this mystery that attracts a disproportionate number of ass violins." He cracked his knuckles. "What next?"

"Now we find out if London has a Plan B."

17

The mototaxi puttered along through the narrow streets of Tarapoto. The odd-looking mode of transportation was an amalgam of a mini-bus and a three-wheeled motorcycle. Maddock and London were ensconced in the back seat while Bones had managed to mostly squeeze his bulk into the front seat beside the driver. After failing to acquire Black Thorn's map, they had been forced to adapt. Now they were pursuing a different line of inquiry, one which London said she had been looking into for many years.

"Where, exactly, are we going?" Bones asked, flashing an annoyed glance over his shoulder.

"It's a place called the Petroglyphs of Polish," London said. "It's not far from town. We don't leave for Iquitos until morning so I thought we would squeeze in a visit."

"And what do we expect to find there?" Maddock asked. "You've been awfully mysterious."

London bit her lip. "If Akakor is the City of the Serpent, which I believe it is, there's another way to find the city."

"Don't keep us in suspense," Bones said.

"The city is guarded by a giant snake."

Bones whipped his head around. "The Yacumama? Are you freaking kidding me?"

Beside him, the driver let out a little grunt and jerked the steering wheel. The mototaxi narrowly missed a group of tourists, who scrambled out of the way, shouting curses and shaking their fists.

"I take it this is another of your pet cryptids?" Maddock asked. Bones ˙ had a fascination with cryptozoology—the search for animals whose existence or survival is unproven or disputed.

"Yacumama is a legendary aquatic serpent that lives somewhere in the western part of the Amazon," Bones said. "The name is Quechuan and translates to Mother of Waters."

"And you think this giant snake really exists?" Maddock asked. It was unlikely, but he and Bones had encountered plenty of unlikely things in their lives.

"This is a recent aerial photo." London took out her tablet and called up a photograph. It was low resolution, but it clearly showed a portion of what was obviously a huge serpent slithering out of the river and into the rainforest. A nearby canoe provided some scale. The thing was massive.

"How can you be sure this is real?" Maddock asked. "This is the digital age after all."

"I had it examined by experts," London said. "None of them could find evidence that it's a fake. And the person who gave this to me has an impeccable reputation." She called up another photo. "This one is from one of those online satellite programs." It was a blurry image of what might have been a giant snake swimming in a river. "I followed up with the company to see if they had any other images from the area. The image of the snake was scrubbed from their site within hours."

"What do you know about this snake?" Maddock asked Bones.

"The stories are fairly sparse. She exists in folklore and some of the stories are way over the top. Some claim she's sixty meters long. Over the years, people have reported catching a glimpse of her in the water or seeing giant snake trails in the forest. Occasionally livestock or even people will go missing, and Yacumama is blamed." He scratched his head. "It reminds me of the Cherokee legend of the Great Leech of Tlanusi'yi. It supposedly lives near my home, but we don't take it seriously."

"Meaning what?" London snapped.

"Look, I'm not saying it's impossible," Bones said. "I know for a fact that some so-called cryptids are alive and well today." An unreadable expression passed over his face. "But there's very little evidence to support the Yacumama legend."

"And from a biological perspective, a two hundred foot long serpent is considered highly unlikely," Maddock said.

"I don't consider that part of the legend to be accurate," London said. "But a giant snake is not impossible. Titanaboa was huge."

Maddock shrugged. Titanaboa was a giant prehistoric snake that reached lengths of over forty feet and weighed more than a ton. It had also been extinct for fifty million years, give or take.

"And there have been reports of giant snakes in the past," London said. "Back in the 1950s, Remy van Lierde, a war hero with an immaculate reputation, had an encounter with a fifty-foot-long snake with a head three feet long and two feet wide. He even got a photograph of it."

"That was in the Congo," Bones said.

"But if it's true, that proves giant snakes can exist. And what about Percy Fawcett? He killed a snake that was over sixty feet in length."

"He made the claim," Bones said. "But he couldn't prove it. He could have at least brought the head back as proof."

Maddock nodded. He was familiar with Percy Fawcett's life, and had heard the tale. "That was also the wrong part of the Amazon."

London was undeterred. "In 1906, Fawcett was commissioned by the Royal Geographical Society of London to map an area of the Peruvian Amazon. He reported coming across snake trails that were five feet wide."

The story rang a bell with Maddock. The expedition to which she referred was connected to a dispute over rubber production, and thus Maddock had not paid much attention to it.

"Any recent accounts?" Maddock asked.

"A father-son team explored the region. They interviewed lots of tribes in the region and gathered plenty of contemporary accounts of the snake. A house on the water was reportedly destroyed by a giant snake."

"Hold on." Bones held up his hand. "Are these the guys who posted pictures of a sandbar and called it a giant snake?"

"I don't care if you believe me. This is the trail we're following. Unless one of you has a better plan." Glowering, London closed her tablet and tucked it into her backpack.

Maddock had no other ideas. They had sent the map to their friend, Jimmy Letson, an accomplished hacker, to see if he could match it to any known landmarks. He had quickly declared it an impossible task. Too much of the Amazon was unmapped, and there was no telling if the lines on the map corresponded with rivers, old Inca Roads, or any number of other possibilities.

"We always keep an open mind," Bones said. "Just don't get your hopes up."

"I'm not hoping to find a giant snake," she said. "I want to find Akakor, and I think the serpent legends and eyewitness accounts will help us get there."

Up ahead, a gate barred the narrow road. As the mototaxi drew near, two unsavory looking men raised the gate and watched them pass through.

"Security guards?" Maddock asked.

"Ronderos. They call themselves law enforcement, but they are not official."

"Just what the world needs. Armed, untrained civilians trying to play cop." Bones turned and stared at the men as the mototaxi bounded along the rough road.

"Not our problem," Maddock said. "We have bigger fish to fry."

Bones flashed a wicked grin. "I think you mean bigger snakes."

18

The Petroglyphs of Polish were located eight kilometers outside of Tarapoto. Given its out of the way location and the lack of public transportation to the site, it was considered one of Peru's undiscovered treasures. London paid the driver and promised him double for the return journey if he waited while they explored the petroglyphs. He was more than happy to wait for the guaranteed fare and settled down in the shade for a nap.

Maddock was surprised by how small the site was. If any secrets were hidden here, a skeptic would assume they had already been uncovered. But he and Bones had plenty of experience with clues being hidden in plain sight. Despite its lack of breadth, the place had an otherworldly vibe that seemed to affect the others as well.

"It's strange," London said. "I know we're only a few miles from civilization but there's something about this place that makes me feel like I've stepped into another world."

"Welcome to the jungle," Bones said. His voice was unusually subdued. "What are we looking for?"

"I'm not sure," London admitted. "My research indicated this place is connected to the City of the Serpent, but I never learned anything definitive. I scoured the web and never found a complete photographic or video record of the site. We don't leave until morning, so I figured why not see if we can find something useful."

"What happens if we come up empty?" Bones asked.

"I thought Maddock was the cynic." London reached up and gave his cheek a condescending pat. "I have plenty for us to go on, including the bits and pieces I was able to glean from Boyd's work. I'm just hoping for a little bit more."

The caretaker was a man of late middle years with rheumy eyes, whiskey breath, and lots of ear hair. He introduced himself as Romario. He seemed pleased to have visitors.

"Few tourists visit here," he said. "We are small and the road is rough." He made an up and down motion with his hand.

"What can you tell us about the petroglyphs?" London asked.

Despite his muzzy demeanor, Romario proved to be a competent guide, giving them a thorough background of the site.

"The petroglyphs were discovered in 1966," he began. "Since that time, the site has been given very little attention. A few archaeologists have visited, but no one has conducted a serious study."

"Why is that?" London asked.

"They do not understand the importance of the site. They look at the petroglyphs and they see only plants, animals, simple shapes, and curvy lines." He made a curlicue with his index finger. "But they ignore the more mysterious images."

"Mysterious? I like the sound of that," Bones said.

The site consisted of five large boulders the color of asphalt. Each was covered in images carved into the surface and highlighted with white mineral pigments. Sheltered by thick vegetation, it was little wonder that they had gone undiscovered for so long.

Romario began by pointing out some of the more obvious petroglyphs—birds, monkeys, and snakes. Maddock raised his eyebrows at the sight of the snakes.

They were all rendered in the same way as the images they had found on the walls of the hidden prison cell in Auguas Calientes. Aside from the visual similarities, though, there appeared to be no significance to the images, which were scattered among other commonplace images. As they continued, the images became more interesting.

One was of a four-legged creature with a humped back, serpentine neck, pointed head, and a long tail. Romario pointed at the image and grinned.

"What does this look like to you?" the guide asked.

"Dude, that is a dinosaur," Bones said.

"Archaeologists say it is a dog." Romario rolled his eyes and Bones did the same. Maddock had to agree with them. This petroglyph was obviously a representation of a dinosaur.

"This one," Romario said, pointing to a figure with a square head, "is what Americans would call..." He paused, ran a hand through his thinning black hair. "Elderly aliens?" He grabbed two handfuls of his own hair and pulled it up, making it stand on end.

"You mean *Ancient Aliens*," Bones said. "The television show. I'm a big fan."

Romario nodded eagerly. "You must see this next rock." He led them to a boulder covered with odd geometric shapes. "You like?" he asked, beaming.

"They're cool," Bones said.

"What do these symbols represent?" London asked. "They don't resemble anything in nature that I can think of."

"These are special." Romario looked around, as if someone might overhear them, and then lowered his voice. "Some people say that they have no meaning, that they are products of too much Ayahuasca."

Maddock nodded. Known as the "Rope from the Dead," Ayahuasca was a brew made from local flora. It was commonly used in native religious ceremonies due to its hallucinogenic properties. In recent years, people had begun using it for its alleged antidepressant effects.

"Give us the straight dope," Bones said. He smiled, but his face fell when his pun fell flat.

"The elders say these symbols were left to us by the gods. They are the key to another world." The guide lowered his voice to a whisper. "The underworld."

London flashed a questioning glance at Maddock. He knew what she was thinking. This was a clue that could potentially bridge the gap between the Akakor and Serpent mythology.

"If these are the keys, where is the door?" Bones asked as London took photos of the symbols.

"You have to follow the map," he said simply.

"Map?" Maddock asked. "Where?"

Romario led them around a stand of palm and fruit trees and past a rectangular stone adorned with a single row of dots running around the top edge.

"What is that?" Bones asked.

"Sacrificial altar," Romario said with an air of disinterest.

Bones frowned. "Who got sacrificed there?"

"American tourists who ask questions." Romario glanced back and smiled. "I have jokes, too."

"I like you!" Bones said.

They stopped in front of a broad, flat stone. A series of wavy lines, loops, curls, and circles covered the surface. Maddock couldn't deny that it resembled a map.

"The straighter lines could be roads," Bones said. "And those looping double-lines might be rivers. Maybe tributaries of the Amazon?"

London turned to Romario. "Has anyone studied this? Compared it to known maps of the region?"

Romario shrugged. "A few have tried. One said these are rivers. Another said it showed old Inca roads. But no one has succeeded."

"That is music to my ears," Bones said.

"Is it possible that this is not a map of something on the surface?" Maddock asked.

Romario frowned and scratched his chin. "I am not sure what you mean."

"Could it be, I don't know, underground?" Maddock tried to keep his tone casual, but Romario blanched.

"I have taken too long. I should go to the gate. You never know. Maybe we will get five paying customers in the same day." He forced a laugh and then hurried away.

"That was weird," Maddock said. "Did he misspeak or was there somebody else here before us?"

"One person was here," Bones said. "I see fresh prints from a pair of hiking boots. About a man's size ten. And the prints are deep. The guy was heavy."

Maddock moved in for a closer look. The two knelt and inspected the prints.

"You can see the tread clearly, even the brand name. These boots were probably purchased recently," Maddock said.

"Not bad for a white dude," Bones said. "But you missed something."

"What's that?"

"The imprints of the left foot are shallower, with little of the heel showing. This person was limping."

Maddock and Bones turned to look at London. She was slowly shaking her head.

"Boyd is alive. That son of a bitch. He must have made a deal with the Amaru." She cursed and kicked at the earth. "I should have suspected. And now he's ahead of us."

"Not necessarily," Maddock said. "Matching this map up to any known location will take some time."

"Considering the way Romario reacted when I mentioned caves, I think it's safe to say Boyd was asking about the underworld."

"Surely we can locate that river. It's large and distinctive in shape." She pointed to a wavy line that ran along the left side of the map, ending in a small lake.

"I don't think that's a river." Bones had followed Boyd's tracks around to the side of the rock. "You guys come and look at it from this angle."

They moved around to stand alongside Bones. He was correct. Seen from this perspective, what he had thought was a river looked like something else entirely.

"Oh, my Goddess!" London breathed.

Bones grimaced. "That is one big snake."

19

They left Tarapoto early the following morning. London had arranged a driver with a Jeep for the first leg of their journey. After that, a boat would take them to their lodge outside of Iquitos, where they would meet their guide and secure provisions for their trek into the Amazon.

The road was bumpy, the air cool and moist. The jungle grew right up to the edge of the road, giving the place an oppressive feel.

While Bones snoozed in the front seat, Maddock and London reviewed the information they had collected.

"I have no idea what to make of these symbols," Maddock said. "They don't correspond to any known Inca symbols I've found. Same with the map."

"I'm surprised your hacker friend hasn't come up with anything," London said.

"It's not like he can scan an image, click a button, and, voila, he's solved an ancient mystery," Maddock said. "That only happens in thriller novels. There's typically a lot of manual comparisons involved. It's time-consuming. Something he loves to remind me about."

"Maddock, it is far too early to start speaking French," Bones said, eyes still closed.

"What time is a good time?" London asked.

"Half past never."

The driver slowed the jeep and Maddock glanced up to see a group of armed men and women barring the road up ahead.

"Ronderos," the driver muttered, bringing the vehicle to a halt.

"These guys again?" Bones complained. Upon leaving

the Petroglyphs of Polish the day before, they had found the gate closed and the ronderos that guarded it had demanded what they called a "security fee." They had only wanted ten Peruvian soles, about three American dollars, so Maddock had paid the fee despite Bones' protests.

"What's our move?" Bones asked.

"Just follow my lead and be ready for anything," Maddock said. Hopefully, like their counterparts in Tarapoto, these highwaymen only wanted a toll. He could live with that if it meant avoiding bloodshed. He wasn't worried about himself or Bones, but he preferred not to put London's life at risk if he could help it.

The ronderos surrounded the Jeep. Only a couple of them carried firearms. The others bore clubs and knives. One of them began barking orders in Spanish. Maddock and Bones understood enough to know they were being ordered out of the vehicle.

One of the men approached London, speaking softly. He reached out and caressed her cheek. Before Maddock or Bones could make a move, London kneed him in the groin. He let out a grunt and his knees buckled. As he sank to the ground, one of his companions pointed a pistol at the back of her head.

"Hands... behind... head," he ordered in slow, heavily accented English.

London complied, staring daggers at their captors. The man she had injured slowly regained his feet. He spat on the ground and then fixed her with a lascivious grin. He tucked his pistol into his belt and began frisking her.

"No way!" London took a step back, then turned toward one of the female ronderos. "If somebody's going to pat me down, I want a woman to do it."

Despite the language barrier, the ronderos

understood. They began to laugh and engaged in an animated argument over who would be the one to search her.

As the argument continued, Maddock noticed that their driver had drifted away from the group. He and one of the ronderos had moved into the shelter of the forest and were chatting amiably.

Scarlet rage burned through Maddock. They had been betrayed.

"Your ears are turning red," Bones said. "That means you're either pissed off or a girl has seen your tiny package."

"Looks like we've been set up," Maddock whispered as the ronderos continued to banter and make crude comments about London. "And I've got a feeling they've got more on their mind than a simple toll."

"I'm ready when you are," Bones said.

Five ronderos stood near London, arguing over who was going to do what to her. Two carried handguns. They had faced worse odds before.

Maddock caught London's eye. "Hit the ground and crawl to the woods," he whispered. She nodded. Maddock glanced at Bones then mouthed a countdown. Three... two...

Earlier, London had secured handguns for them—a Walther for Maddock and Glock from Bones in accordance with their preferencest— and on one, he and Bones drew their weapons and fired. Maddock put two bullets into the rondero who had manhandled London. Bones took out the other man who carried a pistol.

All was chaos. The ronderos scattered into the jungle, leaving their wounded companions behind. Bones squeezed off a shot in the direction of their driver and his companion, who turned and ran. London had followed orders and was down on all fours, scurrying for the jungle's cover.

"We need to get out of here quickly, before they recover." Maddock glanced at the Jeep and saw the driver had taken the keys with him.

"I can hotwire it," Bones said.

Just then, shots rang out. Their driver had drawn a small caliber pistol and opened fire. Maddock squeezed off a single shot that missed, but it forced the man to hit the deck.

"Quickly!" Maddock barked. The ronderos had regrouped. He could hear them creeping forward. A knife flew through the air and just missed him. He scooped up their backpacks, fired off another shot, and made a dash for the spot where London had vanished into the trees.

There were more gunshots, shouts of alarm. A bullet zipped past his ear. And then the forest enveloped him. He found London hunkered down behind the twisted trunk of a kapok tree. She was breathing hard from exertion but was surprisingly calm.

"Nice job," she said. "I didn't think we'd get out of that one." She looked around. "Where's Bonebrake?" she whispered.

"I'm here," a voice said from a few feet away. Bones emerged from the foliage. He had a pair of pistols tucked into his belt.

"Goddess! I didn't even hear you," she whispered.

"I'm very good," Bones said.

"What took you so long?" Maddock asked.

"I disarmed the dudes we shot. I don't think either of them is going to make it, but I didn't want their friends getting any ideas." He glanced at London. "I'll bet you'd like to get your hands on my gun," he said with a smile.

London rolled her eyes. She snatched one of the pistols, a nine-millimeter, from his waistband. She engaged the safety, checked to make sure a round was in the chamber, then popped out the magazine. "Six rounds counting the one in the chamber."

"You know your weapons," Maddock said.

"A little bit." Her cheeks went pink at the compliment. "What do we do now?"

"We're only a few kilometers from where we are supposed to catch our boat. We'll have to hoof it from here," Maddock said.

"They've got a Jeep," London said. "What's to stop them from getting there ahead of us?"

"That thing won't be going anywhere anytime soon," Bones said. "I didn't have time to hotwire it, but if you know what you're doing, it only takes a few seconds to jack up the ignition." He held up a wire.

"Nice one," Maddock said. "We should keep away from the road in any case. As the crow flies, it's the shortest route to our destination, and we won't have to worry about encountering any more ronderos."

"What if they try to follow us?" London said.

"Maddock smiled. "I'd like to see them try."

20

"**Are you sure** we're going the right way?" Bones raised up on his tiptoes and made a show of peering into the darkness ahead. The thick jungle canopy blocked out the worst of the midday sun, but the oppressive heat remained. Bones tugged at his shirt, pulling the damp, clinging fabric away from his skin. It was like hiking in a greenhouse.

"It shouldn't be much farther," Maddock said, slicing through hanging vines with his machete.

"You're imagining those vines are me, aren't you?" Bones asked.

"Only some of the time."

The going had been slow. With no guide and no trail to follow, they were relying on Maddock's orienteering skills to find their way. Their route had taken them through unforgiving terrain, and they'd been forced to carve a path through the jungle. London had kept pace and not uttered a word of complaint.

"I hear a river up ahead," Bones said. "Maybe we're there."

Unfortunately, the river they arrived at was not the one they were trying to reach, nor was it on Maddock's map. And there was no way across.

"Are you freaking kidding me?" Bones said. "Are we going to have to swim for it?"

Maddock let out a tired sigh. The weariness wasn't physical; it was Bones' grumbling. He couldn't imagine how much the man would complain if he had to walk the rest of the way soaking wet.

"We don't have to cross right away. We can check

along the bank and see if there's a better way to get to the other side."

Bones nodded. "Upstream or downstream?"

"Guys?" London said quietly.

There was something in her tone of voice that set off alarms inside Maddock. He turned in her direction and saw she was trembling.

"What is it?" Bones asked, looking back in the direction from which they had come. "Did the ronderos follow us?"

She slowly shook her head. Her eyes were wide as saucers.

"I think we should go upriver."

"Okay, why?" Maddock asked.

London raised her hand and pointed a trembling finger.

"Because in the other direction is a giant snake."

Mayra fanned away a cloud of exhaust as the leaky boat eased up to the pier. Nicknamed the "Capital of the Peruvian Amazon," Iquitos was the jumping-off point for expeditions on this stretch of the Amazon. It was located at the confluence of the Amazon, Nanay, and Itaya Rivers. Peru's ninth-largest city, it could only be reached by boat or plane, making it the world's largest city that could not be reached by road.

Beneath the scorching sun, dugout canoes plied the water alongside luxury cruisers, and on the docks, well-dressed tourists mingled with people who could easily pass for forest dwellers. For all Mayra knew, some of them might actually live in the woods. Iquitos was penned in on all sides by jungle. A person could literally enjoy a meal at a fine restaurant, walk for five minutes, and become hopelessly lost in the Amazon. For all its modern trappings, the city was truly a jungle outpost.

She hired a mototaxi to take her to the lodge where a room had been reserved for her under a false identity. The streets were chaotic, with mototaxis and bicycles weaving around tourists and locals alike. Along the way, she passed mud huts, luxurious homes, and everything in between. She smiled, imagining what a Homeowners Association in the US would say about the local zoning and planning ordinances.

The Casa de Caiman was built on the riverbank near Belen, the floating market district. The décor was rustic, but the room was clean and the water pressure respectable. She treated herself to a long shower and a brief power nap. Her trip to Iquitos had been a series of broken-down trucks, leaky boats, and creepy drivers and pilots who weren't half as charming as they thought they were. She needed the break.

An hour later feeling refreshed, she got down to business. She reviewed the dossier she had received from the contact in Lima.

"London Margaret Thatcher," she read aloud. "Seriously? And she's not even from England."

London was the only daughter of William Thatcher, a powerful businessman. She worked in corporate law but had a passion for environmental causes. She was rumored to have served as her father's agent in the illegal antiquities market.

Mayra scanned down to London's itinerary. She was scheduled to arrive in Iquitos by boat the following morning and would meet their guide, a young man named Giancarlo, at midday. The itinerary also included the name of the pilot whose boat Giancarlo had secured for their journey, and the name of the lodge where they would be staying the following night. She wondered who had provided the information. It would have to be someone close to London.

"Never trust anybody," she whispered. "Especially those closest to you."

Next, she read up on Giancarlo, familiarized herself with his face. Information about him was sparse, but that was all right. She had the name of the bar where he liked to hang out, and confirmation that he was straight. That ought to be all she needed to win him over.

She smiled at the thought. She enjoyed the challenge and the risk involved in extracting information from unsuspecting targets, and she was good at it. She moved to the mirror and stared at her reflection. An hour from now, she would look like an entirely different person.

"Time to get into costume."

21

"There's a giant snake just downriver from here." London's voice was a hoarse whisper. Disbelief shone in her big brown eyes. Her body trembled. "I think it's coming this way."

Maddock turned and looked in the direction she was facing and scanned the forest. He couldn't see much among the dense growth. His eyes scanned the forest floor, but he saw nothing but green.

"See anything, Bones?" he asked.

"No," Bones said quietly. "But out here, a snake could be within arm's reach and we might not know it until it was too late."

"You would know if this snake got anywhere close to you," London's voice still shook. "That thing is massive."

Maddock frowned. To this point, London had given no indication that she was prone to flights of fancy. And she had obviously seen something that had shaken her to the core.

"What are the odds we walk right into the Yacumama on day one?" Bones said, still looking around.

"Even slimmer than the likelihood of its existence," Maddock said. "Mostly because we're a long way from where she's supposed to live."

Bones seized his arm and pointed up ahead. Something was moving through the jungle. Maddock couldn't see what it was, but he saw the tops of low-growing plants and shrubs shake as it came toward them.

"Maybe heading upriver is a good idea." Bones rested his hand on his pistol.

Maddock nodded and the trio began to slowly work

their way upriver. As they walked, they kept an eye on whatever it was coming toward them.

"Can you shoot it?" London whispered.

"We would have to actually see it first," Bones said.

"Firing a handgun at a large predator is seldom the best course of action," Maddock said. "We won't do that unless we have to."

She swallowed hard and nodded. Beads of sweat were forming on her brow and she looked as if she might throw up.

"It'll be fine," Maddock assured her. "Most of the time, wild animals just want to be left alone."

"Unless they're hungry," Bones added.

London missed a step and almost landed flat on her face. "Did that really need to be said?"

"Out here, a healthy appreciation for the food chain keeps you on your toes. But Maddock is right. Disengage whenever possible."

The thing, whatever it was, kept coming. It was far away, but moving in their direction. And then he caught a glimpse of blotchy, olive green scales. And then a large, narrow head with high-set eyes raised up from the undergrowth.

"It's a giant anaconda," Maddock whispered.

"I'll say," Bones added. "It's no Yacumama, but still I would not want to tangle with that thing."

"Told you," London said, a measure of relief evident in her voice. The identification of their pursuer as a known species of snake, and not the giant serpent of legend, had a calming effect on her.

Maddock nodded. The green anaconda, or giant anaconda, ranged up to five meters long, more than fifteen feet, and weighed close to six hundred pounds.

This one was no exception. Its body was thicker than a football. Twigs snapped beneath its weight as it slithered forward, still moving in their direction.

"I say we give it a wide berth," Maddock said. "Let's get the hell out of here."

They picked up their pace, moving upriver as fast as the jungle would permit. But every time Maddock glanced back, the snake was still moving in their direction.

"That thing is persistent," Maddock said.

"Must be female," Bones said. "Chicks of all species find me irresistible."

"Chicks?" London said. "1972 called. They want their idiom back."

Bones bared his teeth in a wicked grin. "I don't use the word because I think it's clever. I use it because it gets a reaction."

London let out a plaintive groan and turned pleading eyes toward Maddock.

"Has anyone ever tried to sand off his rough edges?"

Maddock shook his head.

"You know what they say," Bones began, raising a finger, "it's the sharp edges that make the diamond."

"I don't think that's a saying," London replied, casting another nervous glance over her shoulder.

"It will be when I get one of those Twitter things." Bones paused, giving London a moment to gape before he broke out in laughter. "Just kidding. Twitter sucks. Besides, I like to do my trolling in person."

"I think I'm beginning to hate you," London said. "But not as much as I hate that snake. Why is it following us?"

"I'd follow you," Bones said. "You look good walking away."

London gritted her teeth and drew back a fist to punch Bones. He smiled and moved out of range.

"Maybe right now isn't the best time for a brawl," Maddock said. "It's very rare for an anaconda to eat a human. When they do, it's almost always someone asleep, usually drunk. Easier to wrap around you that way. So, I don't recommend lying on the ground. They're not particularly fast on land, so how about we don't let it catch up to us?" He shuddered at the thought of being wrapped in those massive coils, squeezing tighter every time he let out his breath, slowly crushing the life out of hm.

"I assume swimming for it is no longer an option?" London asked.

"Nope. They prefer to hunt in the water. And they are excellent swimmers." Bones glowered in the direction of the massive serpent that continued to stalk them. His expression brightened. He reached into his pocket and took out his phone.

"Calling animal control?" London asked.

"Just trying something." He tapped the screen a few times and a high-pitched ululation filled the air.

"What is that?" London asked.

"It's a song shamans use to control serpents," Maddock said. "Or something like that."

"Maybe you have to actually sing it," Bones said. Walking backward, he turned toward the serpent, cupped his hands to his mouth, and began to chant. "Huancahuiii, huancahuii…"

The Anaconda suddenly froze and poked its head up from the foliage. It turned a dark, glossy eye on Bones.

"Uh oh," Bones said, backing away faster.

"What's wrong?" London said.

"According to legend, if you don't chant the song

perfectly, the snakes devour you." Maddock hadn't bought into Dakota's absurd snake-charming shaman legend, but the song seemed to have elicited a reaction from the snake.

Bones tried again. "Huanchuii!"

As if on cue, the anaconda lowered its head and made a beeline for them. The trio began to run. Up ahead, Maddock spotted a fallen tree that spanned the river. It wasn't particularly large, but it looked like it would support their weight.

"There's a way across. Hurry!" They made a run for it, crashing through tangled undergrowth. They batted away low-hanging limbs, stumbled as vines snagged their ankles, but they made it to the tree in a matter of seconds. "London goes first. She's lightest."

"Damn right I am." Gracefully, she strode out onto the fallen tree. It was young, recently uprooted, and still retained some of its springiness. It sagged a little under her weight, but it held, and she reached the other side safely.

Maddock told Bones to go next, then turned to watch the anaconda's approach. Unbelievably, it was still on their trail and closing in. It needed some discouraging.

Maddock drew his pistol and took aim at a spot just in front of the snake. He fired a single shot. The report of the pistol was deafening in the quiet jungle. The bullet kicked up a spray of dirt inches from the giant snake. Maddock didn't know if it was the bullet or the sound of gunfire, but the anaconda changed course. Maddock breathed a sigh of relief as the massive serpent slithered down the steep riverbank and into the water.

"Your turn," Bones called. "But take it slow. The tree barely supported my weight."

Now that they had seen the last of the giant snake, Maddock took a moment to catch his breath before stepping out onto the tree. His backpack made balancing on the narrow log a challenge. Little by little, he inched out over the water. With each step, he felt the tree sag a little beneath his weight.

"Too many cheeseburgers," Bones called.

Maddock was too focused on remaining balanced on the log to bother with a retort. Instead, he merely raised his middle finger.

"He's showing you how big it is," Bones said to London. "But he dated my sister and she says there's a lot less girth."

"Sounds like somebody is compensating," London said to Bones.

"Back in the day, they called him Mister Shrinkage," Maddock said. He was halfway across and the tree was holding.

"That was because of the cold…" Bones broke off in midsentence. He drew his pistol and leveled it at Maddock. "Get down!"

Instinctively, Maddock threw himself to the side. A bullet zipped past his ear and clipped a branch over Bones' head. Bones returned fire.

Maddock almost managed to turn his leap into an awkward dive, but it ended up as more of a belly flop. His breath left him in a rush as he struck the water. He struggled to the surface and fought to catch his breath. The strong current was carrying him downstream and he had to fight to swim for the other side.

"Some of the ronderos followed us," Bones called. He and London had taken cover in the forest. "I'll cover you!" Bones fired again and Maddock heard a cry of pain from the other side of the river. "Bullseye!" Bones proclaimed.

From the other side of the river, shrieks of pain intermingled with loud bickering. And then they heard the sound of footsteps heading in the opposite direction. The wounded man was still crying out in pain, but the sound of his wailing faded away as his companions carried him off.

"Shot him right in the package," Bones said. "After that, the others had second thoughts."

Maddock finally managed to suck in a breath of precious air. Rejuvenated, he headed for shore, driving himself forward with powerful strokes.

He had almost reached the other side when something caught his eye. A dark, sinuous form was swimming toward him. The anaconda was back, and it was closing in fast.

The shore was tantalizingly close, but Maddock could tell he wouldn't make it before the anaconda caught up with him. He made a decision. He would have to stand and fight. Rather, he would tread water and fight.

As the huge snake closed in, Maddock fumbled for the machete this hung from his waist. The cold water numbed his fingers and he fumbled with the snap that held it in place.

The anaconda was now only meters away. Its dark eyes peeked up above the surface. Up close it appeared even larger than Maddock had believed. He managed to get the machete free and raise it high above his head just as a shot rang out.

The anaconda jerked and then began to thrash wildly. Blood streamed from a hole in its head. Dazed, Maddock watched its death throes with fascination and a measure of regret as the current swept it away. It had been necessary to kill the snake, but it was a shame to destroy such a magnificent specimen.

"Thanks, Bones. I owe you one," he said, still watching the snake.

"Seriously? You just assume it was Bones?"

He looked up to see London holding her pistol in a two-handed grip. She still had it trained on the dying serpent.

"That was a damn fine shot," he said.

"Thanks. It was more luck than skill. I'm a decent shot, but not that good, and I've never fired a weapon under duress."

"In that case, I'm glad you didn't hit me instead of the snake."

"I'm not that bad!"

Maddock swam to shore and London gave him a hand up as he climbed the steep riverbank. When he reached the top, he removed his backpack and laid down on the soft earth. He took a few seconds to catch his breath as he gazed up at the canopy of green.

"Where's Bones?" he asked.

"He went after the ronderos. Said it was a matter of principle."

"You have got to be kidding me." Maddock stood and peered into the jungle. He couldn't see anything.

"He's going to get himself killed, isn't he?" London said.

"Probably not. Still, I ought to go after him."

There was no need. By the time they reached the fallen tree, they heard Bones call out to them.

"All clear!"

Maddock and London exchanged glances.

"I didn't hear any gunshots," London said.

"He didn't use a firearm," Maddock said. Bones would have wanted to do the thing quietly in case there were even more ronderos within earshot.

"Just how dangerous are you guys?" London asked in wonderment.

Maddock managed a sad smile. The question brought back memories he'd like to forget.

"We're not dangerous at all, unless someone gives us a reason."

22

Boyd was in pain. His back ached, his ankle throbbed, and his ass was sore from riding in the back of a pickup truck. For what must have been the fiftieth time, he cast a dirty look at the two men riding in the cab. Alejandro, one of his new Amaru allies, had explained that Boyd was simply too big to fit comfortably in the cab of the battered old Volkswagen. But once they were on the road, any semblance of compassion had vanished.

The man drove recklessly. Every bump they hit was pain in his back. Sharp turns flung him this way and that until he was forced to cling to the truck bed to keep from being thrown out. Laughter from inside the cab told him that his partners were well aware of his struggles.

"Damn these Amaru. Why do I have to deal with them?"

He knew the answer to that question. He had no choice. When they'd found him injured on the trail to the Temple of the Moon, they had intended to kill him. He had bargained for his life with the most valuable thing he had to offer—the path to Akakor.

He reached into his pocket and took out a folded sheet of paper. It was a printout of a photograph he had taken of Black Thorn's map. It was a good thing he had taken the photo—the original had begun falling apart the first time he unrolled it.

He unfolded the page and smoothed it out. The folds were worn smooth from being folded and unfolded again and again. The paper was dirty from all the times he'd traced his finger over the many squiggly lines as if he could absorb their secrets.

He scowled at the pattern of wavy lines. What did they represent? Roads? Rivers? With so little information at his disposal, there was no way of telling.

"Where are you pointing me?" he muttered.

Day by day his frustration had mounted. When he had discovered the hidden cell where the so-called Blind Spaniard had lived his final days, driven mad by what he had found in the jungle, he was sure he was on the verge of success. Now he had the Black Thorn map. But that map alone wasn't enough. According to the Amaru, London had cut the map off White Flower's body. And then she had died, falling into a booby trap inside the chamber, taking the map with her.

"Dammit!" He hissed the curse between gritted teeth. "She ruined everything."

Now that he was unable to combine the two maps, he had been forced to move to Plan B. It was not a plan in which he had much faith, but unless he could figure out this map, it was all he had to go on.

The truck hit a bump and Boyd went airborne. The paper flew out of his hands and he barely managed to snatch it before it flew away. He came down hard on the rusty truck bed. There was a loud thump and fresh pain tore along his spine.

"Slow the hell down!" he shouted.

The Amaru laughed, but to Boyd's surprise, the driver slowed down. He smiled, a warm feeling passing over him. Some people needed strong leadership, and it would be up to Boyd to provide it on this mission. The truck continued to slow down.

"Hey, I didn't say to stop!" Boyd banged the truck bed with his closed fist. "Let's get going!"

Alejandro ignored him. The truck rolled to a stop.

Annoyed, Boyd turned around and saw the reason for their sudden halt.

A battered jeep blocked the road. A woman was sitting in the shade, smoking a hand-rolled cigarette.

"Tell her to get that thing out of the road," Boyd ordered, but the driver was already speaking with the woman. They went back and forth for a minute, their voices growing louder.

"What is she saying?" Boyd said.

"She's a rondero," Diego said. He wasn't exactly friendly, but he was somewhat easier to deal with than Alejandro "Her truck will not run. She says a red Indian broke it. Her companions went after him but they have not returned."

Boyd wondered if the man was speaking in some sort of code. Then he remembered the man he had encountered on the train, and again at Machu Picchu. "Red Indian" was the name some foreigners used to identify Native American Indigenous Indians, or whatever the hell they wanted to be called this week. Could it have been the same man?

"Ask her to describe the Indian," he said.

Diego raised an eyebrow but asked the question and relayed the answer.

"Very tall and handsome, but she liked his friend better. He had blonde hair and blue eyes."

Boyd's stomach did somersaults. It couldn't be!

"Was there a girl with them?"

This time, the woman scowled. Scorn laced her words. The driver laughed before he translated.

"Brown hair. Pale like a ghost. Shrieks like a howler monkey."

In the driver's seat, Alejandro suddenly whipped his

head around. "Is she talking about the people who defiled White Flower's tomb and desecrated her remains? They survived?"

Boyd nodded, unable to believe it. London was alive, and she had obviously hired the two thugs from the train to help her continue the search. "Jesus, Mary, and Joseph! I can't believe she's alive."

"I hope we see them again," Alejandro said. "I will kill them."

"I don't care what you do to the men," Boyd said, "but the girl has to live."

Alejandro smirked. "I don't want to know what you have planned for her."

"She has information we need," Boyd snapped. "And a rich father who will reward us handsomely if we bring her back to him alive."

23

The sign outside the El Musmuqui bar read, *Especialistas en Tragos Exóticos*—"Exotic Drink Specialists." The bar's claim to fame was a menu filled with amusingly named drinks, such as Levantate Lazaro which translated to "Lazarus Rise Up." According to the reviews, that particular drink was supposed to help a man with his performance in the bedroom.

The joint was packed. Tourists comprised the bulk of the patrons, but she spotted a few locals here and there. Mayra ignored the whistles and clucking noises a few of the tipsier men sent her way. As if any of them would ever have a chance. She had used temporary dye to color her hair purple and wore a pair of tortoiseshell glasses and a simple black cocktail dress that put her trim figure on full display. Her lipstick and eye shadow were black as well.

"A Goth librarian. I like!" said a portly man at the bar.

Mayra ignored the compliment but was pleased that her disguise was having the desired effect. She spotted Giancarlo sitting at a table in the corner. He was a handsome man in his late twenties, with wavy dark brown hair and a strong chin. He sat facing the room but didn't make eye contact with anyone. She sensed that she would have to take the initiative here.

She caught the eye of the bartender, who stopped in the middle of filling a pitcher of beer to come over and greet her. The customer who was waiting for the pitcher threw up his hands in frustration.

"How may I help you, Miss…"

Mayra chose not to fill in the blank. "I was wondering if you could tell me what the guy in the corner is drinking?"

The bartender's eyebrows shot up. "You mean Giancarlo? He's a Cusqueña beer man. It's basic, kind of like him."

"That's not very nice," Mayra said.

"No, he's a good man. I only mean he likes things simple. Down to earth."

"Thanks for the tip. But I am not drinking generic beer." Mayra ordered two shots instead.

"On the house," the bartender said, handing her the small glasses. "So you know I'm not a bad guy."

She thanked him, then took a deep breath. It was time to get into character. She turned, lowered her head, slowly approached Giancarlo's table. She smiled shyly and did not quite meet his eye.

"Um, hi there," she said when she reached the table. "You are him, aren't you?"

Giancarlo sat up straighter. "Who am I supposed to be?"

"I heard you're an adventurer. You take people into the deadliest parts of the rainforest and bring them back alive."

Giancarlo shrugged, but a smile tugged at the corners of his mouth. "I guess everywhere in the forest is deadly. I don't do anything special. Just take tourists down the river."

"I think you're being overly modest. I'd love to hear your stories." She held up the shot glasses. "And I hate to drink alone."

Giancarlo eyed the glasses suspiciously. "What are we drinking?"

"This one is for you. It's called a 'Super Sexy.'" She handed him a glass and settled into the chair beside him.

"And mine is a 'Besame Mucho.'"

Giancarlo blinked. "Do you know what that translates to?"

"Kiss me a lot." She winked, then scooted her chair closer to him. "So, tell me about your adventures."

Like every man Mayra had ever met, Giancarlo responded to gentle flattery and lots of eye contact. She oohed and ahhed in all the right places as he did his best to make his guide business sound like a series of Doc Savage adventures. Soon, she had him speaking freely about his next client and what their plans were. She asked a few questions, nothing too probing. Giancarlo was oblivious, expounding in great detail.

When she was satisfied she had learned all she could from him, she reached out and gently laid her hand on his. "Let's go for a walk." She stood and Giancarlo allowed himself to be led out into the night. The young man appeared to be so surprised by his good fortune that he never asked why she was guiding him out of town and into the rainforest.

They finally came to a stop near a slow-moving stretch of river—one of the many tributaries that fed into the Amazon.

"This is not a safe place," Giancarlo said. "There are caiman here. Large ones."

Mayra already knew that. She draped her arms around his neck and gave him a kiss.

"You'll protect me, won't you?" she asked. She kissed him again, felt him relax. She slid her hands down his chest. Giancarlo let out a low moan.

That was when Mayra made her move. She locked her hands together, squeezed him tightly around the waist, hooked her right leg around his left calf, and drove him backward. They fell into the shallow water with Mayra on top. She shifted to a mount position, pinning him to the soft river bottom, grabbed two handfuls of hair, and held his head underwater.

Giancarlo was physically fit, but he apparently had no experience in hand-to-hand combat. He thrashed around, trying to buck her off him, but in his drunken state, he could do little to resist.

Even after his struggles ceased, she kept his head underwater until she was certain he wouldn't be coming back up. Finally, she rose on unsteady feet and waded out of the river. Hopefully, the caimans would get to his body before it was discovered. If not, the death would almost certainly be treated as an accidental drowning. Giancarlo wouldn't be the first drunk person to fall into the river and not make it back out.

She had hidden a bag nearby with a few needed items. She wiped away the black makeup, changed into conservative clothing, pulled her hair up into a bun, and gave it a quick shot of black touch-up hairspray. When she emerged from the forest, she was confident no one would ever recognize her as the sexy girl with whom Giancarlo had left El Musmuqui.

24

Belen was a floating shantytown and market on the outskirts of Iquitos. Nicknamed "The Venice of Latin America," the community was built on the flood plain of the Itaya River. Homes were built on stilts or floating logs. During the seasons in which the river overflowed its banks, locals and tourists relied on water taxis, floating walkways, and rickety bridges to move through the community.

A breeze blew through the shantytown, carrying with it the dank smell of mud and rotting vegetation. Mayra crinkled her nose.

"It stinks like Venice," she mumbled. Unlike Upper Belen, which was the home of the Mercado de Belen, the floating market, Lower Belen was a residential area.

The people here lived in abject poverty. Clean water and proper sanitation were sorely lacking. Mayra wasn't entirely immune to the suffering, but she recognized it as an inevitable part of the human condition. She believed that most people were fated to live out unremarkable lives and fade away without leaving a mark. That was one of the reasons she had chosen to attach herself to a greater cause. Her work would make a difference.

A gap-toothed man poked his head out of an open door and whistled. She smiled at him and kept moving. He was clearly a pig but an inconsequential one. Let him have his moment of fun. If he tried it again on the way back, a knee to the groin would set him straight.

As she neared her destination, she mentally reviewed her plan. After disposing of Giancarlo the previous night, she had broken into his apartment and obtained all of his notes and records. She had stayed awake until late into the night, familiarizing herself with his plan and preparing herself for the role. She was ready. She just had one loose end to tie up.

The boat which Giancarlo had hired was tied up at the far end of the pier. She could see that the provisions were already loaded. They could depart as soon as London Thatcher arrived, which should be within the hour. A short man with a bowl cut and a round, weathered face, saw her looking at him and scowled. That simply wouldn't do.

"Are you Tito?" Mayra asked. The man nodded. "I am Giancarlo's sister." She held her breath. Tito didn't know it, but his life hung in the balance. It all depended on how he responded right now.

Tito looked her up and down, turned, and spat into the river. His expression softened into a look of curiosity.

"If you are here to tell me that the job is canceled, you can tell Giancarlo he will not get his money back. I have already bought supplies." Tito waved a callused hand in the direction of his boat.

"The job is not canceled, but Giancarlo will not be the guide. I will be."

Tito scratched his chin, pursed his lips, and stared at Mayra. "Why?"

"He drank some bad water. Now he can't get too far from the toilet."

Tito winced, nodded in sympathy. "You know what you are doing out there?" Tito asked, pointing downriver.

Mayra nodded. "Absolutely."

He considered for a moment. "Did Giancarlo tell you the rule?"

"No. He must have been too busy vomiting," Mayra

said.

"The tourists are your clients, not mine. I do not take orders from them."

"This will be the easiest trip you have ever taken," Mayra said. "I promise."

Tito's willingness to accept her cover story made matters easier. She had feared she would have to eliminate Giancarlo's pilot of choice and track down a new one on short notice. She checked the time. London should be arriving soon.

She left the filth and poverty of the residential area behind and headed for the market area of Upper Belen. Popular with tourists, the market offered an eclectic mix of shops and stands. Seemingly anything that walked, crawled, swam, flew, or grew in the Amazon could be purchased here. As she strode through the marketplace, vendors called out to her, offering fish, produce, and indigenous "remedies".

"Good medicine!" a man shouted, holding up a handful of leaves. "Nature has a cure for everything."

Two tourists, a guy with a man bun and a girl with a shaved head, hurried over and nodded sagely as the vendor extolled the virtues of his miracle plant.

"It's true," man bun said. "In the past, people didn't need all these shots and pills."

Mayra rolled her eyes. The advent of modern medicine and vaccines, along with improved agriculture and sanitation, had added thirty years to human life expectancy. Not that facts mattered to some people.

Up ahead, a man caught Mayra's eye. He was Native American, tall and handsome. There was a twinkle in his eye as if he were enjoying a private joke at the expense of everyone around him. He was causing quite a traffic jam.

Some people stopped to gawk at him. Others, mostly women, paused to look him up and down.

As the big Native American drew closer, Mayra saw that he was accompanied by a blond man with blue eyes. He wasn't bad looking either, though Mayra preferred her men tall and dark. Both of them were physically fit and moved through the crowd with a confident air. She was certain these two were not mere tourists.

The crowd parted and Mayra saw there was a third person with them—London. The woman must have hired bodyguards to accompany her. Smart.

"London Thatcher?" Mayra said.

"Yes?" London frowned. "May I help you?"

"I am Mayra, your guide. Giancarlo is ill so I will be taking his place."

"I wasn't notified of a change," London said, her tone suspicious.

"He only called me a few hours ago. He woke up this morning with an extremely high fever and has been quarantined as a precaution, so we had to regroup quickly. I am his sister and we are partners in the guide business. I've been thoroughly briefed on the plans and everything is in place. I'll be happy to go through all the details with you and answer any questions you have. We want to make sure you are comfortable."

London exchanged glances with her two companions. The big man nodded.

"I think you should hear the lady out," he said. "I'm Bones, the handsome one. This is Maddock." Bones leaned in and spoke in a stage whisper. "We allow him to believe he's the brains of the operation, but that's actually me, too."

Mayra smiled. Bones was charming. Too bad she

would probably have to eliminate him before this was over.

"There's a place nearby where we can get a coffee and go over the itinerary if you'd like to follow me."

London and Maddock agreed. Bones, however, was gazing at something in the distance.

"You three go ahead. I'll catch up in a little while." He took off his backpack and set it down by Maddock's feet.

"Everything all right?" Maddock asked.

"There's something that needs seeing to," Bones said. "I'll be back soon."

"I'll stay with London," Maddock said.

With that, Bones moved off along the floating wooden walkway. Despite his size, he weaved gracefully through the tourists and locals who milled about.

"Does he do that a lot?" Mayra asked, wondering what in the hell had caused the man to leave so abruptly.

Maddock grinned. "All the time."

25

Bones wasted no time. He set off, moving quickly through the crowd of tourists. His eyes locked on his target—a man with serpent scaled tattoos on the back of his neck. The man's collar-length hair mostly covered the ink, but not completely. Bones had only caught a glimpse of the man's face, but he was certain he had recognized Diego, one of the Amaru who had followed them into White Flower's tomb.

Diego glanced back over his shoulder and Bones ducked into a nearby stall. Diego frowned, scanned the crowd, then turned and kept moving.

"You must have seen us," Bones whispered. "And now you're going to tell your friends, aren't you?"

"Señor, would you like to buy turtle eggs?" an old woman asked hopefully.

"No, thanks," Bones said, still eyeing Diego.

"They are very popular in France," the woman added, holding up a soft, white orb.

"Screw the French," Bones said. Diego was loitering beside a rack of snake skins, gazing in the direction from which they had come.

"I also have bark from the Chullachaquicaspi tree," she said in a whisper. "Very rare."

The name rang a bell. Something Dakota had said.

"You mean the Teacher Tree?" Bones asked.

"Yes!" The woman nodded vigorously. "My brother found the tree far downriver. He had harvested only a small amount of bark before he was chased away."

Bones loved a good story, even if it was a pile of crap. "Who chased him?"

The old woman cast a furtive glance around, then lowered her voice. "The Chachapoya."

Now she had Bones' attention. "The Cloud People? I thought they vanished a long time ago."

The woman shook her head.

"Can you tell me where your brother encountered them? Maybe show me on a map?"

"I do not sell information," she said with a shrewd expression on her face. Her meaning was clear.

"Fine. How much for some bark?" Bones asked.

"One hundred soles."

Bones calculated that to be about thirty US dollars. A steep price for some crappy bark, but a bargain if her information were of any value.

The woman handed him a paper-wrapped block about the size of a cigarette lighter and he handed over the cash.

"Grind up the bark and put it into boiling water. Breathe the vapors to relieve pain." She made a motion with her hand as if fanning something toward her nose. "Let the water…" She paused, frowned, and inclined her head. "What you do with tea after it boils."

"You let it steep?" Bones said. He wondered when Diego would make a move.

"That is it. You let it steep. Drink it and it will cure sickness." She mimed raising a cup to her lips. "Make a poultice of the boiled bark, and it will draw out any infection or poison."

"Your English is awfully good," Bones said, tucking the bark into his pocket. "It almost sounds like a well-practiced sales pitch. I hope I didn't just get scammed."

"I was married to an American," she said simply.

"So, about these Cloud People. Can you tell me where

your brother saw them?" He took out a few wadded bills and held them out to her.

"I do not sell information," she said, waving them away. "This is all I can tell you." She scribbled a few words and images on a scrap of the same paper with which she had wrapped the bark.

Bones thanked her. Before he could examine the page more closely, Diego began to move. Bones bade the woman goodbye and continued his pursuit.

The farther they went, the seedier their surroundings became. Here, many of the ramshackle market stalls looked as if a stiff wind would knock them down. Some of the vendors had only a few items on display. He wondered if such stands were merely a front for selling illegal items.

"Big man!" someone shouted. "You like snake?" A vendor held up a dead python.

The sudden cry caught Diego's attention. He snapped his head around. Bones dodged into an empty stall, but he was too late. Diego's eyes went wide and he began to run.

"Holy crap," Bones muttered.

They dashed along the rickety walkway, which creaked and sagged with every step. Up ahead, the walkway came to an end. A square floating platform served as a stepping stone to the next section of the market. Diego's feet barely seemed to touch the wooden surface as he hit the platform then jumped to the next walkway.

Bones took the more direct route and jumped over the water. He almost made it. His fingertips touched the opposite deck as he plunged into the foul river water.

He came up sputtering and swearing and hauled himself up onto the deck. All around, people jeered at the sight of the soaking wet Indian. He gave them all the finger and resumed his pursuit of the fleeing Amaru.

Diego rounded a corner and Bones followed. The Amaru looked back and shouted a curse when he saw Bones closing in on him. He passed a fruit vendor, where a pyramid of green dragonfruit was stacked. As he ran by, Diego threw out an arm and sent the fruit rolling across the deck. The vendor let out a shout and shook his fist.

Bones cleared the fruit in a single leap. But he couldn't stop himself from crashing into a man pushing a cart filled with mamey sapote, a melon that resembled a cantaloupe. The vendor flew one way, the cart the other. Bones landed face down, surrounded by rolling melons.

"Sorry, bro," he grunted to the stunned man who lay catching his breath. As he sprang to his feet, Bones fished a few bills out of his pocket and tossed them to the man. "For your trouble."

He looked around for Diego and saw him running along the dock. Instinctively, Bones grabbed one of the melons. Like a quarterback throwing a bomb, Bones hurled the mamey sapote at the fleeing man. It flew in a high arc and struck Diego in the back of the head. The melon shattered and Diego stumbled and fell.

"Yes!" Bones pumped his fist and continued the pursuit.

Around another corner, they found themselves back in the crowded section of the market. Bones followed the angry shouts as Diego fought his way through the throng. He danced around a woman selling brightly colored feathers, then was forced to drop and roll as a man shoved a platter of raw fish in his face.

Up ahead, the dock on which they were running came to an end. Diego didn't slow down. He flew through the air and landed in one of the many boats that plied the waters around Belen. The man piloting the craft shouted at Diego, but the Amaru was already jumping to the next boat.

"This is just great," Bones said. Seeing no other choice, he jumped into the first boat. He landed off-center and his bulk nearly capsized it.

"Follow that guy!" Bones shouted at the pilot, who folded his arms and shook his head. "You are no help." Another boat was passing by and Bones jumped into it. One of the passengers, a guy with a man bun, let out a cry of alarm.

"Just passing through," Bones said before jumping on to the next boat.

He began to hopscotch his way across the water, jumping from boat to boat, following behind Diego, who had commandeered a raft and was frantically paddling his way toward the residential area of Lower Belen.

"I am never going to catch up with him like this," Bones said. He spotted a tour boat carrying three young women. All of them wore matching tops with a large Z on the front. "Sorority girls! Now we're talking." As they approached, he called out to them "Yo, can I get a lift?"

"You can do whatever you want," a green-eyed blonde said. "I'm Carly, by the way." The other two, a redhead and a brunette, laughed and beckoned for him to come aboard.

For a brief moment, Bones considered abandoning the chase and spending some time getting to know these young ladies. But he had to know where Diego was going and what he was up to.

"Can you take me to that dock over there?" he asked.

"You can't stay for a while?" Carly asked.

"I wish," Bones said. "But that dude stole my phone

and I need to catch him."

This caused an uproar among the young women, all of whom agreed that a person's smartphone was sacred.

"If I lost my phone, my life would literally be over," Carly said.

"Help me get mine back and you can text me," Bones said.

Only after she had entered his name and number into her phone did Carly order their guide to take them to the platform where Diego was just now climbing off his raft.

"That is a bad place," the man said. "Not part of the mercado. Just criminals."

"You don't have to get out of the boat," Carly said. "Just take us there. How bad can it be?"

Shaking his head, the pilot fired up the engine and steered the boat toward the dock. They had only gone a few meters when Diego returned flanked by a pair of men. One of them raised a revolver.

"Get down!" Bones threw himself on top of Carly, who was seated closest to him. He heard the whine of the bullet as it zipped past his head, the pop of a small-caliber pistol, the frightened shrieks of the women in the boat. The guide let out a stream of obscenities and turned the boat around. Bullets punched holes in the hull and river water began to pour in. Bones counted six shots and then the weapon went silent.

"Do you not have a protection plan on your phone?" Carly shouted in his ear. "Because I don't think he's going to give it back."

Bones was too busy bailing water as the boat chugged away. Soon, they were back in the middle of heavy boat traffic. He looked back and saw that the Amaru had disappeared. Even in a crime-riddled place like Lower

Belen, shooting at a boat full of tourists was apparently reason enough to get out of sight for a while.

It took all his remaining cash, which wasn't much, to convince the pilot to take him back to Upper Belen. The man clearly would have preferred that Bones swim back, but Carly browbeat him until he relented and accepted payment. Although her two friends were crying and hugging one another close, Carly found the experience exhilarating.

"I wish I had gotten that on video," she said. "It would have blown up on TikTok."

Bones neither knew nor cared what the hell TikTok was. Right now, he was focused on warning Maddock and London.

"Where are you staying? Maybe we could get a drink later," Carly said when they reached Upper Belen.

"Unfortunately, I'm leaving right away," Bones said.

Carly grabbed him by his ponytail, pulled his head down, and kissed him firmly on the lips. Were it not for the very recent memory of bullets flying past his head, Bones might have stayed a while. He gently broke the kiss and pulled away.

"Sorry, but I really do have to go."

"You didn't lose your phone, did you?" Carly eyed him suspiciously. "Are you an FBI agent or something?"

"Not exactly."

Carly stuck out her lower lip. "I don't suppose you will ever find your way to Miami? We're students at the U."

"I live in Key West," Bones said as he climbed up on to the deck. "I'll give you a call when I get back."

"Call, not text? How old are you, anyway?" Carly said. "Might as well send me a fax."

"I'll bear that in mind."

When Bones reached the coffee bar, Mayra was stuffing a sheaf of papers into a backpack.

"Everything appears to be in order," London was saying. "I just wish I had heard it from Giancarlo."

"You can call him," Mayra said, "but reception is spotty where he lives. And he looked like death warmed over."

"There's no time," Bones said. London looked up, surprised by his sudden appearance.

"Did you decide to go for a swim?" Maddock asked.

"We need to get the hell out of Iquitos," Bones said. "The Amaru are here."

26

They reached the village of Gari Gapra just before nightfall. It was a location that London had identified as their first landmark, and her theory was supported by the directions Bones had been given by the shopkeeper in the Belen Market. They were now deep in the Peruvian Amazon, far from civilization, and an eerie sense of foreboding hung over them.

A small dock extended out into the river. Overlooking it was a statue of a Spanish Conquistador down on his knees, his hands pressed to his head. His mouth was twisted in a scream and his eyes were empty sockets.

"That's not creepy or anything," London said.

"That is the Eyeless Spaniard," Tito said from the stern where he was piloting their boat. "Gari Gapra is Quechua for 'Blind Man.'"

"Was he a real person?" Bones asked.

"I don't know," Tito said. "I seldom come this far upriver."

The village was a ramshackle affair with only a small church to set it apart from any other remote rainforest settlement. The villagers eyed them uneasily as they approached.

"Can you two try and look as non-threatening as possible?" Mayra said to Maddock and Bones.

"Trust me, Maddock frightens no one," Bones said. "Unless he takes off his clothes. Nobody wants to see that."

One of the villagers, an old man, was apparently fluent in English. He broke out in laughter, then turned to his friends and translated what Bones had said. The others laughed and a few pointed. One sturdily built woman with a scarred face and a machete on her hip eyed him with interest.

The joke seemed to have broken the ice. Mayra began conversing with the villagers in a mixture of Spanish and English with a few words in Quechua here and there. Finally, she nodded and turned back to the others.

"Giancarlo had planned to meet with a man they call Wilton. He is a wanderer who knows this part of the jungle well. He has not been seen here for about a week, but they told me where to look for him. They have invited us to stay here tonight, and we can continue in the morning."

Maddock was more than willing to call it a day. They had been on the move ever since their encounter with the ronderos. After their trek through the rainforest, they had traveled through the night by boat to Iquitos, and then on to Gari Gapra. He could barely keep his eyes open.

"That sounds great. Where should we bunk down for the night?"

"London and I will stay in huts. They say you two and Tito can bed down in the church."

"Won't that bother the priest?" Bones asked.

"The priest left a long time ago," said one of the villagers, a short, stout woman with snow-white hair. "We work hard all day every day. We did not like spending our evenings being told we are bad people."

"Preach!" Bones said. "No pun intended."

The villagers proved to be generous hosts. They provided a simple but filling meal of fish and vegetables. An old man named Aristotle, the villager who had laughed at Bones' wisecrack, seemed to have appointed himself host. He and Bones hit it off right away, and soon

Aristotle was regaling them with legends and tall tales of the rainforest.

"Tell us about the statue," Bones said. "I'm told he's called the Eyeless Spaniard."

"Ah, yes. The Eyeless Spaniard was a conquistador who came to this part of the jungle many years ago searching for Atahualpa's gold."

Maddock nodded. Atahualpa was the Inca emperor captured by Pizarro in 1532. In exchange for his life, Atahualpa offered to fill a room with gold and two more with silver. To the surprise of his Spanish captors, he delivered on his promise. Pizarro had him killed him anyway, but the emperor's ability to produce so much treasure convinced the famed conqueror that what Atahualpa had given him was only a fraction of his wealth.

"The man heard a rumor that Inca General Rumiñahui had hidden the treasure in a jungle lake."

"How did he make it all this way if he had no eyes?" Bones quipped.

"He had eyes when he came here, but not when he returned."

"What happened to him?" London asked.

"He tore them out himself. Whatever he saw in the jungle, it drove him half mad. The villagers nursed him back to health, but he never fully regained his sanity. He was always talking about finding the 'other map' and 'destroying them.' One day he vanished into the jungle and was never heard from again."

Maddock glanced at Bones, who nodded. Both were thinking of the hidden jail cell at Aguas Calientes. Could the Eyeless Spaniard have learned of White Flower's tomb and made his way to Macchu Picchu, only to be taken captive?"

"Have you ever seen this symbol?" Maddock drew the looping S-shape that represented a serpent.

"It is the ancient symbol of the serpent god."

"I heard a story about a giant snake called Yacumama. Any connection?" Bones said.

Aristotle's gentle demeanor hardened suddenly. "Yacumama is not a story."

"Have you ever seen her?" London asked.

Aristotle nodded. "I was a young boy. She came up out of the water and looked directly at me. Her head was as big as my body."

"What happened?" Bones said.

"I could not move. She looked at me, then swam away. I suppose she had already fed that day." Aristotle shivered and managed a weak laugh. Whatever he had seen as a child had left him so shaken that the mere memory of it still frightened him.

"Does she live in this area?" London asked.

The old man shook his head. "She has been seen close by a few times in my life, but like most animals, she generally avoids the company of humans. Too many people in this village for her liking."

Maddock found the notion that this remote village constituted "too many people" amusing.

"Where does she normally range?" Bones asked.

"You will have to ask Wilton when you find him. He has seen her several times."

"We are archaeologists," Maddock said. "Are there any ruins in this area that other explorers might not have found?"

"Ruins are everywhere," Aristotle said. "Right over there is what is left of an old stone building, but you would not see it unless you knew to look there." He pointed into the jungle. Maddock looked but could not see anything. "That is the way of things out here. The forest devours all."

"What about an entire city?" London said. "Maybe something underground?"

The old man shook his head.

"Are you familiar with the legend of Akakor?" London asked.

Aristotle blanched. He stood on shaky legs. "It is late. I must rest." With that, the old man hurried away.

"What did I say?" London said.

"I think you touched a nerve." Maddock watched the old man hurry into the darkness. "Let's tread lightly around that subject."

"You should not ask about the Serpent City, or even hint that you know about it," Tito whispered.

"I asked about Akakor."

"They are one and the same. Had I known that is where you are going, I would not have taken the job."

London failed to suppress a grin. It seemed her theory had been correct.

"What can you tell us about Akakor?" Maddock asked quietly.

"I know people have been killed for asking where to find it." Tito looked around suspiciously, but their hosts were paying them little mind.

Maddock glanced at Bones who nodded. If the mere mention of Akakor was worth killing over, it meant somebody was hiding something. It also meant they were in even more danger than they had believed.

27

Maddock sat bolt upright. He'd been roused from a fitful sleep by the sound of something moving outside the tiny church. He strained to listen, but Tito began to snore, drowning out all other sounds. He caught a glimpse of movement in the moonlight. A silhouette appeared in the doorway. A voice spoke softly.

"Maddock, are you awake?"

"London, what's wrong?"

"Nothing. I just wanted to talk to you about something. Do you have a minute?" Her voice was tentative, nervous.

"Do I have a minute at two o'clock in the morning? Um, sure."

Bones rolled over and opened one eye. "If you're going to hook up with her, can you be a little more discreet? I might need plausible deniability if Spenser asks."

"I'm not…" Maddock sighed and rubbed the sleep from his eyes. "Go back to sleep, Bones." He pulled on his shoes and t-shirt and slipped out the door.

Even outside, the night air was sweltering. Not a single breeze stirred. London wore a tight-fitting tank top. It was soaked with sweat and clung to her tight curves. He caught him looking and smiled but didn't mention it. He felt his ears burning and hoped the darkness covered it.

What are you doing, Maddock? You've finally met a girl who puts up with all of your crap, and your eye is already wandering. And then another voice, Bones' voice, replied, *There's no harm in looking.*

"Are you all right?" London raised up on her tiptoes

and looked him in the eye. "For a moment there you looked like you were in pain."

"Headache," he said.

"I'd rather not talk in the village," she whispered. "Let's go down by the river. Less likely to be overheard."

Maddock thought the air might be cooler by the river, which was reason enough for him. As they walked, London reached out and took his hand.

"Hope you don't mind. My night vision isn't that great."

"I'll keep you from falling," he said.

"So gallant." She gave his hand a playful squeeze.

A rickety dock extended a few meters out into the river. Half a dozen boats, including the one in which they had arrived, were tied there.

The current in this unnamed tributary of the Amazon was sluggish, and the river flowed past them with barely a whisper. The moon painted a long, silver streak across its surface. Maddock closed his eyes and took a deep breath. The air was a few degrees cooler here, and in this heat, he would take what he could get. They sat down at the end of the dock.

"This is as far from the village as we're going to get," Maddock said.

"Sorry for the cloak and dagger. It's just... I don't trust Mayra."

"I see." Maddock cupped his chin thoughtfully and gazed out at the water. "I know the last-minute switch in guides was unexpected, but she seems competent."

"I know. But there's something about her I just don't trust. She's too pretty to be a river guide in a crappy town in the middle of nowhere."

"So, she's good at her job and she's attractive,"

Maddock scratched his head. "You two are practically twins."

She rolled her eyes. "My gut tells me something's not right. What if she's Amaru? We know they're still after us after that guy chased Bones through the mercado."

"If she's an Amaru plant, then why did they chase Bones?"

"Fair point." She let her shoulders sag. "I'm tired and on edge, but I'm also excited. The way that old man reacted when I asked about Akakor. Maddock, I am certain we are on the right track! Don't you agree?"

"The pieces do seem to be falling into place," Maddock said. "Did you notice that, according to the story of the Eyeless Spaniard, he wanted to find the *other* map and destroy *them*?"

London nodded eagerly. "He must have been the one who found Black Thorn's map. He believed it would lead him to Atahualpa's treasure. After he failed, he made his way to Machu Picchu to find White Flower's map, planning to destroy them both. But how did he end up in that cell?"

Maddock scratched his chin. "I had been thinking that the purpose of a hidden cell would be to prevent the prisoner from being rescued. But what if it was to keep him away from other people?"

"You think he came out of the jungle with some sort of contagious disease?" London asked.

"Or he showed up in Machu Picchu raving about a Serpent God and who knows what else? Given what we know about the lengths to which priests and missionaries back then went to spread and cement their faith, it's reasonable to assume a blasphemer would be locked away to prevent him from interfering with their efforts."

"That would also explain how Black Thorn's map fell into the hands of the church." She bit her lip. "What could he have seen out there in the jungle that would cause him to tear his own eyes out?" She shuddered at the thought.

Maddock didn't reply. Something had caught his eye—a dark shape moving through the water on the far side of the river. He stood up for a better look.

"What is it?" London asked, rising to her feet and peering out into the night.

"There's something big swimming in the river." He pointed.

"Is that a cayman?"

The darkness, distance, and movement of the water combined to make it difficult to estimate the size of the animal that was slowly swimming downstream. He saw a dark, triangular shape cutting a *V* in the surface of the water, saw a flick of what might have been a tail far behind it. And then it was gone.

"I think we should go back," London said. "We've got to be up early."

As they returned to the village, they heard voices. Many voices joined in a low, guttural chant. The sound was coming from the far side of the village.

"What do you think that's about?" London asked. The chanting continued, still quiet, but faster, more intense. "It sounds like they're getting worked up for something."

Maddock agreed. "Get Mayra and meet us at the boats. We're leaving right now."

London nodded and ran off into the night. Maddock hurried to the church and ducked inside.

"Bones! Wake up!"

Bones didn't open his eyes. "Yes, it was the wrong thing to do. No, you're not a bad person; you just did a bad thing. Yes, I would have done the same thing. And no, I won't tell Spenser as long as it doesn't happen again. Now shut up and let me get back to sleep."

"We're bugging out." He quickly described what he had heard in the village.

"Holy crap. Why did you let me go on like that?" Bones began tugging on his clothes. "Tito, move your ass. Vámonos!"

Tito sat up slowly and took in his surroundings through bleary eyes. He cocked his head and then he gasped.

"The Qichuyahuar!" he said.

"What does that mean?" Bones asked.

"The Taking of the Blood." Tito's voice trembled. "It is a ritual of human sacrifice."

28

"**Oh hell no,**" Bones said. "I will…" He halted in midsentence and began frantically searching through his backpack. "Holy freaking crap. My Glock is gone."

Maddock checked his own pack and found that his Walther, too, was missing. He let out a curse. "Mine is gone, too. Nothing we can do about it now. Let's get the hell out of here."

Torchlight flared in the distance. Things were about to come to a head. They grabbed their backpacks and hurried out the door. London and Mayra were coming their way.

"My gun is gone," London said. "I had it in my pack because I didn't want to freak the villagers out."

"Same here. Let's just get to the boat as quickly as we can," Maddock said.

"Thank you, Captain Obvious," Bones said.

London flashed him an angry look as they began to run. "Is this really the time?"

"Gallows humor. I like it." Mayra winked at Bones, who looked surprised but pleased.

Like giant fireflies, torches flared to life all around them. It seemed the entire village was out in full force. They closed in all around. They were all stripped to the waist, their bodies and faces painted emerald green. Black paint ringed their eyes in dark ovals. And painted in white on each villager's chest was the same S-shaped serpent symbol they had first seen in the jail cell at Aguas Calientes.

"I think we've just learned the actual reason there's no priest in the church," Maddock said.

"I wish I had my sidearm," Bones grumbled.

"Maybe it won't have to come to a fight," Maddock said. "The dock is just around that bend."

No sooner had he spoken than two men came charging up the pathway toward them. Each carried a torch in one hand and a pistol in the other.

"Found your Glock," Maddock said.

"And your Walther," Bones replied. "They must have stolen them while Aristotle was chatting us up."

Up ahead, the two villagers stopped running and raised their weapons. Despite the painted face, Maddock recognized one of them as Aristotle.

"Stop!" Aristotle shouted. "We do not wish to fight."

Maddock slowed to a jog and moved as close as he dared before coming to a halt.

"If you don't want to fight, then let us get to our boat. We'll be out of your hair in no time."

"You must not seek Akakor," Aristotle said.

"Why not?" Bones asked.

"You must not wake the serpent!"

In his peripheral vision, Maddock saw the torch-bearing villagers closing in on them. As they slowly approached, he once again heard their low chanting. Tito had claimed the villagers were preparing to make a human sacrifice. That meant that sometime very soon, he and Bones would have to try and disarm these men.

"I like when a woman wakes my serpent," Bones said, inching closer to Aristotle.

"What if we agree to call off the search?" Maddock asked. "We'll go back to Iquitos and never trouble you again."

Aristotle shook his head. "It is no good. You have offended the serpent and you must be punished."

"That's so weird. I was just saying that to London in our hotel room the other night.," Bones said. Aristotle frowned. "I hate it when a joke doesn't land," Bones said to Maddock. Their eyes met. Bones gave a tiny nod. The first one to see an opening would attack.

"If you don't want to fight, then what's your plan?" Bones asked.

Aristotle laughed. The villagers, torches raised high, had them hemmed in. A few circled around to stand behind Aristotle to bar their way to the dock. Maddock looked around and saw that, while some villagers carried clubs or knives, most were unarmed. He saw no more firearms than those that had been stolen from his party.

"Our plan is for you to quietly return to the village."

"No thanks," Maddock said. "We find your hospitality sorely lacking."

"You have no choice," Aristotle said. "If you come quietly, I promise we will let the women live. Such beauty can be put to better use.

"You are a pig," Mayra said flatly. With a blank look on her face and remarkable quickness, she drew a small-caliber automatic pistol and shot Aristotle in the chest. Before his partner could react, she shot him in the throat.

Though surprised, Maddock and Bones moved instantly. They sprang forward and scooped up their fallen weapons. Maddock's hand closed around the barrel of the pistol. Before he could pick it up and reverse it, something struck him in the back of the head. Still gripping the pistol by the barrel, he whipped around and struck one of the painted natives in the temple. The man went down in a heap, only to be replaced by a huge, shirtless woman. Her face and chest were painted in the same fashion as the men. She let out a serpentine hiss and stabbed at Maddock with what looked like his own Recon knife. He leaned to the side and the knife whistled past his ear. He kicked her in the gut and when she doubled over, he clubbed her in the back of the head with the butt of the pistol. She hit the deck, and he hastily retrieved his knife.

All around him were the thuds, grunts, and cries of hand to hand combat. Firelight swirled all around him. Bodies moved everywhere. He wanted to use his pistol but couldn't risk hitting the wrong target.

Bones drove his fist into a man's nose, breaking it. As the man staggered back, Bones drove a push kick into his chest and sent him flying backward. He fell at the feet of two oncoming villagers, who tripped and fell.

One of the men swung a torch at London. She ducked, then punched him in the throat. He let out a gurgling sound and let his torch fall to the ground. She snapped a crisp front kick that caught him square between the legs. He grunted and fell forward. London drew back a foot to kick him in the head.

"London! Run for the boat!" Maddock shouted. He didn't have time to see whether or not she obeyed his order. Another villager, a skinny, gap-toothed man with flyaway gray hair, charged in, screaming, holding a knife high above his head. Within the dark circles that painted his face, his bloodshot eyes reflected the torchlight.

Angry, exhausted, and just plain fed up, Maddock punched the man as hard as he could. He felt the impact all the way up to his elbow. The old man stopped in his tracks and blinked twice. Like cutting the strings on a marionette, he seemed to crumple in on himself as he collapsed.

Maddock heard the pop of a gunshot coming from the direction of the dock. He turned to see Mayra walking through the chaos like Wyatt Earp on his Vendetta Ride, calmly taking aim and gunning down the attackers one by one.

Maddock felt something grab him by the ankle. He yanked his foot free and turned, finger on the trigger.

"Please, Mister Murdock. Don't shoot." It was Tito.

"Come on. We're getting out of here." He grabbed the pilot by the collar, hauled him to his feet, and gave him a shove. "Get to the boat and get us out of here."

Tito took off in a dead sprint. His overstuffed backpack bounced from side to side, and he stumbled but did not fall. Maddock followed along behind.

The villagers' resistance was crumbling. One by one, and then in groups of three and four, they threw down their torches and fled into the jungle.

Maddock caught up with Mayra just as she was taking aim at the back of a fleeing villager. He forced her arm down, and she rounded on him with fire in her eyes.

"What is your problem? They tried to kill us."

"Shoot the ones who are actually trying to stop us from getting away. Otherwise, it's a waste of ammunition."

She looked as if she were about to argue, but then she gave a curt nod and made a run for the boat. They hurdled over the bodies of fallen villagers. Some of them would regain consciousness. Others would not.

They reached the boat only a few seconds behind Bones and London. While Tito fired up the engine, the rest of them hurriedly cut the mooring ropes on all the boats tied to the dock and began setting them adrift. Let the villagers try and follow them without any boats.

"We will go back to Iquitos?" Tito said.

"Do you want to get paid?" Mayra asked.

Tito gazed longingly upriver as if he could see all the way to Iquitos. His lips moved, but he didn't speak.

"We won't force you to go with us," Maddock said. "We can take one of these boats. But make up your mind right now."

"I will go," Tito said.

With that settled, they cut loose the rest of the boats, then climbed in and headed out into the water. They rode in silence for a while, keeping eyes and ears open for more danger. Maddock doubted the natives would try to come after them. Right now, he was thinking about the thing he and London had seen swimming in the river. Had it really been as large as they had thought, or was it merely a trick of the light and the moving water? He hoped they didn't have to find out.

29

"**Do you smell** smoke?" Boyd raised his head and looked around. He saw nothing but river and jungle. Alejandro and Diego had recruited two more Amaru and acquired two boats. Now they were deep in the Amazon, following a combination of clues he and London had uncovered.

"We smelled it half an hour ago," Alejandro said from his seat in the bow. He smirked at Diego, who sat at the stern.

"What do you think it is?" Boyd hated that he had to put up with these Amaru idiots.

Alejandro squinted up at the sky and considered the question. "I think… something is burning."

Diego broke out in a deep, hearty laugh. Boyd's cheeks burned. Screw these guys. Sometime soon he would find a way to remind them who was supposed to be in charge.

They rounded a bend and Alejandro announced that they had reached their destination. Boyd saw an old boat dock and a strange statue a few feet back from the riverbank. It was a kneeling Spaniard with no eyes.

"What the hell is that thing?"

"The Eyeless One," Alejandro said as the boats glided to shore. Was there a note of trepidation in his voice? "This is the village of Gari Gapra," Alejandro continued. "If the woman and her thugs came up this tributary, they are likely to have stopped here."

"How far is the walk?" Boyd asked. His injured ankle was getting better, but it was painful to walk on it.

Alejandro rolled his eyes. He turned and said something to the men in the other boat. They looked at

Boyd and laughed. Boyd regretted dropping Spanish after his freshman year. He forced a smile as if he were in on the joke. Just one of the team.

"Ignorant savages," he said through his false smile. He kept his words soft enough that no one else could hear. Still, saying it aloud made him feel better. "Tell them to go up to the village and find out if London was here," he said to Alejandro. "If she was, then I'll hike up."

"You can speak directly to them. Unlike you, most of them speak more than one language."

"Fine." Boyd turned and repeated the order.

"I said you could speak to my men. I did not say you could give them orders."

Boyd clenched his fists and his body trembled as rage boiled up inside him. He itched to wrap his hands around the skinny man's throat and choke the life out of him. But not until he had found the city.

Silence fell over the group, broken seconds later by the Amaru's uproarious laughter.

"We like to joke," Alejandro said. "We know you are the man paying the bills." He barked an order and two of the men in the other boat went ashore and headed for the village. Each man gave the creepy statue a wide berth.

"Are they scared?" Boyd asked, a note of derision in his voice.

"Of course they are," Alejandro said quietly.

"Why? It's just a statue." That was untrue. The thing was dark and foreboding.

"It is not the statue. It is what the statue means." Alejandro turned and looked him directly in the eye. "The distance a blind man can walk in the jungle."

"Is that some kind of riddle?" Boyd was too hot and tired to puzzle it out.

"That is the distance from this place to the source of an evil so foul that a man tore his own eyes out at the sight."

That bit of trivia was enough to send Boyd into a contemplative silence. The natives had to have it wrong. Akakor was not a place of evil. It was something very different.

A breeze blew in from the direction of the village, carrying with it the acrid odor of smoke. Boyd caught a whiff of burnt hair and scorched meat. Diego muttered something in Spanish.

"What was that?" Boyd asked. He was surprised when the man actually replied.

"When I was a boy, the house next to mine burned down with all of the family inside. That is what this smell reminds me of."

"Maybe someone is having a Darth Vader funeral up there," Boyd said dismissively. The Amaru actually understood and laughed at his joke. He hated how good that felt. He didn't need the approval of his inferiors.

Distant cries broke the silence. Angry shouts rang out from the direction of the village, and then a cry of pain.

"Start the engines," Alejandro said.

More shouts pierced the forest. The sound of many running feet came closer. Boyd unsnapped the safety strap on his holster and drew his pistol. His hands were clammy and shaking. He had spent countless hours at his local range, and he was accounted a fine shot. This, however, was very different.

And then his ears caught a dull, rhythmic song. As the sound drew closer, he recognized it as some sort of native chant. He saw movement deep in the trees. His emissaries to the village were returning as fast as they could. Hot on their heels was a horde of warriors. Their upper bodies were painted green, squiggly white lines covered their chests. They carried spears, clubs, and knives. There were only a dozen of them but to Boyd it seemed like an army. He rose on wobbly feet, nearly capsizing the boat.

"Sit down, man!" Diego said.

Boyd ignored him. He raised his pistol and took aim. When he had taken his oath to the New Dominion, it had been made clear to him that he might someday be called upon to take lives in the service of a greater cause. Now was that time. He had to find Akakor!

Alejandro glanced back and his eyes went wide. "Don't shoot!"

Boyd ignored him. The villagers hurled spears and rocks that fell in a rain around the two fleeing Amaru.

"They need my help!" Boyd aimed into the middle of the throng and squeezed the trigger. The gunshot was so loud that he nearly lost his grip on the weapon. One of the Amaru let out a cry and fell to the ground. Boyd tensed, then breathed a sigh of relief when he saw a spear stuck in the man's back.

Thank God I didn't shoot him.

At the sound of gunfire, the villagers in the lead hesitated and were run down by those who were just a few steps behind. The series of collisions gave the one surviving Amaru the extra seconds he needed to break free of the pursuit.

"Hurry, Shaq!" Alejandro yelled to the Amaru.

Boyd turned, glanced over his shoulder at Diego, and mouthed *Shaq?*

"His mother loves the Lakers."

"So, it's short for Shaquille?"

Diego shook his head. "No. Just Shaq."

Just Shaq had almost made it to the river. The villagers seemed to have recovered from their moment of fear and were once again dogging his steps.

"Get the boats moving," Alejandro said, then raised his voice and shouted through cupped hands. "Shaq! You will have to jump!"

The boats slowly began to back away. Footsteps and chanting filled his ears, gradually drowned out as the boat engines revved up. Shaq took the dock in two steps and jumped. He fell short of his mark but managed to grab hold of the bow of the boat as he hit the water.

"Keep going, Kobe!" he shouted to the man who was piloting the other boat.

"Are they brothers?" Boyd asked.

"No, but their mothers are sisters and rivals."

The villagers reached the end of the dock and began to fling whatever they could find at the retreating boats. A spear flew through the air, coming right at Boyd. He covered his head and ducked. He heard a clang inches from his body. He opened his eyes to see the projectile strike the gunwale and rebound into the water. Another spear flew but fell well short of its mark.

Boyd breathed a sigh of relief. His first time in combat and he had survived! He felt more alive than he ever had before. He felt like taking another shot at the villagers, but that would be a waste of a bullet.

"Why did they come after you like that?" he asked Shaq.

"They were circled around a fire, burning bodies. That was what we smelled. They had already worked themselves into a frenzy, and when they saw us, they attacked. Didn't give us a chance to tell them what we wanted."

"Savages," Boyd muttered. "What's with the weird makeup?"

"It is not to be spoken of," Alejandro said.

"Those squiggly lines painted on their chests are the same as the markings in the Blind Spaniard's prison cell. Was he the Eyeless One?"

No one answered him. As the shouts from the irate villagers faded in the distance, they settled into an uneasy silence. Boyd, however, was excited. He was convinced the natives had, in fact, been engaged in some weird serpent ritual. And that meant they were on the right track. Akakor would be his!

30

"**What is this** place?" Maddock looked around at the rainforest that enveloped them in a curtain of green. Standing among the jungle growth were a series of vine-covered shapes. None of them looked natural to his eye.

"It has no name that I know of," Mayra said. "Giancarlo calls it 'The Ruin.'"

Maddock nodded. Like so many places in the Amazon, nature had devoured whatever had been built here.

"And why are we here?" London asked, looking around nervously.

"If we didn't find Wilton at Gari Gapra, Giancarlo planned to come here next. This is where Wilton goes to commune with nature. And it's where the villagers said to look for him."

"It's also the area where the lady at the market told me the Cloud People had been spotted." Bones frowned. "By the way, Maddock, I've got a present for Dakota." He opened a side pouch on his backpack and took out a small bundle.

"What is it?" Maddock asked.

"Bark from the so-called teacher tree. Grind it up and boil it. The vapors are good for pain relief, the liquid cures illness, and you can make a poultice of the boiled bark to draw poison from a wound. Of course, it's probably all a bunch of crap."

Maddock noticed that both Mayra and London were staring intently at the bundle. He decided to hang onto it. Sometimes, a local remedy proved useful, even if it didn't quite live up to its legendary properties. He tucked it into his pocket, and they began to look around.

"This thing over here looks weird. It doesn't look like it was part of a wall or a dwelling." Bones pointed to a tall object covered in vines.

They moved in for a closer look. As they approached, Maddock began to make out details. The object was a head taller than Bones and carved from light colored stone. Bones began stripping away the layers of plant life. When he finished, they gazed at it in wonder. It was a statue of a scaly hominid with serpentine eyes.

Tito whimpered and took a step back.

"Is it human?" London asked.

"Could be alien," Mayra said.

"Maybe it's Amaru," Bones said.

"I don't know what it is, but I suspect it means we're getting closer to Akakor," Maddock said. Something caught his eye and he moved closer.

There were seven circular indentations carved into the thing's chest. At first, he had taken them for the natural consequence of erosion, but there was something about the way they were arranged that triggered a memory.

"London, can you call up the photos of the Petroglyphs of Polish?"

"Any particular one?" she asked.

"The map stone."

London held the photo up beside the statue. Everyone saw it at once. The same seven-dot pattern was carved into the stone near a sinuous line that resembled the river they had traveled today.

"What is this? It's a perfect match!" Mayra said.

"We think this might be a map," Maddock said.

Mayra frowned. Apparently, she had not been fully

briefed on their expedition.

"We should look around and see if anything else around here matches anything else on the glyphs," Bones said.

"Agreed," Maddock said. "It'll give us something to do while we wait for Wilton to show up."

They began by clearing the jungle growth away from all the structures in the immediate vicinity, but they found only partial walls and a few piles of stone. There were no more statues nor carvings of any kind.

"Let's try treating this as a map," Maddock said. "We'll operate on the assumption that this is the river, and this is the statue." He pointed to the two symbols. "North would be over here. And this weird-looking thing would be to the northeast." He indicated a pictograph that showed spirals connected to sinuous lines.

"Let's check it out," Bones said.

Tito volunteered to remain behind in case Wilton appeared. They left their heavy packs in his care and plunged into the jungle. They were off the edge of any reliable maps of the region. Maddock took care to track their course, and London constantly flipped through a stack of satellite images, maps, petroglyphs, and her own notes. Bones took a more practical approach, occasionally using his machete to hack an arrow shape into the bark of a tree. The arrows all pointed back in the direction they had come.

They had traveled for half an hour when Bones, who had taken point, stopped short. He stood stock-still. The world fell silent.

"What is it?" Maddock asked, moving to stand beside his friend.

"Look at this trail," Bones whispered, awestruck.

It looked as if a steamroller had passed through the clearing, crushing everything in its path, and leaving a smooth trail as wide as a small car.

"What could do this?" Mayra asked.

"This is a snake trail," Bones said.

"Impossible!" Mayra snapped. "It would have to be…" Her eyes went wide. "Are you suggesting Yacumama is real? I mean, not just an exceptionally large variety of a known species, but an actual giant snake?"

Bones turned to London. "You didn't tell her?"

"What was there to tell? We are looking for the ruins of a city that is found in the same region that birthed the Yacumama legend, so we are following clues pertaining to the legend. I don't take the legend as literally true. Although, I can't think of another explanation for this track."

Mayra crossed her arms. "What else have you hidden from me?"

"I haven't intentionally hidden anything from you. Anything I haven't brought up is theory or speculation on our part, or simply hasn't come up yet. I've conducted a lot of research over the past several years."

"How about you begin filling me in while we continue our search?" Mayra asked.

Maddock checked their bearings. The giant snake trail, if that was what it was, ran in the same direction they were headed, so they followed it. It was like a road cut through the jungle, and they were able to move quickly. As they walked, London brought Mayra up to speed.

"You already know, we are searching for the lost city of Akakor. We believe that this is also the City of the Serpent God out of Inca legend. We don't have a complete map; just a portion of an old map without any context to it and no way of connecting it to an actual location."

"Let me see it," Mayra said. She frowned at the image of the map taken from the body of White Flower. "What is this map written on?"

"Mummified human flesh," Bones said.

"You can explain that to me later. Where does the search for Yacumama come in?"

"We're not looking for her per se. Yacumama guards the City of the Serpent, which we believe is Akakor. Our hope was she could lead us there."

"Metaphorically," Bones added. "We're not looking to hire a giant snake as our tour guide."

Mayra considered what they had told her. "These people who are chasing you, the Amaru, I assume the serpent scale tattoos have some connection to all of this?"

"Amaru is Quechua for 'serpent.' That's the only connection we're aware of," Maddock said.

"It is possible that they are working with a man named Boyd," London said. "He works for my father. He's no good."

"That is a lot to take in at once." Mayra took a deep breath and let it out in a rush. "All right. I suppose the essentials of the job haven't really changed. But I want time to review all of your information, even the more speculative elements. It's absurd to hide potentially helpful information from your guide."

"Fair enough," London muttered, not meeting Mayra's eye.

The snake trail followed a winding path that continued to take them in the direction they wanted to go. Maddock checked his watch then glanced at the sky.

"We should turn back soon. I don't want to try and find our way in the dark."

"Just a little bit farther," Bones said. "I've got a feeling." As was often the case, Bones' gut spoke true. They rounded a curve and found themselves standing in a clearing staring at a bizarre sight. Bones scratched his head.

"Would somebody like to tell me what the hell that is?"

31

Before them stood a weathered statue of what appeared to be a giant tortoise with an exceptionally long neck and tail and tentacles in place of legs. The statue was weathered and crumbling. Trees grew upon the back of its shell.

"I have never seen anything like that," Mayra said. She hung back, apparently reluctant to come any closer.

Bones was captivated by the sight. He was well read in the field of cryptozoology, but he had never heard of such a creature. He was, however, convinced that this was the object denoted on the glyph map. The spirals represented the tentacles and tail, and the single, blunt protrusion was the head and neck.

"I think we've confirmed that the glyphs are, in fact, a map," Maddock said.

Bones scratched his head. "I still want to know what this is."

"That is Sachamama," a voice said from behind them. They turned to see an old man with a heavily lined face and thick black hair sprinkled with silver. He smiled at their surprise. "I did not mean to startle you. I learned long ago how to move in the jungle without been heard."

Bones nodded. Taking him by surprise required an uncommon skill set. Bones had sharp eyes and ears, and had spent much of his life in the wilderness.

"Are you Wilton?" London asked.

"I am," the man said simply. "And who might you be?"

London introduced herself and explained that Mayra was her guide and Maddock and Bones her support staff, as she phrased it. Wilton greeted each with a small nod.

"Wilton is an interesting name," London said. "I don't think I've heard it before."

"It means 'place by the stream.' Perhaps that is why I choose to live in the Amazon."

"So, what can you tell us about Sachamama?" Bones said, glancing up at the statue.

"Sachamama is the Earth Mother," he said.

London sucked in a sharp breath. "Sort of like how Yacumama is the Mother of Waters?"

"Precisely. Sachamama comes from the world beneath, and is one with the earth. She can lie in one place for extended periods of time, so long in fact that the jungle sometimes grows on top of her shell. She is a master of camouflage, and despite her great size, she can escape notice by closing her eyes."

"I'm not sure it works that way if you're over the age of three," Bones said.

"Her eyes glow like fire, and she can use them to hypnotize or bless you, depending on whether or not you please her. The earth trembles when she walks, and she crushes everything in her path."

"What happens after she hypnotizes you?" Maddock asked.

"Sometimes you do her bidding. Most of the time she simply devours you."

"Is she a giant river turtle?" Bones asked. That was the creature she most strongly resembled, except for having tentacles for legs.

"Something like that, but she is much more."

"Why do they call her the Earth Mother?" Maddock asked. "Is it because she comes from within the Earth?"

"That is part of it. But she is a mother to all plant life.

Anything that grows, she can imbue it with her power."

London was nodding eagerly. "She's like Mother Nature!"

Wilton scratched his head and shrugged. "Something like that. Inca religion includes a goddess who is similar to your culture's image of a Mother Nature. When the Europeans invaded, they subsumed the story into the character of the Virgin Mary. Some of us believe that all Earth Mother legends have their beginnings with Sachamama."

"Is Sachamama real?" Mayra asked.

"Real?" Wilton frowned, the lines on his brow deepened. "What do you mean?"

"Is she merely a legend, or maybe an Ayahuasca-induced vision, or is there an actual Sachamama stomping around the jungle?"

"Sachamama has not been seen in my lifetime, but others have seen her."

"What about Yacumama?" Mayra pressed. "Bonebrake thinks this is the trail of a giant serpent." She pointed to the track they had followed to this place. It wrapped around the statue and continued on into the jungle.

"Of course Yacumama is real. I have seen her myself."

"You have?" Mayra asked.

"Yes, but never up close." He stood with his hands on his hips and looked at the group of explorers. "I have answered your questions, so perhaps you will do the same for me. How do you know my name?"

"We have been looking for you," London said. "Mayra's brother, Giancarlo, gave us your name. He said you might be able to help us with some partial maps."

"You do not look much like Giancarlo," he said, his

brow furrowed.

"Same mother, different fathers," Mayra said. "My mother was not married to Giancarlo's father when I was conceived, so it's not something we talk about."

"Please forgive me," Wilton said. "I am suspicious by nature. What are these maps you speak of?"

London began with the map stone from the Petroglyphs of Polish, pointing out the details they had already identified. Wilton identified most of the lines as rivers that were known to him.

"What about this fat line that looks like a giant snake?" Bones asked.

"There is a river there as well, though not so large as it is represented on this map."

"Other than the two statues we have already identified, does anything on this map correspond with old ruins? A city, perhaps?"

"No," he said flatly.

Next she showed him the map taken from White Flower's tomb. "This is a partial map. Does it look at all familiar to you?"

Wilton took a long look at the map. He rotated it a quarter of a turn at a time, giving each new perspective a careful examination. Finally, he nodded.

"There is a place northeast of here where several small streams converge. That is what this looks like to me."

Bones frowned, tugged at his ponytail, then his eyes lit up. "Remember the image from the cell that we thought was the setting sun? I think it was this place. Five streams emerging from one side of a circle."

Maddock nodded. There was a resemblance between the two images. He turned to Wilton. "How about a system of underground caverns? Anything like that around here?"

"The streams meet at a sinkhole, where they feed an underground river. Perhaps there?"

Maddock took out a conventional map, unfolded it, and spread it out on a smooth rock. The area they were now exploring was woefully short on details, with only a few rivers marked.

"Is there any chance you could help us locate these spots on our map?"

Wilton took Maddock's pencil and began making notations. He drew in the rivers from the petroglyph map. Further to the northeast, he added those from White Flower's map, leaving a gap between the two.

"Maybe the map hidden with Pizarro would have bridged the gap between the two?" Bones kept his voice low. Maddock looked at him and gave a nod.

Wilton quickly became absorbed with his task, adding landmarks and notes, filling the empty spaces with vital details.

"Dude, you are like a walking satellite photo," Bones said.

"I am better. There is so much the cameras cannot see."

"How about the other photos we've taken?" Bones said to London. "Maybe something else will ring a bell?"

Wilton skimmed through their material, shaking his head as he swiped past each image. Finally, he stopped and uttered out a small note of surprise.

"Found something?" Bones asked.

"I have seen these patterns before." He held up a photo from the Petroglyphs of Polish.

Bones tried to keep the excitement from his face. He could tell Maddock and London were doing the same. If their information was correct, these symbols were the key to the underworld!

"Where did you see them?" Maddock asked.

"At the spot where the river plunges into the earth."

Bones clenched his fists and resisted the urge to let out a cry of triumph.

"Could you show us the way?" Maddock asked.

"I could but I will not."

"Why not?" London demanded.

"Because the river you must travel will take you into the very center of Yacumama's territory."

32

They set out the next morning following the course Wilton had mapped out for them. They floated along in near silence. Up to this point, Yacumama's existence had been theoretical. Now, the discovery of the giant snake trail coupled with the old woodsman's words had turned a scant possibility into a probability.

The river was wide and deep, enfolded on either side by the jungle's thick green arms. This far from civilization, the diversity of life was incredible. Along the way they had spotted sloths, toucans, parrots, howler monkeys, even a few pink river dolphins. Maddock was on high alert, keeping a close eye out for danger. The tributary they followed seemed to take them into another world. They had not seen any signs of human life—no villages, not even a fisherman or a hunter. Ordinarily, Maddock would find comfort in the absence of so-called civilization, but there was a dark, oppressive feel to this place. He was keenly aware of how isolated his party was, and a dark sense of foreboding hung over him despite the bright sun that shone down.

"Is it much farther, Mister Murdock?" Tito asked.

"The map isn't to scale, but judging by the landmarks, we aren't far away," Maddock said. He had given up on correcting the man about his name.

"That is good." Tito had been reluctant to continue the expedition, but had changed his mind once the others made it clear that they would be continuing, with or without him and his boat. In the end, he had chosen strength in numbers over traveling the river alone. "You said the snake trail was wider than an automobile?"

"Not a real car," Bones said. "A Smart Car maybe." He held his hands about four feet apart.

"We don't know for certain that it is a snake trail," London said.

Tito ignored her. "And Wilton said this river is home to Yacumama?"

"According to legend, which I'm sure is all there is to the story," she said.

They entered a long, fairly straight section of river. In the distance lay a fork where two rivers converged.

"We'll take the branch on the left," Bones said. "We want to go northeast." He turned to say something else to Tito and he froze.

"What is it?" Maddock asked.

"There's something back there." Bones pointed downriver. Something was moving in the river. "It's mostly submerged so I can't make out any details. But it's large and it looks like it's coming this way."

Maddock caught a glimpse of an undulating shape twisting through the water. His heart raced.

London took out a pair of binoculars and took a look at the distant object. She let out a little gasp.

"What do you see?" Maddock had a feeling he already knew.

"I'm not sure. It went underwater almost as soon as I caught a glimpse of it. It's definitely a living thing, and not a floating log." She passed the binoculars over to him.

He raised the binoculars to his eyes and focused in on the place where they had spotted the thing moving. The first thing he saw was the V-shaped ripple caused by something large moving beneath the water. It reminded him of alligators swimming underwater in the lakes and rivers of his home state of Florida.

"See anything?" Bones asked.

"Nothing much." And then he saw it! A pointed head just beneath the water, and a serpentine tail flicking back and forth. He let out a sigh of relief. "It's a black caiman."

The others visibly relaxed. Even Tito managed a smile. Maddock handed the binoculars to Bones, who whistled at the sight.

"That thing is huge! I'll bet it's a good seven meters long from nose to tail."

"So, like twenty five feet?" London said.

"That would make it a world record, I think," Maddock added. The typical black caiman measured within the fifteen to twenty-foot range, about five to six meters. This creature far outstripped that. Now feeling more at ease, they took a moment to admire the magnificent reptile in its natural environment.

"If this stretch of river is home to an exceptionally large strain of black caiman, could that be the reason Yacumama is reputed to live here?" London asked.

Maddock doubted it. Wilton had seemed quite certain about Yacumama, and there was no way a caiman had left the giant snake trail in the jungle. But he saw no need to cause Tito unnecessary panic.

"Possibly," Maddock said.

"It's comforting to know there are still places in the world where a magnificent creature like that can live unmolested by humans." London took out a camera and began snapping photographs.

"It's the apex predator out here," Bones said. "What other animal is going to mess with it?"

His question was answered seconds later. There was a rustling at the river's edge, the underbrush shook, and then a vision from hell burst forth. It was a giant snake.

Not merely the largest Maddock had ever seen. This was a monster from his worst nightmares. It was a dark, mottled green. Its head was the size of a coffee table, its body so thick that Maddock could not have wrapped his arms around it.

London let out a scream of sheer terror as Yacumama plunged into the river. Its body was impossibly long, and it seemed like forever before its full length was clear of the tree line.

"Get us the hell out of here!" Maddock ordered.

Tito didn't have to be told twice. He gunned the outboard motor and the boat surged forward. The caiman recognized the danger and began swimming upriver as fast as it could. Yacumama closed in behind it.

"No, don't lead it toward us!" Bones said to the fleeing reptile.

The boat strained against the slow-moving current. Tears streaming down his face, Tito fought to coax every ounce of speed out of the craft that he could. Behind them, the caiman continued to swim upriver with Yacumama in relentless pursuit.

"We'll never outrun her!" Mayra drew her pistol and chambered a round, but Maddock grabbed the barrel of the weapon before she could disengage the safety.

"Do not do that," Maddock said.

"Why not? That thing could eat us alive."

"Which is precisely why you don't want to piss her off," Bones said.

Mayra made a grudging nod and holstered her weapon.

"What do we do?" London asked, her voice trembling.

"We keep running and hope she leaves us alone. If it comes to a fight, we'll give it to her, but we're not going to antagonize her if we can avoid it."

Reluctantly, London nodded. "I hired you two to get me in and out of here safely. If that thing eats me, I'm going to haunt you for the rest of your lives," she said to Maddock and Bones.

"Fair enough," Maddock said. He could not take his eyes off Yacumama as she bore down on the caiman. She moved through the water at a rapid clip, churning up a wake like a speedboat as her undulating coils drove her forward.

The caiman angled off and made a run for the far shore, but it was far too slow. Yacumama caught up with it just as it reached the shallows. Recognizing its peril, the caiman turned to fight. But Yacumama was gone.

"Where did she go?" London whispered.

"She submerged," Bones said quietly. "Could be anywhere."

Three heart pounding seconds of silence ensued, broken only by the whine of the engine and the slapping of water against the gunwale. And then the water around the caiman erupted in a gush of white foam.

Yacumama burst out of the river, jaws open wide, and sank her fangs into the huge crocodilian. The caiman fought with all its might. It thrashed, snapped its jaws, and battered the giant snake with its powerful tail. Each blow struck with a resounding slap.

"That's got to sting," Bones said.

The caiman continued to struggle, but it couldn't break free of Yacumama's powerful jaws, and could not get its head around to bite the giant snake.

"She bit through that caiman's hide like it was nothing," Bones said.

"Can you not point out the obvious?" London said.

"Sorry. I meant to say that pathetic little snake doesn't scare me one bit," Bones said.

"Screw you, Bonebrake."

They watched, mesmerized, as Yacumama wrapped the caiman in its coils and began to crush the primordial beast. Slowly, its struggles ceased, until only the occasional twitch indicated it had ever been alive.

"At least she isn't chasing us anymore," London said.

"Looks like she was just looking for dinner," Bones said as Yacumama unhinged her lower jaw and began to swallow the caiman headfirst.

"I can't watch this." London covered her eyes.

"Better it than us," Maddock said. He continued to stare at the gruesome sight until they rounded a bend and Yacumama disappeared from sight.

33

Boyd was growing impatient. The heat and humidity made him feel like he was living inside a greenhouse. The biting and stinging insects seemed to have no interest in his Amaru companions, and his best insect repellent seemed to have little effect.

"I... am... sick... of... this!" he grunted, swatting at flies with his bare hands.

"You know what they say." Diego grinned. "White meat is healthier than dark meat."

All the men laughed, even Boyd. They would be singing a different tune once they reached their destination. A lot of people thought they knew what was hidden there, but Boyd was confident that only he and those who had sent him knew the truth.

"You just smiled. I did not know you had teeth," Diego said.

Boyd couldn't tell if the native was mocking him or trying to be friendly. At least Diego was willing to talk with him sometimes. The others had plenty to say *about* him, mostly in their own language and under their breath, but they avoided speaking directly to him.

"I'm in a good mood," Boyd said. "My ankle is feeling better, I've lost so much weight that I had to drill a new hole in my belt, and soon I'm going to walk into Akakor."

"Good thing, because I am not going to carry you."

Once again, Boyd wasn't certain if he was in on the joke or the butt of it, but he laughed. "The only thing you will be carrying is your share of the gold." Boyd had told the Amaru about the gold in order to get them on his side. But they didn't know the rest.

"And your mysterious map is still proving reliable?"

"Absolutely. We are definitely on the right track." The Petroglyphs of Polish and its map stone had been a revelation. The moment his eyes fell on it, he had recognized a symbol that also appeared on the Black Thorn map. After that, things began to fall into place, and it was all thanks to London's research. There was still the matter of White Flower's map. He was banking on them catching up with London and retrieving it. But if they did not, he was confident they would be so close to Akakor they could not help but find it.

Something at the edge of the jungle caught his eye. It was large, mottled green, and scaly. His first thought was that it was a snake, but it couldn't be. It was way too large. He had caught only a glimpse, so he couldn't say for sure.

Twenty feet upriver he caught another glimpse of it. Strange that the thing had managed to outrun the boat, yet seemed to be lying still. It didn't make sense. Unless...

London's research had hinged upon the theory that Akakor was the City of the Serpent God, which was guarded by the legendary giant snake, Yacumama. It had seemed academic to Boyd, connecting the dots of serpent lore. But what if it were real?

A rifle lay at his feet, and he snatched it up. His eyes scanned upriver for another sight of the thing. His eyes fell on what he initially thought was a wedge-shaped rock, and he gasped.

"Is there a problem?" Diego asked.

"Do you see that? On the far side of the river?" He pointed at the thing that lay by the river's edge, partially concealed by leafy green foliage.

Diego shielded his eyes from the sun and squinted at the opposite bank. In the span of three seconds his expression went from disinterest to curiosity, then from interest to sheer panic. That confirmed it in Boyd's mind. He was looking at the head of a giant snake. Diego let out a yelp.

"What is wrong?" Shaq called from the other boat.

"Yacumama!" Diego pointed a trembling finger at the giant snake.

Shaq clearly thought it was a joke, as did his cousin Kobe, who was piloting the other boat. A moment later, Kobe shrieked when his eyes fell on the snake.

"Yacumama!" he wailed.

"Quiet!" Alejandro turned and frowned at Boyd. "It looks like she has fed recently. Reptiles are often sluggish while they digest their food. Perhaps she will leave us alone."

Boyd doubted it. Even if they got away this time, they would still have to pass this way coming back. And by then, Yacumama would probably be hungry again. He needed to eliminate the threat. He raised the rifle and aimed down the sights.

"What are you doing?" Diego gasped.

"The thing is lying there sunning itself. It just ate. We might never get another chance to kill it."

"You would need a bazooka," Diego said. "A bullet will only anger her."

"I'll shoot her in the eye," Boyd said. He wasn't great with a handgun, but he could handle a rifle. He'd been squirrel hunting since he was seven years old. He could do this.

"You can't make that shot from this distance," Alejandro said.

Boyd's mouth went dry as doubt began to creep in. Could he make the shot at this distance? Should he even try?

And then Yacumama turned her head and looked directly at Boyd. At that moment he knew what it was like to look evil in the face. Since the Garden of Eden, the serpent had been the manifestation of evil in this world. Boyd had to kill it. God would want him to try.

Alejandro lurched toward Boyd, trying to grab the rifle. The boat wobbled.

Boyd squeezed the trigger.

"No!" Diego shouted, turning the boat hard to port.

The shot went wide and struck Yacumama on the snout. His shot ricocheted off the giant snake's skull but left barely a mark.

"I got her," he said.

Yacumama slowly raised her head. Boyd saw a flash of scales that shone like gold where the shafts of filtered sunlight struck them. Her hiss was like a dry wind rustling the last, dead leaves of autumn.

"You should not have done that," Diego said. He opened the throttle and the boat lurched forward.

"Just keep that engine in the red!" Boyd barked.

"I doubt we can outrun her," Alejandro said.

"We only need to outrun those guys." Boyd pointed at the men in the other boat.

"You are a selfish man," Diego said over the engine's wail as he tried to coax it to go just a little bit faster.

"I'm a pragmatist," Boyd said.

"I do not know that word."

"I see the world for how it really is, and not how I wish it would be. And that's not evil; it's honest."

On shore, Yacumama began to slither forward. Slowly at first, then faster. Boyd fired again and struck the creature in the flank. He held his breath. Diego had been correct. They needed more firepower. Otherwise, it would take a miracle shot to kill the monster.

Remarkably, Yacumama did not come after them. Instead, she turned and slithered off into the jungle. Silence fell over the five men as they stared in the direction she had gone, waiting for her to return. But she did not. Only after they had rounded a bend in the river did Boyd breathe easily again.

"I did it! I drove the damn thing away." Boyd laid down his rifle, closed his eyes, and took time to catch his breath. "Not so scary after all. Just a big, dumb snake."

Shaq let out a scream of sheer terror as a massive head popped up from beneath the water up ahead. Boyd understood in an instant. The snake knew this jungle well. While the boats had followed the winding river, Yacumama had taken a shortcut through the jungle and gotten ahead of them.

As the behemoth raised its head to strike, Boyd realized just how huge the thing was. His throat clenched. He wanted to scream but he couldn't make a sound. Eyes locked on the terrifying sight, he fumbled for his rifle with trembling hands.

The other boat stood between them and Yacumama. Maybe there was a chance for them to get away. He turned to Diego.

"Step on it!"

Diego looked down at his own feet. "Step on what?"

"Just get us out of here as fast as you can!"

Diego glanced at Alejandro, who nodded. The engine roared and the boat leapt forward, the bow rising as it cut through the water.

In the other boat, Shaq and Kobe were so preoccupied with the gargantuan serpent closing in on them that they didn't notice their allies leaving them behind. Spewing a stream of curses, Shaq stood, leveled his pistol at the beast, and emptied the magazine. Boyd watched, mesmerized, as bullet after bullet struck Yacumama's tough underbelly. Some of the slugs pinged off her hard scales. Others penetrated her hide, but the wounds were minor and seemed only to annoy the beast. She let out an angry hiss and then struck.

She snatched Shaq out of the boat. His curses died as the upper half of his body vanished inside her gaping maw. His legs kicked wildly as Yacumama lifted him high. She whipped her head from side to side until the lower portion of his body tore free and flew through the air. The legs were still twitching when they landed in the shallows. Moments later, a pair of caimans closed in. Boyd felt the bile rising in his throat as the crocodilians began fighting over the remains of the Amaru. Like two children pulling the wishbone at Thanksgiving dinner, the caimans began a tug of war over the twitching legs until they finally came apart. Boyd retched and turned away.

Kobe screamed at the sight of his cousin's violent demise. In his panicked state, he forgot all about trying to flee. Instead, he drew his own pistol and began firing wildly. Yacumama dropped the remainder of Shaq's corpse. She closed in, ignoring the bullets that pinged off of her skull. His magazine empty, Kobe hurled the pistol at the angry serpent.

Yacumama struck. Kobe dived out of the way and her jaws closed on the gunwale near the stern on the starboard side. The aluminum was no match for her powerful jaws and giant fangs, and the boat began to fill with water. Kobe grabbed a paddle and threw it like a spear at Yacumama. Remarkably, it found its mark, disappearing into the serpent's open mouth. But Yacumama gave a shake of her head and sent the paddle flying away. She struck again. This time, Kobe barely eluded her snapping jaws by diving into the water and swimming for the opposite shore, screaming all the while.

They rounded another bend and their companion disappeared from sight. When his shrieks turned to a sudden, squelching cry of pain, and then fell silent, they knew it was over.

"What do we do?" Diego asked softly.

"They are dead, and the snake is behind us," Alejandro said. "The only thing to do is go on."

34

They went ashore at the confluence of two slow-flowing rivers. Unable to take their boat any farther upriver, they beached it and hid it at the edge of the jungle before continuing on foot.

"How long do you think it will take to get there?" London asked.

"As the crow flies it's not too far," Bones said. "Unfortunately, we are not crows, so we will have to walk. Wilton gave us landmarks to follow, but we have no idea about the terrain."

"Or what we might encounter along the way," Maddock added.

Bones looked at Maddock and gave him a slow, scornful shake of the head. "Always tossing the wet blanket, Maddock." He held up his hand, palm facing out. "I know. You're just being realistic, because it never occurred to anyone else in this group that there might be something dangerous out there in the rain forest."

"Screw you, Bones," Maddock said.

Before beginning their inland track, they took a break to eat and recover their strength. While Maddock, Bones, and London reviewed their notes and scrutinized their maps, Tito pleaded with them to return to civilization.

"Please, Mr. Murdock," Tito pleaded, hands pressed together in supplication. "Let me take you back. You are making a mistake searching for Akakor. If you continue on this course, we will all die."

"If I had a dollar for every time someone told me that," Bones mumbled, tracing his finger across the map.

"Do you really want to go back right now and maybe

get eaten by Yacumama? I say we wait until she's had time to move along. And as long as we're waiting, we might as well search for the city," London said.

"Yacumama fed today. She should be satisfied for a while," Tito said. "Right now, she is probably sleeping. This will be our best chance to get away."

"I'm not sure we should count on Yacumama behaving like an ordinary snake," Bones said.

"What does Mayra think?" London looked around for their guide and frowned. "Where is she?"

Maddock stood and looked around. Somehow Mayra had slipped away without any of them noticing. A sense of dread filled him. Where had she gone? Had something happened to her?

"Bones, see if you can find her tracks. See where she went."

"You know what, Maddock? You remind me of the Lone Ranger."

"Oh yeah? Why is that?" Maddock asked, still scanning the jungle for any sign of Mayra.

"Because he was always sending Tonto into danger while he sat on his lazy ass until it was time to swoop in at the last minute and take all the credit." Bones made a sideways glance at London. "White dudes, am I right?" he asked in a tone of commiseration.

"Dudes in general," she said punching his shoulder. "How about Tito and I wait here while the two of you look around for Mayra?"

Bones turned to Maddock and grimaced. "I changed my mind. It's not just the dudes."

"Because you're all about blindly following orders," Maddock said, rolling his eyes. "You're just afraid I'll find her tracks before you do."

"You're on." Bones immediately began scanning the area where he had last seen Mayra.

"Too easy," Maddock whispered to London as he followed along.

Predictably, Bones found Mayra's tracks right away. She had left camp, moving in the direction of the river. But halfway there, all sign of her vanished. Not a single footprint, not a leaf pressed into the ground, nor broken twig to show that anyone had passed this way.

"I can only think of one explanation," Maddock said. "For some reason, she decided she did not want to be followed."

"Unless something came along and snatched her," Bones said. And then he froze. His eyes narrowed and his jaw dropped. Slowly he turned his eyes up toward the trees. Maddock's hand went to his weapon as he looked around. Bones chuckled. "Made you look. Did you seriously think these trees could support Yacumama's weight?"

"There are a lot of things I once thought impossible that have proved to be quite the opposite," Maddock said.

"Fair point. Want to keep moving toward the river?"

"You're the boss," Maddock said.

Bones arched an eyebrow. "I'm going to remember you said that."

It wasn't long before they heard a voice in the distance, upriver from where they had left their boat. As they moved closer, they caught a glimpse of someone moving in the forest. Maddock and Bones stalked them, drawing closer until they could make out three armed men wearing heavy backpacks, hiking into the forest. Two of them were Peruvian, one a big, pale redhaired man. Maddock recognized all three of them. It was Boyd and two of the Amaru whom they had fought inside White Flower's tomb.

"That's definitely not Mayra," Bones said. "Hold on. You don't think she's working for Boyd, do you?"

"Working for who?" a voice whispered. They turned to see Mayra crouching in the jungle behind them. Her eyes twinkled and she put a finger to her lips.

"Where have you been?" Maddock asked.

"Gathering fruit." She held up a small sack. "Out here, you never know when you're going to run across something edible. You grab it when you get the chance."

"Why were you hiding your tracks?" Bones whispered.

"I saw a group of natives. They had an uncontacted look about them. I thought it would be best to avoid them." Suddenly she raised up and frowned. "Where are London and Tito?"

"We left them behind while we came looking for you," Maddock said. His heart was racing. He'd been an idiot to leave them alone.

"The two of you go back and see to them," Bones said. "I'll follow Boyd. See if I can figure out where they're headed."

"We know where they're headed. Akakor," Maddock said.

"They've got Black Thorn's map. It won't hurt to follow them for a little while and make sure we are on the right track." He glanced at Mayra. "I'll be sure to leave enough sign for you to follow me if need be."

"We'll catch up with you soon," Maddock said.

They parted ways, with Bones slipping away into the shadows in pursuit of Boyd, while Maddock and Mayra headed off in the opposite direction. They hadn't gone far when they heard a shout coming from the direction of the river. Recognizing Tito's voice, they headed in that direction and found their pilot along with London at the spot where they had hidden their boat. Tito was stalking back and forth, cursing and pulling his hair.

"What's going on?" Mayra asked.

"Tito decided he was leaving with or without us," London said. "I came along to try and talk him out of it, but when we got here, we found that someone sabotaged the boat."

Maddock frowned. "Must have been Boyd and the Amaru." He filled them in on what they had seen, including the presence of natives in the area. "If we hurry, we should be able to catch up with Bones fairly quickly."

London and Tito had brought all the backpacks along, so Maddock carried Bones' bag as well as his own. They moved as quickly as they could while making as little noise as possible. Mayra easily moved through the forest with as much skill as Maddock, maybe even rivaling that of Bones. London also managed to choose her steps carefully without slowing them down. Tito was a different story. The distraught, frightened man moved as if in a stupor. Several times Maddock had to seize the man's shoulders and physically redirect him before he staggered into a patch of brush or stepped down on a dry, brittle twig.

Soon, they began to find the signs Bones had left behind—broken twigs, each pointing in the direction he had gone. Shortly thereafter, they came across deep boot prints in the soft earth.

"He's not being careful, is he?" Mayra observed.

"That's about three sizes too small to be Bones' footprint," Maddock said.

"Must be Boyd." London paused to check her map.

"And it looks like they're following the same path that Wilton lined out for us. We're closing in on Akakor."

Just then, a man appeared in the forest just ahead of him. He was tall and long-limbed, his muscles lean. He had a small, flat nose, large eyes, and an elongated skull. He had snow white skin and no body hair. He carried a primitive bow with an arrow nocked, ready to draw and fire. A strip of hide was knotted around his waist, and from it hung a knife in a leather sheath. Maddock recognized the insignia on the hilt—a swastika against a red and white diamond. He had seen its like before and knew that the words *"Blut und Ehre"* were inscribed on the blade. Blood and Honor. The slogan of the Hitler youth. But how had a tribesman in the depths of the Amazon come by it? Had the Ahnenerbe actually found Akakor?

Out of the corner of his eye, Maddock saw Mayra's hand twitch toward her weapon.

"Don't," he said. All around them, warriors were appearing out of the jungle. All were armed but none appeared hostile. In fact, none of them betrayed any emotion at all. "I'm not certain they mean us harm. Besides, if we tried to fight, I don't think all four of us would get out of this unscathed."

Mayra shrugged and flashed him a doubtful look, but she let her hands fall by her sides. "They seem slow-witted to me."

"All the more reason we shouldn't give these archers an excuse to release."

"Do you think these are the Guardians? The Uhga Mongulala?" London asked quietly.

The warrior in the lead turned a glassy-eyed stare in her direction when he heard the name. He said something in a language none of them understood, then beckoned for them to follow him. The other warriors fell in around them, and they allowed themselves to be led away into the jungle.

35

Boyd stumbled and almost fell but caught himself just in time. He let out a curse and swung his machete at the offending vine that had nearly tripped him up. Neither Alejandro nor Diego seemed to notice. The two had been unusually quiet since leaving the river. There had been no sign of Yacumama but still, they were jumpy, anxious. And it was getting on Boyd's nerves. Couldn't they see he had everything under control?

"You guys don't need to worry," he said. "When we get there, I will do the talking."

Alejandro frowned, glanced at Diego, then shook his head. "Who will you be talking to?"

Boyd's mouth was suddenly dry. Had he said too much? They might turn on him if they knew the truth. He would need to keep that to himself until they reached Akakor. By then it would be too late.

"I misspoke. I only meant to say I've got everything under control. You don't need to worry about anything."

"You shot Yacumama and she did not like it. That is reason enough to worry."

"Reptiles are stupid animals," Boyd said. "They eat, they sleep, they lie in the sun. That thing has already forgotten about us."

Alejandro and Diego exchanged dark glances. They blamed Boyd for the deaths of their friends. That was unfair. Boyd was the only one who wasn't afraid to fight back. Yacumama was an animal. A large one, to be sure, but still just an animal. She had likely had little or no contact with humans, which meant that she had not yet learned that man was the most dangerous creature on the planet. The bullets Boyd had fired had not killed her, but she had felt their sting. Now she knew they could fight back.

They continued on in silence until Boyd finally called them to a halt in front of a large, vine-covered mound. It was completely out of place in the remote jungle. He circled it, frowning, taking in its shape, then consulted Pizarro's map.

"Clear away those vines. I want to see what's under there."

The Amaru didn't like taking orders, but they complied. They used their machetes to hack and chop at the vines, then stripped them away. Bit by bit, the jungle surrendered its secret. It was a face—almost human, but with large eyes, a high forehead, and an elongated skull.

"Aliens!" Boyd gasped.

Alejandro rolled his eyes and said something to Diego in their native language. Diego chuckled.

"Is this on your map?" Alejandro asked.

Boyd took out his copy of Pizarro's map and scanned it. There was a skull drawn at the map's edge. He felt a moment of triumph followed by a sense of foreboding.

"It's on here. We are close." He looked around, a cold feeling rising inside of him. He had been certain that if he could just follow the map to its end, he could search from there until he found Akakor. He had underestimated the vastness and sameness of the rainforest. From this spot, one direction looked very much like another.

"Which way do we go?" Diego said. "We want our gold."

"Remember our deal. Any pre-Columbian artifacts are yours." Boyd wanted to laugh. These men were in for a surprise.

"Yes, yes, and you get whatever the Nazis and the men from Mars left behind." Alejandro smirked. "Show us the way so we can divide the spoils."

Cold sweat dripped down Boyd's neck. What would the Amaru say if they realized he didn't know as much as he had let on? Would they turn on him? Abandon him here in the jungle? He couldn't let that happen. Once they made it to Akakor, the tables would turn in his favor. But he had to get there first.

"I want to go over my notes again just to be certain. Let's take a break." Boyd realized he was holding his breath. Finally, the two men nodded and sat down on the soft earth. Sighing with relief, Boyd found his own seat a short distance away, sank to the ground, and closed his eyes. He didn't have White Flower's map, but he had London's notes and he had the petroglyphs. The answer was there somewhere. It had to be.

36

From his hiding place nearby, Bones watched as the Amaru uncovered the statue. His heart beat double time when he saw it. He couldn't disagree with Boyd. The damn thing looked like a freaking alien to him. Yes, the elongated skull could represent the cranial deformation the Inca once practiced, but the large eyes and tiny chin didn't appear human to him. And was the flat nose by design or had it been broken off or simply eroded over the years? Suddenly the Akakor legend seemed a little less far-fetched.

The Amaru began to press Boyd for directions to Akakor, but Boyd put them off. Bones grinned.

"You don't know where to go next because you don't have White Flower's map," he whispered.

Satisfied, he turned and retraced his path through the jungle. If Maddock and the others caught up with him soon, they would only need to slip past Boyd unseen and follow White Flower's map to Akakor. Boyd and his cronies would be left wandering the jungle while Bones and Maddock made a beeline to the city.

"Screw you, Boyd," Bones said. "I hope the snake catches up with you." No sooner had he spoken the words than he caught sight of something moving. His heart skipped a beat, but he recognized instantly that it wasn't Yacumama. It was a group of people moving in his direction. He melted into the foliage and watched their approach. Through the foliage he could see bare chests, primitive weapons, painted faces. These must be the uncontacted natives Mayra had spotted earlier. "Time to get out of here."

And then he froze.

In the midst of the throng of warriors were Maddock, London, Mayra, and Tito. Bones' hand went to his weapon as he quickly assessed the situation. The warriors had not bothered to disarm their captives nor had they taken away their backpacks. For a moment Bones wondered if he had misinterpreted the situation, but then he saw at least half a dozen arrows trained on the explorers' backs.

"What am I going to do about this?" He knew Maddock would be on high alert, looking for an opportunity to escape. The others were civilians, and he had no idea how they would react in a crisis situation. He determined to follow along for the time being and watch for an opportunity. If things looked like they were about to turn ugly, he would have to make his move and hope for the best.

The warriors were headed in the same direction Boyd had gone. Bones wondered if they might be taking their captives to Akakor. He shadowed them as they marched deeper into the jungle. The going was quick—these people obviously knew the jungle well. It would be difficult to elude them once he had freed the others.

Bones was excellent with a handgun and he was confident he, Maddock, and Mayra based on the way she'd handled a weapon in the fight at Gari Gapra, could prevail against these warriors in a fair fight. But getting things onto an even footing was going to be a problem. The men who were bringing up the rear posed the most pressing problem. Every one of them was poised to release an arrow into the back of one of their captives. Bones refused to take that risk unless it was absolutely necessary.

One of the warriors suddenly whirled around. Bones

ducked behind cover just in time.

Don't get careless, Bones, he chided himself.

The warrior stared directly at the spot where Bones was hiding. He frowned, then said something to one of his companions, who grunted and used his lips to point into the jungle. As the rest of the group continued on, the pair broke away and headed in Bones' direction.

Bones could draw his weapon and end these two in a heartbeat, but that would likely be signing Maddock's death warrant. Bones would have to draw them away, then circle back around to catch up with the main party.

He slipped away into the jungle and began moving on a parallel course to Maddock and the others. He glanced back and saw the two natives searching the spot where he had been hiding. They seemed baffled. Bones grinned. "Still got it."

A high pitched scream and a gunshot wiped the smile off of his face. It had come from the direction where he'd last seen Boyd. Footsteps crashed through the underbrush, coming his way. The warriors who had been searching for him heard the sounds and began running in that direction. Bones was trapped in between the two.

"You have got to be freaking kidding me." With enemies closing in on either side, Bones ducked behind the largest tree he could find. A moment later, Boyd and a pair of Amaru came into sight. The two warriors spotted them.

Arrows flew. One of them missed Boyd by inches, embedding itself into a nearby tree trunk. Another struck the soft earth at his feet. Incredibly, Boyd kept running toward the danger. Moments later, Bones realized why.

He caught a glimpse of a dark shape in the distance, saw a flash of mottled, dark green scales.

"Holy crap. Yacumama!"

The warriors spotted the giant snake at the same time Bones did. They immediately forgot all about the intruders into their realm, and broke and ran into the jungle. That seemed like a good idea to Bones. He drew his pistol and followed behind them, trying to keep out of sight. Out of the corner of his eye he saw Boyd turn, raise his rifle, and fire blindly into the jungle. One of the Amaru, Alejandro if Bones remembered correctly, grabbed him forcefully by the shoulders, turned him around, and gave him a shove.

That was all the help Boyd received from his allies. Boyd stumbled forward, hampered by his injured ankle. The two younger men quickly outdistanced him.

"Come back here you sons of whores! Don't you leave me!" Boyd shouted. He cast a terrified glance over his shoulder as the serpent closed in.

Sucks to be you, Bones thought. Sometimes life really was about survival of the fittest.

Boyd, however, wasn't finished just yet. He dug into a belt pouch and took out a spherical object. A grenade! He fumbled with the pin and pulled it free. Squeezing the grenade tight, he looked back again. Yacumama was almost on top of him. Boyd let out a cry of fright, stumbled, and lost his grip on the grenade.

Bones stopped running, unable to take his eyes off of the scene. Boyd began to crawl on all fours, blubbering madly, before regaining his feet and running faster than Bones would have believed the man capable. Behind him, Yacumama broke into the open. She stopped, raised her head to strike.

The grenade detonated.

The world was fire and smoke. Boyd went flying

through the air. Yacumama let out a hiss. Bones covered his head as dirt and debris rained down on him. When he looked up, he saw Boyd sitting up, staring dazedly into the jungle. There was no sign of Yacumama.

Bones decided to get while the getting was good. He took off in the direction the fleeing warriors had run. Off to the right, he heard the sound of running feet, and the Amaru calling out to one another.

"Alejandro!"

"Diego, where are you?"

Diego's only response was a bloodcurdling scream. Bones spied him just as Yacumama came slithering out of the jungle and into the path of the fleeing Amaru. Diego froze, a dark stain spreading across the front of his pants. Yacumama stopped mere feet from him.

"You don't want to hurt me," Diego said to the snake. "I am like you. Look!" He held out his left arm, displaying his serpent scale tattoos.

Yacumama slowly turned her head, fixing one huge eye on the terrified man.

"That's right," Diego said. "I am a serpent, too."

Yacumama moved with blinding speed. She struck, her massive jaws snapping shut on the extended arm. Diego gaped at the stump where his arm had been a moment before. He screamed and emptied his revolver into the snake. If the bullets had any effect on Yacumama, it didn't show. She let out another hiss. Diego turned and ran. Like a cat toying with a mouse, the serpent let him run a few steps before lashing out with her tail, striking him in the legs and sending him flying through the air. Diego crashed into a tree. His body went limp and he slid to the ground.

Bones' mouth went dry. If pistols, rifles, and grenades

were no good against Yacumama, what hope did they have of defending themselves against the legendary beast? The best thing he could do right now was get himself and his friends as far away from that thing as possible.

37

Maddock heard the cries and sounds of gunfire. Their captors heard it too. They halted, looked around, searching the jungle for the source of the sound. Maddock glanced at his companions. Mayra looked as if she was ready to draw her weapon and go full Doc Holliday. London was calm, constantly meeting his eye, ready to act. Tito was another story. He was sweating bullets, his breath coming in ragged gasps. His knees kept giving way, and the warriors who held them captive were becoming annoyed. One of them barked a sharp command and prodded Tito with his spear. Tito let out a yelp and scrambled to his feet.

"What do you think is happening out there?" London asked.

"Is it Bonebrake?" Mayra asked.

"I don't know, but I think we're going to reach a decision point pretty soon. Be ready to move at a moment's notice. If we are separated, keep moving north until you find the place where the rivers meet."

One of the warriors aimed a bow and arrow at him and barked an order. Maddock didn't speak his language, but he knew he had been told to shut up.

And then an explosion rang out in the jungle not far away. Maddock saw a flash of fire and wisps of smoke. The Ugha Mongulala began talking among themselves, pointing and arguing.

"Was that a bomb?" Mayra whispered.

"Boyd said something about wanting to get his hands on some grenades before we headed into the jungle," London said softly. "Sounds like he might have succeeded.

But why is he setting them off? Is he trying to blast his way into Akakor?"

Voices rang out, then a scream followed by a barrage of gunfire. Footsteps approached. Maddock turned to see two warriors dashing toward them.

"Yacumama!" one of the men shouted.

Everyone ran. Maddock and the others were still encircled by armed warriors, but it didn't feel as though they were captives any longer. They were all mice trying to avoid being the one fed to the boa constrictor.

Off to the right, Maddock spotted something large and dark slithering through the jungle. A cold feeling rose in his gut. Even the glimpse was sufficient to confirm that Yacumama was a behemoth!

No sooner had the thought passed through his mind than the giant serpent was upon them. Her massive head burst from the jungle, jaws open wide. The warrior scattered as she struck at the nearest native. He sprang aside just in time and her head smashed into the trunk of a rotting tree. It exploded, sending shards of wood flying in every direction.

The warriors were already showering the angry serpent with arrows. They concentrated their fire on its eyes and mouth. She didn't like it one bit. She coiled and prepared to strike.

"Let's make a break for it! Head west." Maddock shouted. London and Mayra heard and reacted immediately, dashing off into the jungle. Maddock looked around for Tito and saw the man standing frozen in place. "Come on, Tito! We're getting out of here!"

Tito didn't seem to hear him. His eyes were locked on the battle unfolding before them.

Yacumama struck and again the warriors evaded her

attack. Once again, she just missed. Another volley of arrows, almost all of which bounced off of her hard scales. One struck the soft flesh inside her open mouth and she let out an angry hiss and spun about. As she turned, Maddock saw blood flowing from damaged scales on her underside. He doubted the arrows had done that to her. Maybe the gunshots they had heard, or perhaps the grenade?

As Yacumama turned her head, her gaze locked onto Tito. Everything seemed to move in slow motion. Tito went rigid. Then, with robotic movements, he began to walk toward the snake. Maddock dashed toward him, but it felt like one of those dreams where he was running in deep sand and couldn't make headway. Arrows floated through the air. Out of the corner of his eye he saw someone running toward them. Maddock reached out to grab Tito and caught him by his shirt tail.

Yacumama struck.

The world returned to full speed with a jerk as Maddock was yanked off his feet. He found himself flat on the ground holding a chunk of fabric. He looked up to see the bottom half of Tito sticking out of the snake's mouth. He rolled up onto one knee, drew his pistol, and fired a shot at Yacumama's eye. He hit his target and the snake let out an angry hiss. She turned away but didn't release her prey.

"He's dead," a voice said from behind him. "Nothing we can do for him now."

"Bones. Late to the party as usual," Maddock said, rising to his feet and holstering his weapon.

"Looks like you chased her away," Bones said.

Yacumama had turned away and was headed back in the direction from which she had come. Tito's legs, sticking out from her mouth, still twitched. Maddock's stomach did a somersault at the sight. The warriors were harrying her flanks as she retreated.

"I think she lost interest in the fight and decided she wanted to go somewhere and eat in peace. After all, the reptile brain is even smaller than yours."

"Screw you, Maddock." Bones looked around. "Where are the girls?"

"Running that way. Let's catch up with them before our native friends decide they want to recapture us." He still didn't know what the tribesmen had planned for them, but he had no intention of letting them take him again.

38

London sat with her back against a fallen tree and took stock of her injuries. Lots of scrapes, cuts, and bruises but nothing too serious. The worst were the insect bites. Several were red and puffy and itched like crazy. The local bugs loved her fair skin. A wave of embarrassment passed over her when she remembered Maddock had hung back to face Yacumama. He was risking his life and she was worried about infected bug bites.

"You want some insect repellent?" Mayra asked. "I've got the best there is." She took out a tiny black cylinder the size of a cologne sample. There were no markings on it save for a tiny, interlocked SG engraved in the cap. "Just a drop behind each ear."

London doubted there was any repellant on the market that could turn back the constant onslaught of flying, crawling, biting, stinging misery. But this was the friendliest gesture Mayra had made and it would be rude to refuse. She unscrewed the cap and took a whiff. It smelled like a delicate blend of citrus, pine, and something pungent she couldn't quite place. It tingled a little when she dabbed it behind her ears.

"Give it about two minutes. I'm not even kidding," Mayra said, accepting the vial and tucking it back inside her pack. "It's rated for twenty-four hours but I find it wears off after about sixteen, so you'll want to dose yourself again in the morning."

A pleasant tingling sensation spread across London's scalp, out over her shoulders, and down her spine.

"What is this stuff made of?"

"Believe it or not, it's one hundred percent organic, all

sourced from the Amazon. It's a brand new product."

"I wish more people understood just how many remedies are just waiting for us here in the Amazon." The thought brought tears to the corners of London's eyes. Her fingertips began to tingle. She held up her hand and remarkably, the insects swarming around her flew away. Soon, they were gone.

"Works fast, doesn't it?" Mayra asked.

"I have got to get my hands on this. Who makes it?"

"I'll have to ask my brother," Mayra said, turning away.

"What other healing plants have you heard about here?" London said.

Mayra smiled. "All sorts. Obviously, a lot of the stories are crap, but some prove to be true. There are miracles here just waiting to be discovered."

London felt a sudden kinship for the guide who shared her respect for and trust in nature.

"Our encounter with Yacumama has driven home the very real possibility that we might not get out of this alive."

"That's a very real possibility any time you go into the rainforest. Yacumama is just the cherry on top of this expedition," Mayra said. She was so calm, serene even.

"I want to tell you something," London said on impulse. "There are still some things you don't know, and I want to share it in case something happens to me."

Mayra cocked her head, frowned. "Go on."

London bit her lip, suddenly nervous. "My father has cancer. He's got some time yet, but it's a death sentence nonetheless. That's what led me to delve into natural remedies from the Amazon." She paused, but Mayra merely nodded and gestured for her to continue.

"That sort of research tends to lead you into the realms of the esoteric and the really 'out there.' Since I was handling my father's black-market archaeological acquisitions, it was easy for me to dig into old legends from the region. I found many accounts of people being cured of all sorts of diseases, infirmities, deformities. All of the stories which were considered most reliable were centered on this part of the rainforest. The farther I dug, the more incredible the stories. One man born with one arm went into the jungle and came back with two."

Mayra raised her brows. "What kind of plant would do that?"

"It wasn't a plant." She hurried on. "The deeper I probed, the more connections I made between different legends and phenomena."

"Like the City of the Serpent."

"The City of the Serpent, Yacumama, Akakor, unusual animals, plants with remarkable benefits, and stories of healing so incredible that they could only have been performed by something of incredible power."

"So, not a plant?"

"I think the place that some call Akakor, others call the City of the Serpent, is home to something beyond our wildest dreams."

"I'm all ears," Mayra said.

"Mother Nature." For a stomach-churning moment she feared Mayra would burst out laughing, but the guide merely frowned.

"Convince me," she said.

"I can't do that, but I know she's there. There was a time when Mother Nature was alive in the world. All the ancient religions worshipped the Earth Mother. She once touched the world with her healing, cleansing power.

Now she has retreated and disease and death are running unchecked."

"And you think you can bring her back." There was no judgment in Mayra's tone. That was something.

"If at all possible. I'm not claiming I know exactly what she is or what the full extent of her powers are. But I am convinced that people have visited her home and experienced genuine healing. I couldn't bring my father into the depths of the Amazon without knowing exactly where I was going and being certain it would work. At minimum, I want to accomplish that much." She looked into Mayra's eyes and tried to read her thoughts.

"I'd be interested in seeing your research… about the plants mostly, and the healing stories, too."

"Everything is in my pack," London said, relief flooding through her. "You're welcome to take a look. Maybe if we find a safe place to stop for a few hours?"

Mayra nodded. A thoughtful look flashed across her face. She looked around, then drew her knife.

"What are you doing?" London asked.

Mayra turned and her eyes were suddenly cold, emotionless. London tensed. And then Mayra whirled around as quiet footsteps sounded nearby and Maddock and Bones appeared.

"I thought I heard someone." Mayra hastily sheathed her knife. "I should have realized it was you."

"Where's Tito?" London asked.

Maddock shook his head.

"What happened?" Mayra said.

Bones grimaced. "You've heard the phrase, 'belly of the beast'?"

"Enough said. Obviously, Yacumama didn't follow you, so how about we find a place to rest for a few hours?

I think we could all use some rest." She turned to London and flashed a smile that did not meet her eyes.

"Absolutely," London said. Privately, she vowed to keep as close to Maddock and Bones as possible. She couldn't escape the feeling that Mayra was up to something.

39

Bones was keeping watch when Mayra sat down beside him. He wasn't sure quite what to make of her. She was capable, easy to work with, and even easier on the eyes. But there was a distance there that he couldn't explain.

"You ought to be sleeping," Bones said.

"I wanted to speak to you alone," she said quietly. She looked in the direction of Maddock and London, both of whom were sleeping nearby. "What do you think of London?"

"I haven't had a problem with her if that's what you mean. She seems all right."

"You don't think she seems a bit…unstable?"

Bones tuned to look at her. "Why do you say that?"

Mayra took a deep breath and held it. She stared off into the darkness as if making up her mind about something. Finally, her shoulders sagged and she exhaled.

"I feel bad saying anything. She didn't tell me *not* to repeat this but it sort of felt like she was confiding in me."

Bones tensed. All along, he had sensed that London was stingy with her information. It always felt as though she was holding something back. Any time something came up that she had not yet shared with them, she always excused it by saying she had so much research that she couldn't possibly share it all. So far, nothing had caused him to mistrust her.

"Spill," he said.

"She's doing this because her dad is dying of cancer."

"She's not the first to look for a cure for cancer in the Amazon. I'm afraid she's going to be disappointed, though."

"But that's not what she's looking for. She thinks she's going to find Mother Nature."

"You mean Sachamama, the Earth Mother?"

"I mean she's some kind of New Age pseudo-Pagan who believes in an actual Mother Earth deity who lives underground out here."

Bones mulled over this new bit of information. He was undisturbed by it. London's belief system wasn't a common one, but it wasn't exactly unheard of.

"To be fair, there are probably a lot more religions that believe in Mother Earth than don't. It only seems weird to us because it's not part of Judeo-Christian tradition."

"She's doesn't revere the Earth as a mother. I think she's expecting the woman from the old margarine commercial to come walking out of the jungle and hand her a cancer cure."

Bones blinked. "Margarine commercial."

"You know? 'It's not nice to fool Mother Nature!'" Mayra raised her hands and made sounds like thunder booming and lightning crashing.

"How old are you?" Bones asked.

She elbowed him in the ribs. "I saw it online. It's part of pop culture."

"Pop culture changes too fast for me to keep up with it."

"Back to the subject at hand. Doesn't it bother you at all that she kept that a secret?"

Bones shrugged. "I know what it feels like to keep some of your beliefs to yourself because you know how they'll be received and what it will cost you in credibility. The way Boyd treated her, I can see why she wouldn't want us to think she's…" He searched for the word.

"A flake? Out there?"

"Something like that." Bones laughed.

"What's funny?" Mayra scooted in a little closer to him. It felt nice.

"I was just thinking you should meet our friend Dakota. That dude takes it to the next level."

"You'll have to introduce me." Mayra was so close that he could feel her breath on his cheek.

He glanced up. The sky was turning gray. It was almost time to wake the others. Almost. He leaned in for a kiss, and jerked away immediately as a mosquito the size of a dragonfly flew up his nose.

"Holy freaking crap! I am so sick of these damn bugs!"

"I have got the best insect repellent in the world. And if you're good, I might be persuaded to share it with you."

"I'm always good," Bones said.

Mayra produced a small vial, uncapped it, and dabbed a bit of the contents behind each of Bones' earlobes. He immediately felt a tingling sensation that spread down his spine and all over his body. He was about to remark on its potency when he saw the logo engraved on the cap. A wave of shock ran through him.

"Where did you get that stuff?" He tried to keep his tone casual.

"My brother got it from somewhere. It looks like a sample. I just hope he can get more."

Bones made a show of looking at the sky. "It's later than I thought. I need to wake Maddock."

"Are you sure we can't give them ten more minutes?" Mayra stuck out her lower lip.

"That's not nearly enough time for me." Bones forced a grin.

"Promises, promises," Mayra sighed. "I'll gather my

things."

Bones strode over to where Maddock was sleeping. He opened one eye as Bones approached.

"Already that time?" Maddock sat up and rubbed his eyes.

"We need to talk about Mayra."

Nearby, London rolled over. "Mayra acted really strange yesterday," she whispered. "I can't explain it. I just had a weird feeling, like she wanted to hurt me."

"That's not what I'm talking about," Bones said.

"And what about Gari Gapra? She seemed to relish gunning down those villagers."

"Villagers who were trying to kill us," Maddock said.

"Will you two shut up?" Bones whispered, looking around to make sure Mayra wasn't within earshot. "Mayra is carrying what looks like a test sample of some uber bug repellent."

"What's the problem with that?" Maddock asked.

"There's a ScanoGen logo on the cap."

40

"The sinkhole is just up ahead." Maddock paused at the edge of the clearing and looked around. Mist rose from the deep hole in the jungle floor where five rivers spilled down into its depths.

"I guess we climb down inside it and look for the symbols Wilton told us about. The ones that match those from the Petroglyphs of Polish?" Mayra asked.

They had decided to give Mayra a chance. ScanoGen was a multinational corporation of whom Maddock and Bones had run afoul on a few occasions. But ScanoGen also produced a variety of legitimate products which were distributed all over the world. Mere possession of one of their products did not necessarily mean Mayra was connected to the corporation. Still, they intended to keep a close eye on her.

They made their way to the sinkhole and peered down into it. Sheer walls plunged straight down into a churning pool ten meters below.

"I see the markings." Bones pointed to a spot near the water line. Petroglyphs identical to those found at the Petroglyphs of Polish—images that were symbols of the underworld. "But I don't see any way to get down there."

"We've got rope. We'll have to climb down and check it out," Maddock said.

"And by 'we' you mean I'll be the one to scout it out, and then the rest of you will follow," Bones said.

"I'll go if you don't think you can handle it," Maddock said.

"Screw you, Maddock. Your reverse psychology doesn't work on me."

"Most of the time it does," Maddock said.

"Cut the banter. Somebody's coming!" Mayra hissed.

There was movement in the jungle on the opposite side of the sinkhole. Maddock saw white figures moving in the trees. The Guardians were back.

The group found a nearby place to hide and watch. There were fewer Guardians now, and some were nursing injuries, but they had managed to add two to their number. They had taken Boyd and Alejandro prisoner. This time, they had relieved their captives of weapons and backpacks, but they were not bound in any way. Maddock found this puzzling. The warriors did not seem to be completely in control of their faculties. The captives were herded to the edge of the sinkhole where they stood staring down into the water.

One of the tribesmen pointed into the hole and said something in a language Maddock did not understand.

"Is this supposed to be some kind of sacrifice?" Boyd said. Again, the warrior pointed down and repeated the command. Boyd shook his head. "No way. You'll have to kill me first."

Exasperated, the warrior threw his hands in the air, turned, and jumped into the sinkhole. From their hiding place, Maddock could not see to the bottom, but a few seconds later, he heard the warrior again shout a command to Boyd.

"I guess the way in is by water," Bones said.

Boyd continued to protest until one of the warriors prodded him in the buttocks with his spear.

"Okay, I'm going," Boyd said. He inched toward the ledge, his sunburned face growing paler, until the toes of his boots were sticking over the edge. "Just give me second." He licked his lips, shifted his weight, and took a breath.

The warrior grew tired of waiting and gave Boyd a hard shove in the back. He flew through the air, cursing as he fell. Moments after Boyd vanished from sight, Alejandro followed of his own volition. And then, one by one, the Uhga Mongualala followed suit until the clearing was empty.

Maddock and the others rushed to the ledge and cautiously peered over. The natives and their captives swam to the petroglyphs and dove beneath the water. None of them returned.

"I guess that's the way in," Bones said.

"We should wait a little while so the coast is more likely to be clear when we get there," Mayra said.

Maddock let his gaze wander across the forest as he considered the situation. If there was only one way in, there was a good chance they would encounter the Guardians along the way. But unless they had come all this way only to turn back, that was a risk they would have to take.

"But how long do we wait?" London asked.

A flicker of movement in the distance rendered the question moot.

"We go right now," Maddock said, rising to his feet.

"Why?" London asked.

Maddock pointed into the jungle. Beams of morning light cut diagonal slashes through the mist, and danced off shiny, dark green scales.

"Because Yacumama is coming."

41

Yacumama was making a beeline for them. She twisted through the tangled jungle, crushing the undergrowth beneath her massive body. She would be on them in a matter of seconds.

"Think she'll follow us into the sinkhole?" Bones asked.

"I don't know, but I'm certain she'd follow us into the jungle if we tried to run," Maddock said.

No one needed to be told twice. First Bones, then London and Mayra took the plunge. Maddock waited to make certain all three made it back to the surface before he jumped feetfirst into the sinkhole.

The water was icy cold and delivered a shock to his system the moment he submerged. Down he went, deeper and deeper until he wondered if there was a bottom to this thing. And then his feet touched bottom. His foot sank through a layer of muck and landed on solid stone. He braced himself and pushed off for the surface.

The others were treading water in front of the petroglyphs. Maddock swam over to them.

"We thought we'd let you go first," Bones said. "In case the Guardians are waiting on the other side."

"Thanks for that," Maddock said. "Any sign of Yacumama?"

"She's right above us." Mayra pointed overhead. "There are handholds in the wall if you want to climb up and say hello."

They all looked up to see Yacumama's giant, triangular head poking out over the ledge.

"She looks confused," London said.

"Let's keep it that way. Come on." Maddock dived beneath the surface and immediately spotted a gaping hole in the sinkhole wall a few meters down. He swam for it, a gentle current pulling him along.

He swam through the opening and ascended into an air pocket inside a small underground cave. He climbed out onto solid ground and helped London and Mayra out of the water.

There was only one way forward—a broad, gently downward-sloping tunnel that plunged deep into the darkness. No one spoke. They could hear distant footsteps and an angry voice. It seemed Boyd was still being held captive.

Maddock and Bones quickly added red lenses to their Maglites to lessen the chance of being spotted, and then moved on down the tunnel, following the sound of Boyd and his native captors.

After a short distance, the way leveled out and they reached a fork in the passageway. They paused, listened, but they could no longer hear the Guardians.

"Which way?" Mayra asked.

"We can do like the old drinking game where you flip a coin every time you come to a stop sign," Bones said.

London frowned. "That's a driving game."

"You play it your way, I'll play it mine."

They went to the left. A series of twists and turns brought them to a place where a wall of rubble partially blocked the entrance to a low-ceilinged chamber. As their lights swept around the cave, London let out a gasp and Mayra cursed.

Lying among the stalagmites were the skeletal remains of soldiers clad in World War II era German uniforms.

"That explains how an Amazon warrior got his hands on a Hitler Youth knife," Bones said. "I'll bet these guys were part of the Ahnenerbe."

They moved into the cave for a closer look. A few of the skeletons, those nearest to the rubble pile showed signs of violent deaths. They had been stabbed, hacked, and clubbed. There were no firearms lying near the fallen soldiers—only knives and makeshift clubs. Farther into the cave lay a few more bodies. These lay on rock shelves, their arms folded across their chests.

"What do you think happened?" London asked.

"Looks to me like the Germans holed up in this cave for a while. These guys died first and were laid to rest by their companions, who eventually died fighting the Uhga Mongualala."

"They fought with hand weapons at the end," Bones said. "I guess they hung in there until their ammo ran out."

"I'd rather not suffer the same fate, so how about we get out of here?" Mayra said.

"How about you stand sentry for a minute? I want to have a quick look around," Maddock said. "We might find something important in here."

Mayra rolled her eyes. "Not unless you collect vintage belt buckles and scraps of moldering fabric."

"We'll be along in a minute."

While Maddock, Bones, and London made a quick search of the cave, Mayra returned to the rubble pile to stand guard. They found nothing of interest on the cave floor. There were discarded tins that had once contained rations, bullet casings, and little else.

They moved on to the remains of the soldiers who had passed away before the final battle. One man clutched a book which Maddock assumed to be the Bible, but proved to be a thick journal. A quick glance confirmed that it was written in German. Maddock tucked it into his pack. He would translate it when they had time.

"Check this out," Bones said. He had moved to the far end of the cave and was inspecting the body that lay there. "The dude is using a bag of crystals for a pillow." He held up an old leather bag, which immediately split, spilling the stones all over the floor. "Dammit!"

London hurried over and began scooping up the rocks. Maddock picked one up and shone his light on it. Gold flecks danced in murky, translucent stone.

"Don't bother. It's just quartz with bits of iron pyrite." He tossed the rock back onto the floor.

London paused, looked at the rocks in her hands, and then continued scooping them up and shoving them into her pockets. "Quartz has healing properties," she said. "Maybe these are extra special."

Maddock doubted it, but there was no harm in letting her collect them. They were visually appealing. He picked one up and tucked it into his pocket.

"What's that for?" Bones asked.

"If quartz has healing power," he resisted the urge to put air quotes around the phrase, "Dakota will probably love to have one from the City of the Serpent."

"I wouldn't do that," Bones said. "He'll probably take it as a suppository."

Maddock guffawed, but the moment of mirth was cut short when something flew through the air and clattered across the floor.

"Grenade!"

42

Maddock bore London to the ground, covered her body with his, and braced himself for the detonation. When it came, he knew from experience it was not a concussion grenade but a chemical grenade.

"Don't breathe, don't open your eyes," he said to London as he hauled her to her feet and ran for it.

The cave filled with a green mist. His eyes began to water and his lungs burned as he continued to hold his breath. He looked over his shoulder to make sure Bones was coming.

Bang!

Something struck him hard in the temple. Bright light and hot pain flashed through his head and he involuntarily sucked in a tiny breath. He tasted peppermint and caught a whiff of jasmine and coconut. He smiled at the pleasant smell. What had he been worried about?

"This is nice," London said dreamily. "Goddess, I need a nap."

"No, you don't," a gruff voice said.

Maddock was aware of a powerful arm wrapped around his waist. He was floating. The mist cleared and he realized Bones was bundling him and London out of the cave.

"Thanks," he said, regaining his feet. "I only got the tiniest whiff and it nearly knocked me out."

"I'm going to go out on a limb and say yes, Mayra is working for ScanoGen," Bones said. "I'll bet she vandalized the motor on Tito's boat. He wanted to go back but she had to complete her mission."

They moved farther out of the cave until they were well clear of the gas, then stopped for a breather. London took off her backpack and took out a vial of essential oil. "Eucalyptus," she said. "It will clear your sinuses."

"Dakota uses that stuff," Maddock said. "His place smells like kitchen cleaner."

"It's strong. That's the point." London held the cup under her nose and inhaled deeply. She passed the vial over to Bones who shrugged and took a whiff.

"That actually does help," Bones said.

"It purifies your sinuses," London said.

Maddock gave it a try. It was a strong scent, pleasant on the verge of being acrid, and it did seem to clear his head. He handed it back to London, who smiled.

"New Agers aren't entirely full of crap," she said as she replaced the vial in her pack. "And that includes your friend, Dakota."

Maddock shrugged. He had other things on his mind. Foremost was ScanoGen's agenda. What did Mayra expect to find down here?

"I don't get it," Bones said. "Boyd thought he was going to find Nazis and gold and alien tech. For us, it's an archaeological expedition to find the City of the Serpent. What do you think ScanoGen is after down here?"

London bit her lip. "In my research, I uncovered accounts of people who ventured into this area and returned having been healed of various infirmities. The stories must be true! That has to be it!"

"You think this is a plot to kidnap Mother Nature?" Bones asked.

London's cheeks turned scarlet. "Go to hell. First of all, let's not forget I was right about Yacumama. Second, irrespective of what I believe, there's obviously something at work here. The healing stories, the Guardians, who appear to be physically fit but not quite right." She tapped the side of her head. "With the abundance of natural products coming out of the Amazon, isn't it obvious ScanoGen is looking for something like that?"

"The attorney in you is showing," Bones said. "But fair enough. I take it back."

"Don't worry about it."

They moved quietly and kept a sharp eye out for Mayra, but she didn't appear. They returned to the fork in the passageway and this time took a right. The way down was steep, and their boots slipped and skidded as they made their descent.

"This is going to be a pain in the ass to climb back up," Bones said.

"You're welcome to stay down here," Maddock said.

Finally, they heard sounds, faint at first, rising in volume as they approached. Soon, the strains of chanting resolved into a steady pattern, one Maddock recognized.

"We've heard this before," Maddock said.

"The Qichuyahuar," London said.

Maddock nodded. "The Taking of the Blood."

"That does not bode well for your friend, Boyd." Bones didn't exactly smile, but the corners of his mouth twitched.

They rounded a corner and saw light up ahead. Soon, they no longer needed their flashlights.

"What could be making that much light all the way down here?" Bones asked.

"It's almost supernatural, isn't it?" London said, a note of sarcasm in her voice.

They came to a hole in the wall that looked out onto a large cavern. The walls slanted inward, giving the space a pyramidal shape. At the top, where the walls met, the space was open to the world above. They could just make out a few patches of blue sky through the trees and jungle growth that mostly obscure the hole in the earth.

"No one would ever spot that from the sky," London said. "And if the jungle around that spot is dense enough, it's not like someone would be likely to stumble across it. Not that outsiders come this way very often."

"And those who do have to make it past Yacumama," Bones added.

The thin beams of sunlight that steamed down from the opening cast the space in gloomy twilight. As Maddock's eyes drifted downward, he saw that dwellings had been carved into the lower portion of the cavern walls, giving it the look of a beehive. Many showed signs of habitation, but most were empty. The sign of a dying population.

An underground river cut through the cavern, flowing around a small island upon which grew small trees and tufts of jungle grass. Where the light struck the river it sparkled gold. Maddock frowned. That wasn't right.

"Do you see that?" he whispered to Bones.

"There's gold under the water. I think we should check it out."

"I assume that's where the Guardians are taking Boyd, and probably where Mayra is headed. We should proceed with caution."

Bones grinned. "Caution is my middle name."

They followed a winding path that led them to a domed chamber covered with line after line of script, the like of which Maddock had never seen.

"What is this?" London said, turning in a slow circle.

"Alien writing," Bones said. "I'll bet every penny of Maddock's money on it."

"But not your own?"

"Life is short. I spend what I earn."

"It's definitely writing," Maddock said, "and even if it's not the work of people from another planet, it's certainly alien to us."

"Part of the Akakor legend is the recording of knowledge. I'll wager this is the source," London said.

They took time to photograph every inch of the chamber. Perhaps it could be deciphered. When they finished they moved into the next chamber.

"Holy crap!" Bones said.

Standing at the center of a small chamber was an obelisk of the same translucent stone from which the pyramid in White Flower's tomb had been constructed. It glowed pink when the red beams of their Maglites struck it. But what was inside the crystal captivated Maddock. And then the others saw it.

"What is that thing?" London asked.

43

Encased in the crystal obelisk was a hand. It was not a human hand, but long with sharp claws and scaly green skin. Its fist was clenched as if clutching something precious. Maddock felt a sudden hunger to know what, if anything, was inside.

"I told you," Bones said "Aliens. Either that, or the sinkhole took us to the Land of the Lost."

"I didn't love that movie," London said.

"The movie sucked. The television show was the bomb. Worst green screen effects in history."

"How did it get inside there?" London said. "And don't say alien technology."

"I was going to say Sleestak crystals."

Maddock moved in for a closer look. The skin was dessicated, the fragments of bone jutting out were the yellow-brown of parchment.

"The crystal must have formed around it."

"Which means this thing is insanely old." Bones frowned, tugged at his ponytail. "Break glass in case of emergency?"

"It's tempting, but it looks like someone has already tried." He pointed to chips on one side of the obelisk.

Somewhere nearby, the chanting they had heard earlier resumed.

"The chamber must be close by," Maddock said.

Five passageways branched out from the room in which they stood. They followed the sounds of the ritual until they reached the cavernous space they had spotted from above.

Boyd and Alejandro were being led around to the far

side of the chamber. At the center of the island stood a tree-topped, rocky mound, shaped like an army helmet. The mound was no more than a hundred feet long and about two thirds that in height and width. In seconds, the Guardians and their captives were out of sight. There was no sign of Mayra.

"This is our chance," Bones said. He hurried to the edge of the lake, reached in, and drew out a golden gauntlet inlaid with turquoise.

"That's an Inca artifact," Maddock said.

Bones arched an eyebrow. "Really? I thought Thanos dropped by."

"Screw you, Bones." Maddock saw a glimmer of gold near the edge of the water. He pulled it out and held it up. It was a golden pipe, its stem engraved with a feather pattern and the bowl shaped like the head of a condor. "This is Inca as well." They looked at one another. "Atahualpa's treasure?"

"According to legend, the general dumped the treasure in a jungle lake," Bones said.

They looked up. The hole in the ceiling of the cavern loomed directly above the lake.

"That's one way to make sure the Spanish never got their hands on it," Bones said. "How about you, London? Find anything good?"

She didn't answer. They looked around and saw her wading into the water.

"What are you doing?" Bones asked.

"I'm going to the island. If there's anything of medicinal value growing in this place, that's where we'll find it."

"Might as well check it out," Bones said, tucking the gauntlet into his backpack. "It's not like we can carry all this treasure out of here."

They made their way to the small island. The shore was coarse gravel and glimmering crystalline sand. London was already climbing the rocky hill.

Maddock frowned. It was unlike any hill he had ever seen before. The shape was too round, too regular. The stone was dark brown and glossy, and engraved with deep grooves in the shape of hexagons.

"I don't like the look of this," Maddock said. "It doesn't look natural."

"Looks like they turned a chunk of rock into a work of art," Bones said. "There's probably not much else to do here. Besides, the grooves are the perfect size for climbing."

With that, they began scaling the steep mound. The surface was slippery and twice they had to grab London to prevent her from falling.

A cluster of stunted trees grew at the top of the mound. London walked toward them as if in a trance.

"I wonder how she's going to react when she finds out Mother Nature isn't living in a hut at the top of this hill," Bones said.

"It would have to be a small hut," Maddock said.

On the other side of the trees, the chanting continued. Boyd began to shout. It seemed as if things were coming to a head.

Within the shelter of the trees, London let out an anguished cry. They ran to her and found her down on her knees, uprooting plants and flinging them away.

"There's nothing here," she sobbed. "Just cat's claw, huasai, sangre de grado trees, and jungle grasses."

"Nothing with any special healing properties?" Bones asked with an unusual note of kindness.

"They're all useful as remedies, but there's nothing special here."

"I'm sorry, London," Maddock said. "I know what it's like to lose your father."

"I was wrong." London slowly shook her head. "There's no cure, no Mother Nature."

Maddock knelt and put his arm around her.

"For what it's worth, you were right about a lot of things. You found the City of the Serpent, and we discovered Atahualpa's treasure in the bargain."

"No amount of treasure will save him now." She stood, briskly brushed the shredded bits of green from her clothing, and scrubbed away her tears. "Let's get out of here."

They headed back the way they had come. Bones came to a sudden halt.

"Can't go that way," he whispered.

"Why?" London asked.

"There's something in the water."

Maddock spotted a dark shape moving sinuously beneath the surface of the lake.

"I don't believe it," he said.

"How did Yacumama get here?" London asked.

"Must be connected to the sinkhole," Maddock said. "But she's so calm. Why isn't she attacking the Guardians?"

No one had an answer.

The chanting reached a crescendo. Boyd began to shout. "No! Don't you dare!"

They dashed across the top of the hill and stopped at the edge of the trees where they could watch what transpired.

The Guardians they had seen on the surface were only

a fraction of the population who resided down here. There were at least a hundred, including women and children. They saw no elders among the group.

Boyd and Alejandro stood at the water's edge, surrounded by a host of pale-skinned Guardians. They stood frozen in place, staring at something at the base of the hill, out of Maddock's line of sight.

The ground shifted beneath their feet. Maddock grabbed hold of one of the trees to steady himself.

"Is it an earthquake?" London asked.

"It doesn't feel like any earthquake I've experienced," Maddock said. The ground moved again, and then something else moved. They caught a glimpse of a giant, blocky head, narrow eyes, and a beaklike snout.

"What is that?" London gasped. "It looks like the head of a giant tortoise."

The pieces fell into place. The unnatural appearance of the mound, the hexagonal markings. This wasn't a hill at all.

"We are standing on top of Sachamama!"

44

Maddock gazed in wonder as Sachamama raised her head. It was so obvious now. They were standing upon the shell of a giant tortoise. Sachamama lurched forward and they clung to the trees to keep from falling.

"Remember what Wilton said? She comes from the world beneath, and can lie in one place for so long that the jungle grows on top of her shell."

London's eyes practically shone. "Sachamama is Mother Nature!"

Maddock was barely listening. Yacumama had circled around the small island and stopped in front of the Guardians and their captives. She raised her head and let out a hiss. Boyd and Alejandro began to scream. The Guardians banged their spear butts on the ground and continued to chant.

Yacumama tensed to strike, but Sachumama let out a sound like an avalanche. Maddock felt the vibrations of her rumbling cry through the soles of his boots. Yacumama snapped her head around and hissed at the giant tortoise. From head to tail, the two legendary creatures were almost of equal length and their heads roughly the same size, but in terms of sheer bulk, the giant snake would be punching above her weight in a battle with the tortoise.

Sachamama opened her mouth and breathed out a cloud of fine mist that engulfed Yacumama. The serpent immediately calmed down and resumed swimming.

"The legend also says she can hypnotize or bless you," London said.

Two of the Guardians limped to the water's edge.

Both had gashes in their legs from the fight with Yacumama.

"Why is Yacumama their ally down here but their enemy on the surface?" Bones asked.

"It's got to be the influence of Sachamama," Maddock said.

Sachamama wrapped two giant tentacles around the warriors and drew the men close to her. They threw their heads back in ecstasy as they were engulfed in a cloud of mist. When the mist dissipated, the Guardians had been healed.

"It's true!" London said. "Sachamama is a healer!"

Out of the corner of his eye, Maddock saw movement. Someone was creeping through the shadows at the river's edge, just out of the Guardian's eyeline. It was Mayra! She was wearing a mask and carrying a contraption Maddock had never seen before. It was cylindrical with a fan at one end and a transparent bag at the other. The others spotted her.

"Are you freaking kidding me?" Bones said. "She came prepared."

Mayra strode into the cloud of mist and clicked a switch on the device. It made a whirring sound and a few seconds later, drops of liquid appeared inside the bag.

"It's an aerosol collection device," Maddock said.

When the cloud cleared, Mayra removed the bag, closed the seal, secured it inside a protective case, and tucked it inside her backpack.

Bones drew his Glock.

"You can't shoot her," London whispered.

"Do we really want ScanoGen to tap into whatever sort of mind control Sachamama has at her disposal?" Bones said.

"But she's one of us," London protested.

"That was before she threw a grenade at us."

"Maybe she was only trying to knock us out. She could have put on her mask and waited around to kill us once the gas had done its work."

The decision was taken out of Bones' hands when a tentacle shot out and grabbed hold of Mayra. She let out a scream of sheer terror as Sachamama lifted her high into the air. Mayra shrieked and thrashed, but her arms were pinned to her sides and she could scarcely move. Her eyes fell on Maddock and the others.

"Help me, please!" she cried.

Maddock's hand went to his weapon, but he knew it would be utterly useless against the giant tortoise. Sachamama let out another cloud of vapor and Mayra relaxed.

Her eyes went wide and a beatific smile spread across her face. "I can see it all. It's magnificent! My mind… it's expanding to the size of the universe! I know everything!"

London let out a gasp of delight and took two steps forward before Maddock caught her by the belt. She drew back her fist to take a swing at him, but Maddock caught her by the wrist.

"Get a grip, London!"

"She is the true Mother of the Earth. I have to commune with her."

"You don't know what that thing will do to you."

Tears streamed down London's cheeks even as a crazed smile painted her face. "You saw her heal those men."

"At what cost? You said yourself, they aren't right in the head."

Mayra's tone suddenly changed. "Wait! It's too much!

My brain can't hold it all!" She let out a shriek of sheer agony.

"There's got to be something we can do," Bones said.

Other than a well-placed bullet, Maddock couldn't think of anything he could do to help her. Nor could he figure out a way the three of them could get past a hundred Guardians and a giant snake.

Giant snake!

"Do you guys remember the song of the Huancahui?"

"The Shaman song that is supposed to let you control serpents?" Bones asked "The last time we tried that all we managed to do was piss the snake off."

"That's what I want."

The three of them began to chant, "Huancahuiii! Huanacahuiii!"

Mayra's cries had ceased. Her eyes were glazed and drool trickled from the corner of her mouth. Sachamama sat her down the midst of the Guardians, where she stood, staring at nothing.

"It's not working," London said.

"Louder!" Maddock said. "She probably can't hear us underwater."

Next, the giant tortoise wrapped a coil around Boyd's waist. She turned her head to the side and held him up before one of her big, golden eyes, as if taking his measure.

"Put me down you…" Boyd jerked and gasped. Lines of putrid green like creeping vines spread out across his face and arms. "What are you doing to me?" He began to thrash and then twitch. Slimy foam poured from the corner of his mouth, and then he was still. So, the creature was not entirely benevolent.

Finally, Yacumama reappeared. Maddock and the others continued their chant. The giant snake perked up.

She looked at Maddock and for a moment it seemed their minds touched. He caught a glimpse of the chamber from her eyes, a flash of infrared chaos. He saw three figures standing atop Sachamama's giant shell. The connection broke in a split second and Yacumama went mad.

She burst forth from the river and into the midst of the Guardians. She struck at the closest warrior, biting his head clean off. His body, unaware that it was already dead, managed two steps before collapsing. Yacumama whipped her tail around and sent Guardians flying like bowling pins. Sachamama bellowed and lurched forward.

"That's our cue," Maddock said.

They made a run for it, half-sliding, half-falling down the side of Sachamama's shell. Maddock felt a jolt of pain from his heels all the way up to the base of his skull as his feet hit the ground on which the giant tortoise had lain for an eternity.

A tentacle whipped toward them. Maddock and Bones had their weapons ready and opened fire. Bullets shredded the tip of the giant tortoise's writhing limb. Blood and tissue flew. Sachamama let out another of her deep rumbles. Maddock wondered if this might be the first time the creature had ever felt pain.

Maddock let out another cry of, "Huancahuii!" at the top of his lungs. The giant snake turned and attacked the first thing she saw—Sachamama. She struck at the tortoise's exposed neck, but her fangs found little purchase in the tough hide. The giant tortoise tried to bite Yacumama, her jaws snapping shut like a steel trap. Maddock knew what kind of damage something as small as a snapping turtle could do, and couldn't imagine what Sachamama was capable of.

The fight between the two behemoths continued.

Sachamama blew a cloud of mist, but it had no apparent effect on Yacumama's maddened reptile brain. Maddock and the others seized on the opportunity to cross the shallow lake and run for the passage that led back to the surface.

But Sachamama wasn't finished with them. She lashed out with her long, powerful tail. Maddock managed to hurdle it, but London didn't see it coming. Bones shoved her out of the way, but in doing so, put himself in danger. The tip of the giant tail struck him across the shins, upending him. He did a faceplant on the hard stone and didn't get up.

"Bones!" Maddock shouted, hauling his friend to his feet. "You've got to move!"

Bones looked at him bleary-eyed through a mask of blood. "I'm okay." They continued to run, Bones limping along, Maddock and London helping him.

A group of Guardians broke away from the fight with the giant snake and ran after the fleeing explorers. Arrows flew, but none found their mark. Maddock fired on the run, emptying his magazine and taking down three Guardians.

Bones had regained a measure of his wits. He opened fire with his Glock. His aim was not as precise as usual, but he took down one guardian and injured two more.

Maddock ejected his magazine and reloaded on the run. The surviving Guardians abandoned the fight with Yacumama and took off in hot pursuit.

London had drawn her pistol and was firing wildly into the crowd. Bones was struggling with his own weapon. His spare magazine slipped from his fingers and he let out a curse.

"Leave it," Maddock said. "We're almost there."

"My hands won't do what my brain wants them to," Bones grumbled.

"You're probably concussed. Just try to stay on your feet."

The sounds of battle and running feet chased them out of the chamber. They ran past the obelisk that held the strange, scaly hand, through the chamber of petroglyphs, and reached the steep passageway that led back to the surface. When they reached the first turn, Maddock stopped.

"You two keep going. London, give me your weapon."

She handed it over without question.

"What are you doing?" Bones asked.

"Of all the corridors we passed through, this spot is the narrowest. I'll get them coming around the corner."

"Let me," Bones said. "I'm in bad shape anyway."

"Didn't you get the memo? It's the white guy who makes the last stand. Not the Indian." He turned to London. "Keep him moving. Don't stop and whatever happens, do not let him come back for me."

She paled, grabbed Bones by the elbow, and steered him along.

Maddock checked both magazines. He had a dozen bullets, plus one more reload for his Walther. It would have to be enough. He could hear the Guardians approaching. They were almost on him. He chose a concealed spot a short distance away, adopted a shooter's stance, and waited.

The first Guardian who rounded the corner got a bullet in the heart. He was dead before he realized he had been hit. The next guardian stumbled and fell over his fallen comrade. The tangle caused the others to slow down, giving Maddock ample time for some well-placed shots. He emptied London's pistol, then switched to his Walter. The Guardians kept coming. They were now forced to climb over their dead and dying comrades.

What I wouldn't give for one of Boyd's grenades right now.

The Guardians did not falter, nor even cry out. Whatever Sachamama had done to them had deprived them of fear. Maddock was running out of bullets and out of time. He kept fighting until his bullets were exhausted. Dead and dying Guardians lay in a heap. A few twitched in their death throes. One particularly resilient warrior began dragging himself across the floor toward Maddock, leaving a trail of blood behind.

"Why won't you die already?" Maddock said, backing away.

Another warrior appeared around the corner and began clambering over the fallen bodies. Maddock sighed and drew his knife. It would be hand-to-hand fighting from here.

Their eyes met and the Guardian stood up straight and let out a grunt. His eyes rolled back in his head and he collapsed, revealing Alejandro standing behind him, holding a rock.

"I won't try to harm you, I swear," the Amaru said, letting the rock fall to the ground and holding up his hands. "I just want to escape.

"Come on then, but know that my patience is almost at an end."

They made their way up the passageway as fast as their flagging strength allowed. There was no more pursuit. When they reached the window overlooking the chamber, Maddock glanced down. The fight was over. Yacumama was once more placidly swimming a circuit around Sachamama's island. Fallen Guardians lay scattered across the chamber. Most were dead, but a few still moved. As Maddock watched, Sachamama picked one of them up and performed her strange healing on him. Rejuvenated, the warrior picked up a spear and took off running.

"They do not give up," Alejandro said.

"For an Earth Mother, Sachamama really doesn't value the lives of her children, does she?" Maddock said as they resumed their climb.

"I was wrong" London said. "I am so sorry for all the harm I caused."

"All that matters now is getting out of here."

By the time they topped the steep corridor and stumbled to the fork in the passageway, Maddock was running on fumes. Bones and London were just ahead. Bones looked even worse than he had before. There were dark circles under his eyes, and blood soaked one of his pant legs.

"I don't know if he will be able to swim out of here, much less climb out of the sinkhole," London said.

"I can make it," Bones growled.

"He's going to need help," she said sharply.

In the distance, they heard footsteps. The surviving Guardians had almost caught up with them. Maddock doubted there could be that many more of them, but he didn't know how much fight he had left in him.

"You help him. I'll be right behind you."

"I can't do it alone," London said, tears welling in her eyes "And this is all my fault."

"Give me your knife. I will hold them off," Alejandro said.

"But why?" Maddock asked.

"I have done terrible things because I believed that finding the City of the Serpent would herald a new age of the Inca. Instead I have disturbed a terrible evil. I must make recompense for the sake of my soul."

Maddock was too tired to argue. He reversed his Recon knife and handed it to Alejandro.

"Good luck. And for what it's worth, any debt between us has been paid in full."

"Thank you." Alejandro turned and marched down the corridor to meet the Guardians.

Maddock turned to London.

"Let's get out of here."

45

The sky was growing dark when they finally emerged from the sinkhole. Bones had summoned his last reserves of strength to make the climb back out. He had operated on instinct at the last, relying on muscle memory formed from decades of recreational climbing, as well as climbing under duress.

He rolled over and looked up at the first glimmer of starlight. His thoughts were slippery things, his body sluggish. He held up a hand in front of his face and turned it over. It was almost as if the appendage belonged to someone else.

"Bonebrake, you've got to get up," London said.

Bones tried to sit up, but his body wouldn't obey. He tried again. Nothing.

"I'm really sorry, guys, but I can't do it."

"Yes, you can," Maddock said.

"Just drag me away from the sinkhole. I'll feel better after I get some sleep."

"Sleep is not what you need," Maddock said. "You have got to keep moving."

"Look at my leg."

Maddock ripped open Bones' pant leg and let out a curse. Bones looked down with detached curiosity. The blow from Sachamama's tail had made only a small cut in his shin, but his leg was already turning green.

"Venom," London whispered.

"No point in whispering. I can hear you."

"We'll have to act fast before it spreads any farther." Maddock began unbuckling his belt.

"What are you doing, pervert?" Bones said. His own

voice sounded foreign, distant.

"Making a tourniquet. I'm sorry, buddy, but I'm going to have to take the bottom half of your leg. It's the only way to save your life."

"You're not taking my leg."

"If I don't, the venom will spread."

"It already has." Bones held out his arm, revealing green streaks running along the inside. "I don't suppose London has any new age treatments to counteract venom?"

Maddock frowned and then his eyes lit up. He turned to London.

"Let's move him away from the sinkhole. I've got an idea."

"If his idea involves taking his pants off, don't let him do it," Bones said.

London smiled and patted him on the cheek. "You're going to be fine."

"I'm not a child." His tongue was thick and his words came out slurred.

"No, you just act like one." She leaned down and tenderly kissed his forehead. "I do have some herbs that will help with your fever."

"Let me guess. Essential oils."

"You're the one who asked if I had any 'New Age' treatments," London said as she and Maddock lifted Bones and carried him into the shelter of the trees.

"News flash. I'm a sarcastic person."

"What did he say?" London asked.

"He said George Strait sucks and modern bro country music rules."

"Screw you, Maddock." That was what Bones tried to say but it came out in a jumble.

"Now he's saying he prefers skinny women to curvy."

"I just like women," Bones tried to say, but his mouth wouldn't cooperate. Darkness closed in around the edges of his vision. He swam in and out of consciousness as Maddock took out his wing stove and boiled a cup of water.

London rested his head in her lap and trickled water onto his tongue. Swallowing even a few drops was a Herculean task, but he managed. She crumbled up some dried leaves and placed them under his tongue.

"This will bring your fever down and help you rest," she said, smoothing his hair back.

Bones smiled. He had always said he wanted to die in the arms of a beautiful woman. He had pictured a more amorous situation than this one, but it would have to do. He closed his eyes and faded away.

"We're losing him," London said.

"Hang on, Bones!" Maddock felt a lump forming in his throat. This couldn't be happening. Bones had his flaws, but the man was unbreakable. This had to work.

Maddock opened up the side pocket of his pack and found the bundle he was looking for.

"I've given him burdock, dandelion root, and echinacea. All are effective against toxins," London said. "I don't know if it's helping."

"I'm sure it is. You're doing a good job." Maddock sensed that the woman was on the verge of being overwhelmed by guilt and could do with some praise right now. He couldn't have her shutting down.

He opened the bundle and took out the dried root of the teacher tree. At least, that was what the vendor in Belen had said it was. He felt foolish as he crushed it between two stones and sprinkled it into the boiling water. What were the odds this would actually work?

"What is that?" London asked.

"A Hail Mary pass." Steam boiled up, carrying with it a riot of aromas. Maddock smelled ocean breeze, rum, teak, and tobacco. One whiff and all of his pain and fatigue melted away. Hope rose anew. Maybe this would actually work.

He picked up the wing stove and metal Sierra Cup and sat them on the ground next to Bones' head. Then, he stripped off his shirt and used sticks to form a small tent, capturing the steam. Bones' breathing slowed, his short, sharp gasps were soon replaced with deep breaths.

"It's working," London said.

"We're not out of the woods yet," Maddock said. He poured the liquid into another cup and smeared the boiled root directly onto Bones' wound. Bones let out a cry of pain and tried to sit up, but he was as weak as a newborn baby and London had no trouble holding him down.

"Would you care to be more specific about what, exactly, this is?" she asked.

"Root from the Teacher Tree. I didn't say because I had my doubts about its authenticity, and whether or not it could live up to its advance billing."

"What are the claims again?"

"Allegedly, the vapors relieve pain, the tea cures sickness, the poultice is supposed to draw out any poison."

"At the risk of jinxing us, I think it's working."

Thick green liquid was oozing from the wound. Maddock nearly retched at the foul smell. He tore off a section of his tented shirt, wet it, and used it to wipe away the viscous, foul-smelling goo.

London dipped her finger into the cup of liquid and let a few drops fall on Bones' tongue. He let out a low rumble of contentment. The dark circles under his eyes were fading away. The green lines on his arm receded. London looked at Maddock, her eyes bright.

"It really does work!"

Maddock barked a rueful laugh and shook his head.

"What's so funny?"

"I was just thinking, between the Teacher Tree and the song of the Huancahui, Dakota saved our lives.
"

EPILOGUE

Maddock sat up slowly and rubbed his eyes. He looked around at the strange room, trying to collect his thoughts. Every inch of his body ached, and he could scarcely keep his eyes open.

Gradually, the events of the past few days unfolded in his mind. The laborious hike back to the river, where they had repaired the fuel line on Diego's boat. The trip back down the river, and finally, their arrival in Iquitos.

The door opened and Spenser peeped inside. "Finally awake? I've been checking on you every hour."

"For how long?"

She took out her smartphone and glanced at the screen. "Twenty-two hours." She climbed onto the bed and snuggled up next to him.

"I still can't believe you were here waiting for us," he said, closing his eyes and enjoying the feel of her next to him.

"Waiting, my ass. We were trying to find a guide who would help us search for you. Good thing you showed up when you did. We were making final arrangements.

"We? You were going to bring Dakota with you into the jungle?"

"The feminist in me is pleased that you're more worried about his ability to survive in the jungle than mine. The girlfriend in me is deeply hurt."

He kissed her gently. "Trust me, it's a compliment."

"Whatever. But no, I was not about to leave my brother here unsupervised. Goddess only knows what kind of trouble he'd get himself into."

"Goddess? Tell me you haven't adopted London's

weird Earth Mother religion."

Mischief sparkled in her blue eyes. "Hardly. I just say it because it annoys Bones."

"Good girl. Speaking of, where are the others?"

"In the Belen, looking for the woman who sold Bones the Teacher Tree root. London thinks it might cure her father's cancer."

"I wish her all the luck in the world, but I am not going back into the Amazon any time soon."

"Damn right you're not. You skipped out on our vacation, so you owe me."

"Understood. So, what have you been doing while I hibernated?"

"Trying to translate the journal you found. It's been slow going. My German isn't great."

Maddock perked up. "Learn anything interesting?"

"Between the language barrier and some really sloppy handwriting, the results are patchy, but I think I've pieced things together with a fair amount of accuracy."

"I'm all ears," Maddok said, slipping an arm around her waist and resting his hand on her hip.

"Behave yourself. I worked hard on this." She opened the drawer on the side table and took out a notebook. "In a nutshell, the Ahnenerbe sent a squadron of soldiers into the jungle in search of Akakor. It was 1943 and Hitler's invasion of Russia had failed. The Nazis were desperate for anything that might change their fortunes. They expected to find powerful crystals and alien tech."

"And instead they found a giant turtle."

"Shut up. I'm telling the story." Spenser returned to her notes. "As far as I can tell, they never actually encountered Sachamama. They found a crystal obelisk and tried to smash it to get at 'the horror inside,' whatever that was."

Maddock nodded but didn't interrupt.

"The Guardians of Akakor trapped the Germans in a cave, where they held out as long as they could."

"Pretty much what we had surmised, but it's good to have confirmation," Maddock said. "Anything else of interest?"

"The last entry is weird. *I regret that the quest that began at Al Ubaid ends here, but I die in the knowledge that I was right about the lizard men.*"

"Lizard men?"

"That's the literal translation. Any idea what that means?"

Maddock frowned. "The object inside the obelisk was a hand covered in reptilian scales. I can show you photos."

Spenser nodded eagerly. "I did some checking and Al Ubaid is a Sumerian site where archaeologists recovered artifacts depicting human-reptile hybrids."

Maddock closed his eyes and let out a low groan.

"What's wrong?"

"Whatever you do, don't tell Bones about this until we're back home."

The End

FROM THE AUTHOR

One of my favorite things about writing the Dane Maddock Adventures is the research that goes into the books. (Don't tell my younger self that). I love making use of "real" mysteries and legends, as well as actual people and places. Contest is loaded with these, and I would be remiss if I did not acknowledge the work of author M.L. Behrman, whose book, *Mojave Mysteries*, provided a wealth of story material.

ABOUT THE AUTHOR

David Wood is the USA Today bestselling author of the Dane Maddock Adventures and several other books and series. He also writes fantasy under the pen name David Debord. He's a member of International Thriller Writers and the Horror Writers Association, and also reviews for New York Journal of Books.

Learn more about him and his work at www.davidwoodweb.com or drop by and say hello on Facebook at www.facebook.com/davidwoodbooks.

Manufactured by Amazon.ca
Bolton, ON

34083214R00178